Hot Girl

Sonia Lermo

For all the party girls;
you were always enough.

Preface

♥

"[Hot Girl Summer is] just basically about women—and men—just being unapologetically them, just having a good-ass time, hyping up your friends, doing you, not giving a damn about what nobody got to say about it. You definitely have to be a person that can be the life of the party, and, y'know, just a bad b*tch."

—*Megan Thee Stallion*

This book is only for those over the age of legal adulthood due to its graphic sexual content. There are themes such as anorexia, body image issues, off-page rehab, off-page sexual assault, off-page drink spiking, alcohol usage, mention of divorce, mention of gaslighting, age play, light bondage, mention of sucide, mention of mental illness, on-page minor road collision, and swearing.

Chapter One

♥

"WHAT'S YOUR POISON?"

"Fuckboy tears." I am this close to losing my shit. For the past ten minutes, Mr Won't-take-no-for-an-answer has seriously been invading my personal space, and my patience is wearing thin.

"Sorry, I'm fresh out of those."

In his umpteenth attempt at making small talk, I finally snap. When is Prince Charming going to come and save the day? That's right, never.

That sort of thing only happens in books and movies. Never does it happen to the jaded party girl who has given up on anything more than casual dating, and if this guy isn't careful, he's going to feel the wrath of my fiery Italian side.

He meets my death glare, the one I save for the particularly obnoxious men, and I sincerely hope that I won't be teaching guys like him in the fall when I press play on my career as a yoga teacher. Taking the leap from cosmetology to teaching is already a huge, scary step, and I don't need any additional man-shaped drama upheaving my life.

I scan the room for a means to escape, cursing the no table service policy while I try to make eye contact with one of the bar's mixologists, and make sure that once I order my drink, I'll watch my glass extra carefully.

There's no doubt in my mind that this wannabe Casanova is after one thing, and he sure as hell isn't getting it. All I want to do is celebrate my friend's birthday without any hassle from a horny man child, but that's obviously too much to ask.

Squaring my body, I lean across the bar to further avoid Randy Lusterson's advances, silently hoping he takes the oh-so-obvious hint and leaves me alone.

My large dose of the silent treatment must be working, because without another word or terrible joke, Thirsty Terrence soon gets bored and leaves.

Another one bites the dust.

"Hey, Sophia, stop scaring my customers," Luke says, leaning across the bar.

"Then tell them to stop terrorising me," I reply.

I can always rely on Lilura's bartender and resident womaniser to put me in my place. Luke is easily the hottest guy in the vicinity. At six-foot-something, he trumps my petite five-foot-two frame, and his broad shoulders, deep brown eyes and chiselled features are enough to make any hot-blooded female succumb to his charms. Well. Anyone, but me. With our similar strict Catholic upbringings and Italian roots, we're one and the same, and I sure as hell don't want to be hooking up with someone like that.

My phone chimes with a text from my Flavour of the Week.

Alex: You up?

I check the time. It's almost the following day. I text back. *I'm out.*

Luke lines up five shot glasses on a tray and fills them with Tuaca. After knocking one back, I tap my card on the machine in time to the beat of Miley's Midnight Sky.

"Anyway, last I checked," I say, "this isn't your bar."

"One day," he says, pouring orange liquid into four hi-ball glasses. He tops them with prosecco and slides the tray across the bar.

Alex: Come over.

I roll my eyes and slide my phone into my bag.

"Who's that?"

"Alex."

Luke sobers.

"Are you leaving?"

"No, I'm sure he has ten other girls he can call."

I know I'm right, and Luke's silence tells me all I need to know, as does the ache in my chest. I can pretend that Alex's indiscretions don't bother me, but deep down they do. It's not even like we're together—we're friends with benefits, and I like it that way—but nobody wants to be used. I just need to accept that it's the way things are.

"I'll bring those over," Luke says, cocking his head towards the tray of drinks.

Anxiety rises in my chest. I learned the hard way never to leave my drink unattended, and the thought of the tray sitting idly on the bar fills me with dread.

"I'm good," I say, gripping the sides of the circular tray and eyeing the crowd of Luke's adoring eighteen-year-old fans waiting to be served. "You have customers."

I wink in jest, and turn on my heel to leave.

With the tray balanced in both hands, I expertly manoeuvre through the dark interior of the large, Edwardian building, past mirrors and bricks and crowds of young professionals and budding entrepreneurs, swerving large, black Chesterfield sofas while huge, modern chandeliers gift me with the little light I need to navigate the ground floor.

Lilura is like stepping into a swanky New York lounge, but its exclusivity means expense that my salary can barely keep up with. I usually manage to attract some nameless guy in a suit who's more than willing to keep my drink topped up. Nobody likes to be used, but I'm better at it than any man.

After making it back mildly unscathed, with minimal spill, and, most importantly, with my peace of mind intact, I set the tray down on the dark wood table, smooth my tight, black mini-dress and sink into the leather couch beside my roommate, Stefan. His husband, James, is too busy flying aeroplanes to join us, so no doubt he'll be trying to fix me up with someone tonight in an attempt to distract himself.

"Ooh, it has glitter. Is it vegan?" Stefan asks.

"I have it on good authority that no actual fuckboys have been harmed," I say, taking a sip and savouring the taste. Luke's Fuckboy Tears cocktail invention is basically a glorified Porn Star Martini, something much sweeter than how I've always imagined real fuckboy tears to taste—bitter, salty, and disappointing.

"Honey, you embrace your hot girl summer."

"'Tis the season," I say, with a wink.

"It's a full moon. Anything could happen."

"I thought Scandinavians didn't believe in astrology?"

"Traditionally, we believe in fate. But I'm not your average Swede." Stefan takes a shot and winces. "Did I tell you I started reading tarot?"

"Ooh, maybe I should have my cards read," I say, a sardonic smile playing on my lips.

Most of the time, I feel like a fraud. I'm not the average yogi. For starters, I like to party, and I don't care much for things I can't control, like the lunar cycle, tea readings, and tarot. How can someone let a few cards dictate what they do with their lives? I would rather sip cocktails at Ocean Beach Ibiza and rub shoulders with celebrities than go on a yoga retreat, and the thought of foregoing my monthly waxing sessions makes me feel anything but natural.

I don't see why I should have to fit into a neat little box of stereotypes and limit myself to people's expectations of me. I'm not flighty, or into all that 'love and light' stuff. I don't have a superiority complex, either, like some yogis do. My body type is all wrong, and I am the most materialistic future yoga teacher to ever exist. But yoga is more to me than an advanced, spiritual version of Simon Says. Yoga saved me when I needed saving, and I owe it to myself to give that salvation back to whoever needs it. But that doesn't mean that I need to turn to anyone—or anything—other than myself to do so.

"How is Alex, anyway?" he asks, swiftly changing the subject.

"I came, I saw, I came again. That's how the saying goes, right?"

"I don't know, min älskling. We don't have that phrase in Sweden."

His bright blue eyes twinkle with mirth, and we both laugh.

"What are you two giggling about?" April asks, approaching the table. The birthday girl and wing woman extraordinaire takes a seat beside me, but changes her mind instantly. "Never mind. I have something to show you," she says, waving a hand dismissively.

"If it's a dick pic, I don't want to know," I say. Secretly, I'm intrigued.

"Are you sure? It's a good one?" she says, raising her eyebrows.

"I can vouch for that," Stefan adds, raising his glass.

"You've seen it already? You are such a pervert," I say, pausing to sip my cocktail. "Speaking of dicks and perverts, has anyone heard from Ryan?"

Stefan retrieves his phone and reads the screen. "They're on their way."

"Wait, Chrissy's coming? I totally forgot to get her a drink. Please don't make me go back up there," I say, my eyes on the crowded bar.

April and Stefan shoot each other a pointed look.

"Sure, you 'forgot'," Stefan says, making quotation marks with his fingers.

"It's okay, I would've forgotten on purpose, too. I got you girl," April says, with a wink.

April and I have an unspoken language when it comes to mean girls. April's copper hair and fair skin made her an easy target at school for bullies like Chrissy—who makes Regina George look like Mother Teresa. Sure, she's pretty, but she's also pretty awful. She took the easy ride her looks gave her, and instead of helping others up, she shot them down and gave them a hard time. Cruel jibes and gaslighting for comedic purpose being her weapons of choice.

To say I still can't figure her out would be an understatement, but I was glad to see the back of her when we left school ten years ago, until my ex-boyfriend, Ryan, brought her back into our friendship group a year ago.

"Fine, let me see it," I say.

"I knew it. You're such a perv," April says, showing me the screen.

"Nothing like a cock shot to de-stress," I say. My eyes widen as I zoom in to admire the faceless, naked man in the photo. "Wow, good job. Have you met him yet?"

April shakes her head.

"No. We only matched yesterday."

"And he's already showing you the goods? Well aside from the obvious, he's very well groomed...and confident," I say.

"I was going to state the obvious, but we'll go with that," April says.

I raise a shot glass and the others follow.

"Happy birthday, little bean. Welcome to the twenty-six club."

"Cheers," we all chime, and knock the shots back.

"And congratulations, Miss DeLuca," Stefan adds.

I raise my glass again to revel in my friend's praise.

"Excuse me," April calls, catching the attention of a passer-by. "Do you mind taking our picture?"

"Sure," the man says.

He's good-looking in a generic sort of way, not classically handsome like Luke, and he doesn't give off that boy-next-door vibe like my wannabe bedfellow Alex does. He's shorter than my usual type, but still taller than me, and even though he's less muscular than the bodybuilder fitness model types I usually lust over, he clearly knows how to rock a slate grey Henley and dark skinny jeans.

Day-old stubble peppers a sharp jaw, an exact shade match to his grown-out short back and sides haircut, and a small smile drives shallow dimples in his cheeks, but doesn't reach his hazel green eyes.

"Shit, my battery is drained," April says, unlocking her phone.

I smirk, knowing my friend's not-so-secret bathroom nudes are responsible for the lack of juice.

"Here, take mine."

When I hand over the device with an obligatory smile, I catch the scent of clean, sophisticated citrus and woods, with a hint of white florals. It's sexy, subtle, and masculine, and unlike anything I've ever smelt before. His hands are as warm as mine are cold, but he doesn't flinch as I cool his touch, nor does he maintain eye contact, or a smile that reaches his eyes, or any of the other obvious signs of attraction. If anything, he seems bored, like his emotional gearstick is stuck in neutral.

As conceited as it sounds, I'm not used to people being anything less than attracted to me, and I can't understand why I find it so offensive that he hasn't automatically made bedroom eyes at me, especially as he's far from being the hottest person in the room. But these musings of mine only serve to make Mr Barely Interested seem a whole lot more interesting.

After an extremely short photoshoot, he hands the phone back, and we all chime a 'thank you' as he walks away. We lean in to review the single imperfect shot on the screen, in which I can barely make out my own smile. The photo's blurry, and completely unusable. What's the point in taking night out photos if they aren't good enough for the 'gram?

"Excuse me," April calls, but he's already too far.

In a moment of haste, I slide past my friend and catch up with Moody Photographer, and a group of men surrounds him. After demanding his attention with a tap on the shoulder, he turns around, meeting my gaze with a passive expression.

"Hey, I'm so sorry to bother you again, but—" I show him the photo. "—would you mind taking another one?"

He inches closer, and studies the screen.

"Looks fine to me," he says, turning to give me a view of his back once again.

What the heck just happened?

I tap him again. He turns around again, eyes narrowed and lips tightly closed.

Don't unleash the wrath, I repeat in my head. But I'm gradually seeing red. "It's blurry."

"And?"

"And I was asking if you could take a few more that don't leave me squinting." I take a moment to adopt my fail-safe technique for getting my own way. First, a deep breath to calm and centre myself. Second, direct eye contact. If those two things fail, I can always fall back on flirting.

"There are over one hundred people in here, go ask someone else."

Maybe not.

He turns back to his friends once again. I stand there, not moving, for what seems like an age. I look towards April and Stefan for reassurance, but they're engrossed in animated conversation. I'm on my own with this asshole. Taking another deep breath, I summon the courage to tap him again, and this time when he turns around, his jaw is clenched tight and I can almost see the hot steam rising from his ears.

"Look, I'm trying to be polite here," he says. "But your camera sucks."

"Well, I'm sorry if my Android doesn't live up to your superior iPhone, or whatever it is you have, but there's no need to be rude."

"I apologise," he says, laying a hand to his chest. But something tells me that the gesture is far from sincere. "I can take some on mine and send them to you if you want?"

So that's his game. Feign contempt, but have my picture on his phone to use for a pathetic little rage wank.

"Nice try, perv," I say.

He laughs in disbelief, then shakes his head. "I don't know what you think this is." He gestures between us, "but don't flatter yourself."

"I don't think this is anything. All I'm saying is you might want to brush up on your photography skills."

"My photography skills are just fine, thanks. You need an upgrade."

"Wow, a middle-aged white man who thinks he's above me. How original."

"Middle-aged?" he scoffs. "I'm thirty-nine, actually. So technically I'm a millennial. Maybe it's hard to decipher what's old and what isn't when you're an entitled, sophomoric child who measures her worth from Instagram likes. Are you even old enough to be in here?"

That's it.

Raging heat floods my face and my heart threatens to burst my ribcage apart.

We stare each other down, locked in a staring contest for what seems like minutes. In all my twenty-six years I have never felt such a myriad of emotions in one moment. Anger, hurt, hatred, but I won't dare move. The first to retreat is the loser, and I refuse to back down.

Chapter Two

♥

"**H**EY."

April's calming voice resonates in my ear, and I snap my gaze away from those hazel green eyes. Without my tunnel vision, I remember where I am. April links my arm, tearing me away from possibly the rudest man I have ever met as he turns back to his friends.

"That guy. The fucking audacity."

"What happened?"

"Honestly, I don't know. I asked him to take another photo and he just—"

"Forget about him. We're supposed to be celebrating, right?"

In my absence, Ryan has taken up residence on the couch between Stefan and April, where I had originally been sitting. Scooting onto the end, I lean into the soft leather arm.

"Where's Chrissy?" April asks.

"Outside, with her friend. She'll be in soon," Ryan says.

"Everything okay?" I shout. It's so damn loud in here, I can barely even hear myself.

Ryan shakes his head. "Just the usual," he says, and takes a sip of his drink. He grimaces. "We had an argument before we went out. She didn't want to come tonight, but I managed to convince her."

He pauses to admire the two girls he's sandwiched between. Myself, and my gorgeous flame-haired bestie. Lucky guy. "You both look amazing, by the way."

"We know," April says.

Ryan stands all six foot-something of dark skin, tattoos and sculpted muscle. Even though that ship has long sailed, there's no harm in appreciating his great looks. I'm not usually one to stay friends with my exes, but Ryan is the exception. He's had my back since we were teenagers, and he's one of the only straight guys I know that I feel safe with. I trust him.

"I can't drink this, it tastes like medicine," he says, standing. "Anyone want another?"

"I'll come with you," I say.

After my heated encounter, I crave another shot, or ten. We approach the bar, and I peruse a cocktail menu without taking anything in.

"What did you fight about?" I ask him.

"Nothing we haven't fought about a thousand times before."

He sneaks a glance towards April, and I follow his gaze.

"April? You had a fling two years ago. You weren't even with Chrissy back then."

"I know. It isn't just her."

He shoots me a pointed look.

"Me? We were together for like six months in secondary school. It wasn't even a real relationship. Is she serious?"

He shrugs. "She has this notion that since you were my first, I'll always hold a torch for you."

"Well that's probably true. I *am* unforgettable." I flick my long dark waves over my shoulder, then remember the reason for our breakup. Ryan was, and still is, a serial cheater.

"You're something else, Phi—that's for sure," he says. "But she has no reason to be jealous. I mean, look at her."

I conjure up an image of Chrissy in my head, but I can't see what Ryan sees in her. Sure, if I didn't know her I'd probably be a little envious of the long-legged, pretty, tanned blonde. But, unfortunately, I do know her and her toxic personality. Chrissy is the one person I fail to see the good in.

"No Alex tonight?" Ryan asks.

"Apparently not," I reply.

"Are you two a thing, yet?"

I screw up my face as I down a shot. "Fuck no."

"Why not?"

"Because he's the type of guy who would show his dick to anyone if they asked. Because I find hair extensions in his bed. False nails. Used eyelash strips. None of that shit is mine."

Ryan's deep brown eyes widen. "Whoa...okay. So he's not boyfriend material. I get it."

"Call me wild, but I'm happy as I am."

And I am.

I'm more than capable of looking after myself. I value my freedom, and the last thing I want is to be tied down. Besides, I have enough to focus on in my new role without having to juggle some boy's emotions and needs as well.

After another few rounds, we lose ourselves on the dancefloor in an alcohol-fuelled haze to hip hop throwbacks and club classics. Drinks flow freely and the atmosphere sparks with the electricity of a summer storm, and hours pass before anyone notices there is still no sign of Chrissy.

After Ryan calls a search party, we split up. He takes the outside areas, Stefan flees to the roof terrace and April guards the drinks and seats, while I check the bathroom. Princess

Plastic is sure to turn up somewhere, but I don't expect to find her so soon.

On my way to the bathroom, I check my reflection in one of the many mirrored walls and reapply my deep-toned beige lip shade. Behind me, I spot Chrissy and two of her fellow long-limbed mean girls—both of whom I recognise from school—perched on a Chesterfield around a low glass table.

"Ryan's looking for you," I say, approaching the table. My voice carries the same level of disdain that I have always been met with by her.

For a moment, Chrissy narrows her eyes, maintaining eye contact but saying nothing as one of her minions leans into her ear and whispers something inaudible. Then she turns her attention back to her friends, laughing at whatever's being said, and completely disregards me.

I am seething. But logic tells me there's no point in getting angry, or even trying. It would only entertain somebody like Chrissy, even if I am sure as hell done trying to be nice. Not even nice, civil.

I turn on my heel to leave, counting my breaths to try and slow my racing heart as I make my way upstairs. This is turning into a night I would rather forget, and the only thing that gives me comfort is the drink waiting on the other end of my cash card.

I order two shots of Tuaca and knock one back, savouring the delicious fire in my throat as soon as the bartender sets it down. With cosy seating areas overlooking the downstairs bar, it's the perfect place to people watch and contemplate my next move after being subjected to Chrissy's cruel attempt at humiliation. I know that Chrissy heard me loud and clear, and as far as I'm concerned, she's Ryan's problem.

I'd spent most of my teenage years being grossly overlooked. My appearance was nothing like the pretty, blonde, willowy creatures the boys pursued—girls like

Chrissy. Funny how perceptions change. How the media defines who or what is pretty, attractive, or hot. Body types. Nose shapes. Eyebrows. Preferences have changed so much since I was a girl.

Once the Kardashian hype took over, the attention I gained was astounding, like my thick thighs, Roman nose, and wide hips had suddenly earned me hot girl potential.

After that, my confidence grew rapidly, but I always hated that my boobs stayed so small when everything else expanded. Over the years, men seemed to gravitate towards me, and I didn't waste any time making up for all that was lost. Still, I'm grateful for the quiet moments here and there.

I smirk at the thought that I've probably scared off my quota of men for the evening. I guess I'll have to buy my own drinks from now on, or so I think.

"Two gin and tonics, please," a male voice says. "Bombay Sapphire."

My favourite.

My gaze skims across a lean forearm adorned with dark hair and a fancy-looking watch. Catching the familiar, unique scent of clean woods, I turn towards his irritatingly smug face. My smile wanes.

"No, thanks. I can buy my own drink," I snarl.

"Consider it a peace offering."

I turn my eyes back towards the bartender, paper straws, napkins on the bar top, condensation on a glass, anything to avoid that annoying half smile thing he has going on.

After the bartender places the extra drinks in front of us, Mr Fancy Pants taps his card on the machine and hands her a tip.

"How bougie of you," I mutter, loud enough for him to hear.

I study the drinks in front of me, torn at the defeat of accepting his olive branch. But it doesn't take long to convince myself that he owes me an apology, and, despite my best efforts, I'm not going to turn down a free drink from this guy. Fuck it, I might even try and squeeze another one out of the prick.

Raising my eyebrows and the cool glass to my lips, I knock back the second shot, then chase it with a long pull of the gin and tonic, when all I really want to do is throw it straight onto his crotch.

"Bougie? Because I tip the bar staff?"

I cock my head to one side. "Some of us don't have the luxury to throw cash around."

"That appears to be true," he says, openly checking me out, "judging by your lack of clothing."

Is this guy for real? I open my mouth to say something, then close it again. I have absolutely no words for this douchebag.

"Enjoy your drink, Princess."

When he dares to raise his glass and walk away, I manage to think of one word: asshole.

He has no business being that cocky. My eyes fall to my completely impractical outfit. Okay, it isn't the most comfortable piece of clothing I own, but it makes me feel confident. That, and the fact that the residents of Brighton are currently experiencing a heatwave. I have every right to wear whatever the heck I want without some man policing my outfit.

Somewhere between my musings, my body sets itself to autopilot and I follow him, clearly determined not to let him have the last word.

"How would *you* suggest I dress?" I say, claiming his attention again. "And isn't it a little sexist, expecting me to justify the clothes I wear?" He fixes his gaze on my thighs as I size him up, taking a long pull on my drink. If I typed men's indie fashion into Pinterest, I'm confident that his Henley and jeans combo would make an appearance.

"Anyway, it's not my fault you're too old to appreciate style."

"Again with the old?" he asks.

I cock my head to the side and smile sweetly. Eyes narrowed, his gaze fixes on mine for a little longer than I deem comfortable, and it steals my breath away. This guy has a way about him, like he knows exactly how to make me feel self-conscious. I don't like it. A beat later, as if he can read my mind, he breaks contact. I exhale sharply.

"Have a seat," he says, cocking his head towards an empty seating area.

"Why would I want to sit with you? All you've done is insult me."

"Because I'm ridiculously handsome and charming."

Inside, I'm on the floor laughing. He forgot to mention grade A douchebag.

"You mean, you actually *want* to talk to an egotistical airhead who measures their worth in Instagram likes. That *is* what you said, right?"

"Actually, what I said was—"

I raise my eyebrows, daring him to continue. He clears his throat.

"Never mind. Are you always this—"

"Assertive?" I ask.

"Salty," he replies.

My eyes narrow. "You don't even know me."

"You're right. I don't. But I know that I'm enjoying the hell out of arguing with you." He sobers. "And I'd like to chat with you some more, if you're interested."

Before I have the chance to answer back, he takes a seat on a vacant Chesterfield sofa by the glass balcony. Why does he keep doing that? Like he can't keep still long enough to wait for an answer. He's either extremely impatient, weirdly nervous, or it's just how he's wired. Maybe it's all of the above. Still, I'd be lying if I didn't admit mild curiosity.

I try to make sense of the unusual turn of events, of the way I'm acting. Submission was never my jam, and usually I would never allow myself to play right into someone's hands like this. But here I am, seriously considering his offer.

I am sick to death of cocky fuckboys, but there's no harm in seeing how this one might embarrass himself. At the most, he's nice to look at, and at the very least, it might be a good story to tell my friends.

"See that guy down there?" he asks, after I join him. His eyes never leave the downstairs bar.

I follow the direction of his gaze to a lone man nursing a glass of amber liquid, while a bottle of champagne sits in a bucket of ice front of him, along with two empty glasses. I can't help but wonder why this is supposed to be interesting.

"What about him?"

I sink into the Chesterfield sofa beside Mr Impertinent. The well-worn leather dips in the centre as it takes my weight, bringing our bodies closer. He's warm, and I don't hate it.

"Every time I come here, there he is. Always with the whisky, always with the champagne. Hoping he'll get lucky, and get to take somebody home."

I pretend not to notice my bare thigh brush against his denim jeans as a pretty blonde woman walks up to the bar downstairs, and takes up residence beside the lone ranger.

Rising anxiety grips my stomach as I watch the exchange between the two strangers, and I find myself eyeing the woman's drink. It's nerve-wracking to watch, but I force myself to keep an eye on that glass. It never hurts to be vigilant, and I view any man as a potential threat.

We watch together, not saying a word as the scenario plays out. After trying and failing to engage the woman in conversation, the man downstairs cuts his losses and nurses the amber liquid once again. Instantly, I relax, relieved on the woman's behalf, but I still keep a wary eye on him.

"It's pretty pathetic if you ask me," I muse.

"Coming from someone who's clearly never been rejected."

I meet his honey-green gaze. God, those eyes are gorgeous.

"I think," he says, taking a sip from his drink, "that it's incredibly brave."

"He could be happy on his own," I say.

"Or, he could share that happiness with someone else."

He draws his gaze towards my mouth, and my pulse quickens. I suck in my bottom lip, and his eyes fall to the floor.

"Loneliness is dangerous," he says, quietly.

His expression becomes increasingly sombre, and if I don't switch the mood soon, I'm pretty sure we'll both be crying at the bottom of a bottle within the hour—and not in a good way.

"I think there's something kind of beautiful in a little danger, don't you think?"

He answers my rhetorical question with a smile that fails to reach his eyes. I want to fix it.

"So who are you here with, Mr Bougie?"

I cross my legs towards him, hoping a little human contact would lift his spirits. It's a reach, but it never fails.

"Just my band mates. And it's Danny—if you don't mind. Are you going to tell me your name?"

I contemplate telling him my real name, but I haven't worked him out yet. Although he doesn't give off major creeper vibes, I can't risk it, so I go for the safer option.

"I'm Summer."

It's my alter ego, my alias—the name I use to deter potential creepers and weirdos so that they can't find me on social media.

"Nice to officially meet you, Summer."

I instantly feel bad for lying, but on the other hand, it's unlikely I'll ever see him again.

"So, you're in a band? That's cool. Like swing? Or jazz? Or—"

He laughs, taking a sip of his drink. "No, nothing like that. I guess you could put us in the "indie rock" genre," he says, making quotation marks with his hands. "Like Kings of Leon, I guess. But with a lot less talent."

I smile approvingly. His indie boy aesthetic makes perfect sense now. "What do you play?"

"I'm just the guitarist."

"Hey, don't sell yourself short. Everybody knows the guitarist is the real frontman." I wink, then regret it instantly. If he was interested at all before, he sure as hell isn't after that move. I clear my throat, blame it on natural behaviour, and move on. "Is your band on Spotify?" I ask, retrieving my phone.

"Yeah."

I hand Danny the device, with the logic that it's better to have him follow them on my behalf, instead of being shouted at over the already deafening music. As he navigates the device, I try not to notice the size of the palm wrapped around it.

I fail miserably.

Large hands and long fingers are on my list of kryptonite, and I've come to the realisation that this one is dangerous, and not the beautiful kind. Musicians are notorious for being womanizers and at the top of the fuckboy food chain, and I let myself play right into those perfect hands.

Even though he's older, I would bet the money I don't have that his musician status is the reason for his unmatched confidence. That, and the fact that he has probably done his fair share of sleeping around. I push the thought away, and focus on his face, studying the white strands that pepper his dark brown hair. Every fine line around his eyes softens his features, telling a story that only makes him more attractive.

"Here," he says, passing the phone back.

I desperately hope that he didn't catch me staring.

"The Wandering Dragons," I say, pressing the follow button.

"That's us," he says. "Are you on Twitter?"

"I mean, I have it. But I don't really use it. I'm not even sure I remember my password."

I know damn well the game would be over if I gave my handle using my real name. I place my phone face down on the table and take a long pull of my drink. "You were right to assume my 'gram girl status."

"But of course. We're not pretty enough for the 'gram, as you can see."

"Oh come on. You're not seriously fishing for a compliment right now?"

The lines around his eyes deepen as the corners of his mouth curl up, treating me to a full set of dimples that make me blush. I can't help but smile back.

"There you are," Stefan says, approaching our table.

Perfect timing.

He eyes up a tense Danny and introduces himself, then he turns a pointed look in my direction. I brush Danny's arm, where soft, ribbed cotton meets his skin, and he eases under my touch. I know how intimidating Stefan's strong, Scandinavian looks can be, and how they can be misinterpreted.

"Chrissy's gone."

I mentally kick myself. I had completely forgotten about that vile she-devil. "What do you mean?" I plead ignorance.

"We've looked everywhere."

"The roof terrace?"

Stefan nods.

"What about the beach?"

He huffs out a sigh, then nods again. I sit back and pretend to think. Is it really so awful if I fail to mention the incident?

"Maybe she went off with her friends. Didn't you say it was a full moon? I'm pretty sure if you look up at the sky she'll be riding a cold, shiny, hard plastic broomstick," I smirk.

Stefan is unimpressed to say the least, but I'm delightfully entertained.

"She isn't answering any of Ryan's calls or messages. We're going to head out, see if she's at his place." He looks at Danny again, and the most ridiculous smile spreads across his face. "But you can stay here if you like?"

Yes, I would like that very much, is how I want to reply, but instead I opt for, "I'll be down in a minute."

Stefan winks, we exchange goodbyes and he leaves. He can be so childish sometimes, but my god, do I love him.

"I guess I should probably try and find my friends too." Danny says, hesitating. "But if you don't want to leave just yet, you're welcome to stay with us. Don't worry, I'm not a creep or anything. We're pretty decent guys."

I side-eye him. "That's what all the creeps say."

Standing, I fix my outfit and consider his offer. Giving him a final once-over, I tuck the image in my mind with the intention of using it for my drunk 3am orgasm-induced slumber, but when my eyes fall to his hands, I throw it straight in the trash.

There's no mistaking the silver wedding band on his finger, or that I was right all along. He really is the worst kind of human.

"Thanks, but I, uh, better go help my friends."

"Take care of yourself, Summer. I hope you find your friend."

"She's not my friend, but that's a whole different story. I'll tell you some time, if I ever see you again."

I walk away, hoping I'll never have to.

Chapter Three

♥

THE LAST SATURDAY IN June is as busy as any other weekend at Ivy Rose Organics. They're a small skincare company who pride themselves on their green credentials, and high quality, cruelty free and sustainable ingredients. It's harder work than people give any of us who work here credit for, but I adore my job.

My regular clientele consists of mostly middle-class, middle-aged women hoping to recapture their youth, whilst simultaneously trying to save the planet. They tip well, and they always have interesting stories to tell.

The back room is dark and quiet, a stark contrast to the warm, sunny weather outside. I find my rhythm in the mundane task of washing makeup brushes. I knew as soon as I committed to April's birthday night out, I'd have to work extra hard the following day through a hangover and a distinct lack of sleep.

Water runs over brushes, and the ochre-stained fluid renders me hypnotised as I watch the continuous stream spiral down the plughole. The click-clacking of heels across the hardwood floor pulls me out of my spellbound state, and

I jolt as my manager, Lauren, strides through the swing door, and almost knocks it off its hinges.

"Somebody's here to see you," the tall blonde says, cocking her head towards the door.

"Who?" I ask.

Lauren presses her hands into her hips. "I don't know, some guy."

I place the brush in a pot to dry and set the dirty ones aside to return to before I investigate the mystery caller. Moving towards the door, I spy Ryan through a small pane of glass.

"Ugh, it's my ex."

"He's hot."

A hot fucking mess.

I excuse myself to visit Ryan on the shop floor. I could do without a Chrissy-induced headache on top of the one that's already threatening to explode my brain. A message to our friends' WhatsApp group early that morning confirmed that, after our rocky night out, Chrissy was alive and well, and had spent the evening catching up with the mean girls. Maybe I should have mentioned our exchange, after all. Then again, maybe not.

"Hey, Phi," Ryan says. "Any chance you can help with this?"

He hands me a small sheet of paper, and my eyes skim over the names of our three bestsellers scrawled across the page.

"Sure."

Without effort, I navigate the shop, and within moments, I have them rung up, bagged and ready to go.

"Is that everything?" I ask.

He's hesitant. Even though his hands are in his pockets and his gaze on the floor, I know him well enough to know that guilty look. It's the same expression he wore when he told me he kissed his French exchange student when we were fifteen, which ultimately ended our six-month relationship, and fed my wariness of fuckboys in the process. I decide to change the subject. Even after all we've been through, I hate to see him upset.

"Hey, you know what? We have this great new product that I'm sure Chrissy would love." Even though I despise his girlfriend, I can't bear to see one of my oldest friends hurting, and I figure it's probably all down to his inferior half. I walk over to the store's most recent display and pick up a round, glass pot as Lauren re-enters the shop floor. Perfect timing to show off my sales technique.

"It's a powder that mixes with moisturiser, and gives a gorgeous, dewy glow. It's expensive, but it will last forever."

I try to unscrew the cap, but it won't budge.

"Here, let me do that," he says, holding out his hand.

"That's okay, I've got it."

I am determined to open this jar if it takes all day. It's pure luck that I manage to unscrew it on the third try. I tip a little of the iridescent powder into my palm and show it to Ryan.

"See...it's really pretty."

His blank expression registers loud and clear. There's no way in hell I'll ever get him excited about skincare or makeup, when all he cares about is basketball and banging.

Suddenly, the pot slips from my hands, and a puff of pink smoke descends into a sparkly trail amongst shattered glass. We stand there, frozen, with our mouths wide and eyes wider, watching it unravel in slow motion.

Nice move, karma.

I don't know whether to laugh or cry. Mortified, I cover my face with my hands, hoping that when I return to reality, the spectacle was all in my imagination.

It wasn't.

After the realisation hits that I'm chief of clean-up duty, I sink to the floor, gathering the larger, broken shards.

"I'll deal with this," Lauren says, kneeling beside me. She's already armed with a dustpan and brush, and I hope to god she doesn't hold me fully accountable for my clumsiness. I should have accepted Ryan's help from the start. "Can you see to that gentleman over there, Sophia?"

She cocks her head to the side, and I can tell by the tone of her voice she's pissed. I follow her direction to a man with his back turned, browsing the eye care display.

"Sure," I say. I drop the shards into the dustpan, then turn to face Ryan. "I'll catch up with you later."

Flustered and rosy cheeked, I stand and dust myself off, leaving a trail of shimmery pink powder over the front of my black sundress.

Fantastic.

After taking a breath to centre myself, I clear my throat, ignore the stain, and approach the customer, hoping he won't notice.

"Can I help you, Sir?"

Heat turns my cheeks magenta as soon as he spins around and my gaze locks with the familiar glistening hazel-green hue.

"You."

Him.

"Hi."

Danny's eyebrows curve, and a slow smile spreads across his face when his gaze falls to the smudged handprints on my dress.

"You work here?"

I wonder what gave that away? "No, I don't. This is how I like to spend my weekends. Hungover, and pretending to be someone I'm not. Excuse me, I need to wash my hands."

When I return, Danny is the last customer standing. How typical that the first quiet moment we've had all day at Ivy Rose is when the worst possible person is in here. Especially as the remnants of the stain is staring him in the face. I know he'll never take me seriously.

"Sorry about that. How can I help?"

"I met someone last night."

"I don't need your life story."

"She was perfectly pleasant, albeit a little rude."

"Seriously?" Who *actually* uses 'albeit' in a sentence?

"She kept implying that I was old."

"She was onto something."

"You think so?"

I cock an eyebrow and size him up. Still hot. Still an asshole.

"So anyway, I figured what better way to reverse the ageing process than to load up my bathroom with a bunch of fancy creams. Or something."

"I'm good, but I'm not a magician." I shoulder past him to the till in an attempt to create a barrier between us.

"Ego much?"

"My ego is a perfectly normal size, thank you." I fold my arms across my chest, and remind myself of that beautiful little word, patience. "Do you need something or not? I have real customers waiting."

"Where?"

I follow his gaze around the empty shop.

Bravo again, karma.

"I'm serious. I need some cream or something...for my fine lines."

"Your fine lines?" I scoff. "Did you read that in GQ, or something?"

"No. Men's Health."

There is no doubt in my mind that this guy is still most definitely an asshole, but that shouldn't stop me from earning commission on what will most likely be an easy sell. From the look—and the smell of him—he likes nice things, and I'm sure as hell going to try my best to bleed his credit card dry. I cock my head towards a vacant beauty counter.

"Have a seat."

He complies as I navigate the store, filling a basket with tester pots whilst still contending with my raging hangover. Every now and then, I sneak a glance in his direction, and in my territory, he looks completely out of his comfort zone. To my surprise, Mr Cocky is actually starting to resemble a human being.

Awhile later, I take a seat beside him, and proceed to ask the relevant questions regarding his current skincare regimen, water intake, exercise and skin type.

"So, these are your three basic items. Moisturiser, retinol and serum. Are you allergic to nuts?"

"Nope. Are you?" he asks, with a glint in his eye.

I deadpan. I am neither amused, nor impressed.

"Luckily, no. Otherwise I would probably be dead."

As I explain the directions of each product, my curiosity steals a glance towards his hand, but there is no ring on his finger. Its absence completely throws me off my game, making me think that he's playing some obscure version of spot the difference.

I find myself repeating steps of the recommended regimen, and generally getting muddled with my advice. Once I finish stumbling over my words, I finally close the sale. "Give it six weeks, and make sure you use factor fifty. Any problems, come and see me."

"Thank you."

"You're welcome."

"I mean, not just for your help."

There it is, the reason for the missing ring. I wouldn't be surprised if it's hiding in his pocket so he can fool me into being hit on.

"I wanted to say I'm sorry for last night. I acted like a complete dick. I wasn't in the best mood, and I took it out on you."

"It's okay, I'm used to being judged. Thank you, though." Keep it short and sweet.

"It's not okay. I should never have made assumptions on who you are because of the way you look. I was wrong, because you clearly have a lot going for you."

He leans towards me, and Summer, my reckless alter ego, welcomes him into my personal space. I don't completely hate it.

"I mean it."

I have to hand it to him; this guy is pretty good.

We share a fleeting moment of awkward silence, and I'm not quite sure how to feel when his gaze lands on my mouth. I bite my lip, and he suddenly straightens his posture.

"So, how do you know all this stuff?" he asks.

"It's my job, for starters. But mostly training and experience, like everyone else in this industry. Beauty and skincare has always been my passion. Ever since I was little, I used to raid my mum's makeup bag, and..." I trail off, pulling myself back from where he's leaning in, listening. "And I don't know why I'm telling my life story to a total stranger, especially when I just told you I didn't want yours."

Most people I know have zero interest in what I have to say. People don't listen; they wait for their turn to speak. So, I usually keep my thoughts to myself. It's a quiet existence, but I'd rather not waste my words on someone who doesn't care.

"For what it's worth, I find you interesting."

"Thanks," I say, quietly. For whatever reason, I find it difficult to accept compliments when they aren't aimed at my appearance. Maybe it has something to do with a lack of attention when I was young. Ever since I can remember, I have always been praised for my looks, but never anything else. I've never been super smart or talented, I don't know how to play an instrument or knit or play golf. I was always that kid in the background, never really excelling at anything but what was only skin deep. My looks are the only reason people want to get to know me. On that awkward note, I change the subject. "Anyway, I'm sure I couldn't do whatever it is you do, assuming you have a job outside of music?"

"I'm a wealth management advisor."

"That explains a lot."

"About?"

"You."

Danny's brows knit together. He pauses, giving me scope to continue.

"Pushy, over-confident corporate big shot. Used to getting what he wants, and won't stop until he has it. Borderline obsessed with money and power, most probably a narcissist."

He asked for it. I'm surprised when a wide grin spreads across his face, along with two adorable dimples. He folds his arms. "Now who's making assumptions based on stereotypes?"

Touchez.

"It's not an insult. I can barely manage my own money, let alone other peoples." It's true, I spend half my life in an overdraft.

"It's challenging at times, but the majority of my clientele are widowed women whose husbands were responsible for the cash flow." He leans back and smiles.

"How...retro."

"That's how it was back then. All they need is some guidance, and a sympathetic ear. I treasure my coffee dates with Doris."

I smile at the image of him sipping frothy cappuccinos with cute old ladies.

"So, that guy earlier, him of the shattered glassware, is he your boyfriend?"

How predictable. I shoot him an unbelieving glance. "Definitely not. I mean, we used to go out. We're friends."

"Oh, I thought he'd be your type. I saw you two dancing last night; you seemed pretty close."

I don't know whether to be flattered or creeped out. Especially since every memory I have of the night before is filled with hostility.

"I prefer men over boys," I say, casually.

His eyes fall to my lips for a moment too long, and I wonder if I missed something.

"How about you?"

My words sit there for a moment before he answers.

"Do I prefer men?"

"I mean, are you married?"

There is no subtle way to ask about the missing ring without being forward. He pauses, and his sombre expression from the night before returns for a millisecond.

"I was."

"But last night you were wearing—" I backtrack, based on the assumption that he doesn't want to elaborate, and I leave it at that. I don't want to pry. Once I ring up his bill and fill a paper bag with his purchase, I hand him the receipt.

"I thought you said your name was Summer?" he says, examining the tiny square of paper. I know exactly what he's looking at on the receipt:

You were served by: SOPHIA

One hundred percent busted.

"I did."

"It says Sophia right here."

There's no point in lying now.

"Well now you know my real name, you can think of it as a gift with purchase." My words from the night before resurface in my mind. "I'll tell you the story sometime, if I ever see you again."

This time, I secretly hope I will.

Chapter Four

♥

AFTER WORK, I HEAD to The Ethical Coffee Co, Brighton's latest hipster hangout, for a much-needed caffeine fix. Rich, roasted coffee grounds and baked goods perfume the air as I spot Stefan sitting by the window looking every inch the sophisticated style icon that he is. He looks right at home here, with his mass of long curls flipped to one side, slouchy mauve tee, and ripped denim shorts.

"I've ordered you a coconut caramel iced coffee," he says, not looking up from the book he's reading.

"My hero," I say, pulling up a chair.

He turns a page and finishes what he's reading before he closes the book and lays it on the table as I savour the rich, creamy sweetness of my first sip. "So, how was your day?"

"Eventful. Remember that guy from last night?"

"Is he balls deep in your DMs yet?"

I almost spit out my drink. "Not quite. He came into my work, and now he knows my real name, so I guess it's only a matter of time before he finds my socials."

"Is that really so bad? He seemed nice."

"With a side of asshole."

He shoots me a pointed look. Stefan always likes to give people the benefit of the doubt, and he's right of course. Danny had shown that he could be a decent human being, and that perhaps there could be more to him than I initially thought.

"Nice isn't my brand, Stefan."

"Well, maybe it should be."

I navigate the Spotify app, and slide the phone across the table.

"That's his band."

Stefan grabs the phone, and after a brief inspection followed by tapping, typing, pausing, scrolling, swiping, and more tapping, a suspiciously proud smile spreads across his face. "Daniel Pearce."

"How did you...?"

"Twitter. You can thank me later."

On the outside, Stefan is every hipster Viking-lover's dream, but on the inside, he's that secretly nerdy kid you see in movies. I should start calling him Joe Goldberg.

He shows me the phone screen, which displays Danny's bio and a photo that must have been taken ten years ago.

Catfishing prick.

Before handing it back, he hits the follow button.

"Stefan!" My voice raises an octave as I snatch the phone from his hand. "I can't believe you just did that."

"You can't unfollow him now, because he'll know, and you'll look like a stalker."

And he'll be calling *me* Joe Goldberg.

"You're such an ass."

"Hee-haw."

"Very funny," I deadpan. "Somehow, I feel like you want his sausage more than I do."

He cocks an eyebrow.

"Well you're spoken for, so whatever weird crush you have on Danny, don't," I say. God, I really do sound like a possessive stalker.

My phone chimes with a text, and the sound triggers a shot of anxiety through my chest. The tiniest part of me is hoping for a follow back from Danny, but when I check the screen, it isn't him.

Alex: Are we still on for later?

I try to downplay my frustration and send a quick reply to confirm, but I know I can't hide anything from Stefan. "It's so much easier to have disposable dick, am I right?" I say, in an attempt to offset the disappointment.

"You won't get anywhere with that throwaway mind-set, look what it has done to our planet," he says, dramatically. "Maybe it's time you invested in a reusable dick."

"That's what rechargeable dildos are for," I say.

We laugh and I down the rest of my coffee, trying to ignore the little voice in my head that's telling me Stefan's probably right.

Three hours later, after a shower and a fresh face of makeup, I knock on the door to Alex's apartment. Luke answers.

"Hey, Phi. Alex is taking a shower. Come in."

"Mmm, something smells good," I say, following him into the lounge.

"Can I get you something to drink?"

"Water's fine," I say, taking a seat on the couch.

"Seriously? You have not one, but *two* mixologists at your disposal."

"I'm good. Really. I drank far too much last night."

My hangover had worn off with my shower, but I know I can't go through that for the second night in a row. It's much safer to stick to good old-fashioned H2O, at least until after I've eaten something. After a rummage in the kitchen, Luke hands me a large glass of water and sits down on the adjacent couch.

"So, what are you doing tonight?" I ask.

"I have a date," he says, with a wide grin.

"Taking someone out on Tinder does *not* qualify as a date. Everybody knows what it's there for."

"Call it what you want, but it's a date to me."

"Anyone I might know?"

Luke swipes and taps his phone, then hands it to me.

"She's cute," I say, swiping through photos of the same girl I've seen a thousand times before. Luke doesn't have a type per se, but he does seem to have a penchant for petite, doe-eyed brunettes. After he lights some candles and sets the table, Alex emerges freshly showered, with a strategically placed towel hung around his waist. He looks every inch the model that he is.

Steam practically emanates off him, and tiny droplets glisten on his tanned, muscular chest. He smells like soap, and his damp, messy hair looks effortlessly perfect. Aesthetically, he has all the makings of a romance novel hero, but I feel nothing above the waist.

"I'll be out in a minute, babe. Dinner's almost ready," Alex says, flashing a bright white smile before disappearing again.

Once Luke leaves for his date, Alex and I take a seat at the small dining table by the open bay window. Outside, the sound of families making the most of the balmy summer evenings spark nostalgia and warm the cockles of my cold, dead heart, and I can't tear my eyes away from the incredible moonlit view of the ocean.

"This is amazing," I say, polishing off my meal of chicken parmigiana, garlic bread and a mixed salad. "Who knew you could navigate a kitchen so well?"

"That hurts. No dessert for you," Alex says, pouting.

"I didn't want it anyway."

"You don't know what it is yet."

Standing, I cock a brow, and clear the plates. "I'm sure I can take a guess."

Is it really so bad that all I want to do is fuck him and get the hell out of here?

Alex takes the plates out of my hands and sets them down on the table. "The washing up can wait," he says, stealing a kiss.

A soft groan escapes his mouth, and heat emanates from him as he gently grasps my hair. Hot, hungry lips trail along my neck and collarbone, and I arch my body in response, mainly for his benefit, as his fingers find the hem of my top.

Slowly, he traces a line up my spine, and as he does, I find myself picturing Danny. His face, the width of his palms spanning the small of my back, and the thought of him instantly spreads heat between my legs. Fuck.

"No bra?" Alex asks, pulling me back into the present.

"No need," I say, and follow him to the bedroom.

Awhile later, I am spent, satisfied and ready to leave. Outside of sex, we have next to nothing in common, and the dinner Alex made that served as foreplay is over. There's no reason for me to stay.

"What's for dessert?" I ask, pulling the sheets over in an attempt at modesty now that the heat between us has dissipated.

"That was dessert."

"Disappointing," I smirk.

Alex climbs off the bed and grabs a box of tissues. After wiping himself down, he hands me the box and leaves the room to discard the condom while I clean myself up.

"Shall we get some ice cream on the pier?" he calls.

"I'm good, thanks."

I would rather go without. Ninety-nine flake ice creams and summer evening walks along the pier are forever etched in fond childhood memories, and encroaching on them with someone I barely even like would taint them.

Once my breathing slows, I swing my legs around and jump off the bed, instantly wishing I hadn't.

Sharp pain tears through my heel, and reflexes send me yelping and hopping backwards. Perching on the edge of the bed, I inspect the tender point, then lean down to the floor and pick up the offending implement—a hot pink acrylic nail which doesn't belong to me. I desperately hope I don't catch something from it.

After I'm dressed and ready to leave, I take the nail into the kitchen to discard. Flipping the lid of the bin open, I toss in the plastic shard, and it ricochets off a chicken parmigiana ready meal packet. I knew it was too good to be true. Alex isn't the type of boy to make anything from scratch. But the fact that he didn't try to hide the evidence makes me realise that his opinion of me is even less than my own. This is the actual—and the proverbial—nail in the coffin. He's sloppy, and I'm done.

From behind, Alex snakes his arms around my waist. I jolt, quickly closing the bin, and turn around.

"Everything okay?" he asks.

"Actually, I'm not feeling too good." The people pleaser in me would still rather lie than risk bruising his ego.

"You know ice cream is the answer to everything."

When he tries to embrace me, I tense, instinctively rubbing my temples. The thought of being anywhere near him makes me nauseous.

"All that cheese has given me a headache. I think I'm going to go home." Like a dodgeball champion, I body-swerve, and make a beeline for my things.

"We have painkillers somewhere."

"It's okay, really. I just need some rest." I force a smile as I open the front door.

"Thanks for dinner."

He goes in for a kiss, but I step back into the communal hallway before it has a chance to land, and practically fly down the stairs. Outside, relief sweeps over me. On my cycle home, I make a pact with myself. No more notches, no more bedposts. At least not for a while.

When I arrive at the sage green door of the townhouse I call home, I head inside and lean my bike against the wall in the hallway, grateful that the promise of sleep finally beckons.

Through the darkness, I bypass the open plan lounge-diner into the kitchen to make a cup of tea. On the way out, I'm startled with the image of a sleeping Ryan sprawled across the tiny sofa, his long legs dangling off the edge.

Holding my breath, I creep across the parquet floor, being careful not to wake him, and pray that the old floorboards stay silent. His phone chimes, and I jolt, splashing burning hot liquid onto my top.

"Shit," I curse under my breath, and he stirs. When I look back at him, he's bolt upright with wide eyes, his forehead damp with sweat.

"Phi?" His features instantly soften. He lets out a long breath, and melts back into the couch. "Did you just get home?"

I nod, then blow on my drink, taking a tiny sip. It burns my tongue, but it's the only way I can drink it.

"Sorry, I didn't realise you were here." I pause. "Why *are* you here?"

He sighs, and buries his head in his hands. "Chrissy ended it."

"Oh no, what happened?" I feign surprise. This isn't the first time they've broken up, and it won't be the last. I've lost count of the times I've helped mend his broken heart, but it's never easy to see him upset.

"I fucked up. Again."

I take a seat next to him. "So, she threw you out, huh?"

His gaze falls to the floor. "April and I. We...we slept together again."

Why am I not surprised? "Fucking hell, Ry. I mean this in the nicest possible way, but you need to learn how to keep your dick in your pants."

"It was just once," Ryan says, raising his hands in defence.

I don't back off. Not for a moment. "Look, you know how I feel about Chrissy. But you also know how I feel about cheating. If she doesn't make you happy, then it's best you go your separate ways."

Marie Kondo that bitch out of your life once and for all.

I realise how insensitive I sound, but it's been a long day, I'm exhausted, and the last thing I want to be doing is dishing out relationship advice, especially as I'm hardly an expert in the field.

"Thanks, Phi," he says, meeting my gaze. "You always have my back."

"What are friends for?"

I try to remember a time when our roles were switched, but I fail to think of one.

"I need to go to bed," I say, hopping off the sofa. "You going to be okay?"

He nods, and a kind, reassuring smile spreads across my face.

"I'll see you tomorrow." Mug in hand, I start towards the staircase.

"Phi? Can I ask one teeny-tiny favour?"

I pause, waiting for him to carry on.

"Can I stay in your bed? This sofa isn't doing my back any favours."

Turning, I size up his 6-foot-something frame, and then the modest two-seater couch. I roll my eyes. Where's the harm in letting him stay with me? Ryan is one of the few people I trust, and I don't want to be responsible for a pro basketball player's back injury.

"Fine. But don't for one second think about touching me. I don't even want to hear you breathe. And I want fresh juice in the morning."

"How kind of you," he says, half joking.

For once in my life I want to be terrifying, but I know the reality. Being small has its perks, and being taken seriously isn't one of them.

Once we're upstairs and under the covers, I switch off the light, close my eyes and try to tune out the sound of Ryan's annoyingly loud breathing as I clutch the duvet to my chest. After a failed attempt to sync our breaths, my hopes of tricking my body into thinking I'm alone diminishes, and the more I try to ignore him, the louder the noise becomes.

I lose track of the time I spend tossing, turning, and willing myself to sleep. I'm not used to sharing a bed, and I don't like it one bit.

"Phi? Are you awake?" Ryan's deep, silky voice cuts through the silence as he shifts his weight to face me.

"Mmhmm," I hum. My eyes are still closed.

"Do you ever think about us?"

"It was a long time ago."

"That's not an answer."

"Sometimes," I muse, and a smile crosses my lips. "But then I remember that time you cheated on me with your French exchange student and broke my heart. Goodnight, Ryan."

After my outburst, he doesn't dare move or breathe, and I sleep soundly the entire night.

Chapter Five

♥

WHEN I EMERGE IN my gym clothes the following morning, a jug of fresh green juice and three tall glasses lay on the kitchen counter. Stefan's husband, James, has clearly beaten Ryan to his late-night promise.

"Mate, what are you wearing?" Ryan asks, stifling a laugh.

James' blue floral kimono barely covers his modesty, but it's his loungewear staple, and he wears it well.

"Good morning, you two," James says, throwing a pointed look in Ryan's direction over round-rimmed glasses. "And where did *you* sleep last night?"

"Chill, Miss Marple."

"That's Jessica Fletcher to you, Sir."

"It's not my fault your couch is from the children's section of IKEA," Ryan says. "I slept in Phi's bed to save my back."

James cocks an eyebrow, then divides the juice between each glass, and hands one to Ryan, then me.

"I think I'll give it a miss, man," Ryan says, curling his lip.

"Oh, go on. It's kale, cucumber, celery, lemon and ginger. I promise your body will thank you."

"Coach makes us drink beet juice before a game. That's enough for me." Ryan checks his watch. "I should get home, get some things—if Chrissy hasn't changed the locks. What are you guys doing today?"

"I'm flying this afternoon." James says.

"I'm meeting April at the gym," I say, gesturing to my black crop top and high waist leggings ensemble. I actually have a day off on a Sunday for once."

"Best not say anything about this little rendezvous, then," James says, peering over his glasses again. He turns to Ryan. "And as for you, my friend. I hope for your sake that Chrissy isn't there. But if she is, send her my regards."

The men bro-hug goodbye, then Ryan turns to me, circles an arm around my waist, and plants a kiss on my cheek.

"Thank you, again, for being such a great friend," he says.

"Anytime."

He gives me one last smile before he picks up his things and leaves.

With a new found smugness as a direct result of Ryan's appreciation, I slide up onto the kitchen counter and savour my drink, letting the cold, green goodness coat my throat. Nothing can touch me. I am wonder woman.

I pull out my phone and check it, and my stomach does a victory backflip when I see the one notification I have secretly been hoping for.

Danny Pearce followed you back!

Gulp.

Since the follow-back this morning, I've received exactly one message thanking me for my skincare guidance yesterday. I'm trying not to make something out of nothing, because he's probably being polite, but at the same time, I can't contain the smile plastered across my face.

"Oh, come on. I know a look when I see it," April says.

Nothing gets past her. She's been bugging me since I turned up. Said I was glowing, or some shit like that. Girl, that's just the green juice I had this morning. And Danny. Definitely maybe Danny.

"I told you, I saw Alex last night."

I conveniently miss out the part where I ended things in my head.

"No, that's not it."

I check my form mid-squat while my friend stares me down in the mirror.

My rest time between sets are spent in fake conversations in my mind with Danny, and I can't very well divulge that information to my wing-woman.

"Oh my God. It's that guy from the other night," April says.

"What guy? No, it isn't," I say, springing to my defence a little too quickly.

Busted.

But she doesn't hear me. Her gaze is fixed towards the edge of the room.

April huffs and lightly nudges me, nearly knocking me backwards, and she points towards the water cooler. "That's him, right?"

Kitted out in full branded tennis whites, Danny fills up a bottle from the machine. From that angle, outfit number three isn't looking so bad.

This has to be a record number of coincidences. Either that, or he's stalking me. God help him if it's the latter.

I slam the barbell down on the rack and grab my water bottle, then I make my way over to him and clear my throat. He turns to meet my death stare.

"What are you doing here?" I ask.

He makes a meal out of sizing me up, making no effort to hide the fact that he's staring. Starting from my trainers, he follows the curve of my legs, stopping for a full second when he reaches my thighs. He pauses to take a breath, while I hold mine, as his honey-green gaze brushes over my bare midriff, chest, and lingers on my neck before locking eyes with mine. My stomach flips.

"The same thing you are," he says, calm, collected and completely infuriating.

"You don't intimidate me."

In an attempt to showcase my best defensive stance, I fold my arms across my chest, and narrow my eyes. In reality, I wouldn't fare well in the apocalypse, but right now in my head, I'm fucking Wonder Woman.

He smirks, and it infuriates me. "Oh, really?"

Again, I have entered the world's longest staring contest, but I refuse to back down. I can think of worse things to focus on. Mr Cocky has obviously made a comeback, but this time, there is a soft playfulness to his demeanour.

I won't lie, I'm a little turned on.

The longer I spend locked in that hazel-green gaze, the more dangerous this game is becoming. After a few moments, he rolls his eyes and gives in, and I'm almost disappointed that it doesn't last longer.

Almost.

"I play tennis here every Sunday. I have since I was five. So, no I'm not following you. If that's what you were thinking."

I feel ridiculous at how conceited I seem, even more so because at some point, I forgot to breathe. Heat spreads across my cheeks, and my lungs deflate. If I cared, I might wish for the ground to swallow me, but I don't.

"Are you following *me*?" he asks, quirking a brow.

"Why would I do that?"

"Oh, I don't know. Because girls love musicians, right?"

"Not all girls."

While taking a swig of his drink, he sizes me up again, then he notices the bottle I'm holding. The bottle which is almost full to the brim. A rookie mistake on my part.

"Well, you weren't just coming over to fill that up."

In my mind's eye, I pour the entire bottle of water over his head, and wipe that incessant smirk off his face, but in reality, I decide it would probably be a dick move. Either way, the mental image is fun, and I've already decided I'm having the last word.

I shoulder past him, top up my water with the smallest bit of liquid, and mutter under my breath. "Such a smartass."

"I'm sorry, what's that?" He pushes his ear forward with the tip of his finger. "My hearing isn't what it used to be."

I'm not sure why I'm still standing here, but I'm not quite ready to admit out loud that I want to talk to him. He intrigues me, and for an incredibly long time I've felt nothing. But it scares me to think that there's a reason why this guy keeps being dangled in front of me. Stefan and his belief in fate must be messing with my head.

I shake the thought away.

But even so, I struggle to think of anything to say, let alone anything remotely witty. I take a long pull of the liquid. Ignorance is bliss.

"Nice to see you again, Danny. Goodbye."

Before I turn to leave, my gaze falls to his hand. Still no ring. Maybe it's tucked away safely in his gym bag, or maybe I imagined it the first night we met. Still, something doesn't quite add up. For some unknown reason, I have every urge to prize him open. But first, I need to trust the process. I need some sort of game plan.

"What was that about?" April asks, once I return.

"Oh, nothing. Has he gone?"

April nods, and I take a seat on the bench, shifting my gaze towards the water machine. "I think you left him pretty speechless."

"That's the plan," I say, resuming my position in the squat rack. "Anyway...I have a Ryan-shaped bone to pick with you."

A tiny laugh escapes from the redhead's mouth. "I'm not proud of it. But that bone was delicious."

Gross.

"I can't believe you didn't tell me," I say, setting the barbell on the rack. I give April a playful nudge with my elbow. "Do you like him?"

April bites her lip, hesitating. "It breaks all kinds of girl codes."

"If you're referring to *our* girl code, you are more than welcome to him. I just want you to be careful," I say.

"Be careful about what?" Stefan asks, creeping up behind us.

Sweat drips from his brow, his usual afterglow from teaching a HIIT class, and a purple headband barely contains his mass of curls. I am in awe at how he still manages to look pristine.

"Ryan," I say.

"The same Ryan who slept in your bed last night?" Stefan says.

"What are you talking about?" April asks.

"He stayed over last night." Stefan says.

"Are you kidding?" April asks.

"Nothing happened," I say.

"If nothing happened, why did you hide it from me? You can't keep your hands to yourself, can you?" April says.

"I didn't hide it from you. I just didn't tell you because it's a non-issue."

"Right. I'm welcome to him now because you fucked him last night. That's why you seem so happy this morning."

Storm April grabs her keys and water bottle, and makes a beeline towards the exit.

"April, that's not even," I shout.

In haste, I grab my belongings, then rush to follow her out of the exit, through the coffee shop, past the stairs leading to the racket sports and out of the sliding doors by the reception.

"April, can you stop? Please."

An elderly couple armed with tennis rackets walk by and watch the exchange with open mouths. I struggle to keep up as April power walks to her car, almost pulling the handle off its hinges when she opens the door.

"Can we talk about this?" I ask, breathless.

"I can't believe you would bare faced lie to me like that. I —" April leaves the rest of the sentence hanging in the air as she climbs in and turns on the engine. "Stefan can take you home."

She slams the door closed, and within moments, she's gone.

Exasperated and defeated, I start towards the entrance of the building, where Danny stands sporting the most infuriating Cheshire cat smile. He's the last person I want to see.

"Can I get you some popcorn? Or a camera, perhaps?" I ask, shouldering past him.

"Actually, I thought you could use a ride."

I pause, exhale, and turn to face him.

"That was your lift, right?"

"I'm not in the mood for games."

He raises his hands in defence. "I'm not playing one, I swear."

"Then why are you being nice to me?"

"Because despite your opinion of me, I'm a nice guy. And honestly, I'm not buying into this persona you have going on. I know a defence mechanism when I see one."

His final sentence strikes a nerve, and it's enough to almost reduce me to tears, but I blink them back. I hate how I'm seemingly so transparent to him, when I can usually fool everybody, even my parents. All I know is that I don't deserve his kindness right now, but I'm too tired to argue.

"I'm sorry. You're right."

"It's cool, I don't offend very easily. But I wouldn't mind hearing that last part again."

I manage a small smile. "Don't push it."

"I'm sorry, I didn't hear you," he says, flashing those two perfect dimples.

"I said you're right. And I'd love a ride home, just don't kidnap me, okay?"

He laughs. "You're too much trouble," he says, sobering when his eyes land on my face.

I curse my heart for its involuntary backflip, telling myself to get a grip, it's only a ride home.

He leads the way through the car park, to flashing headlights of a grey metallic sports car.

"Of *course* this is what you drive," I say, attempting to sound unimpressed.

"What is that supposed to mean?"

"Nothing. All I'm saying is there's a certain type of person who drives an Audi."

He feigns a shocked expression.

Approaching the passenger side, I open the door and pick up a woven belt from the quilted honeycomb seat before sliding in. The scent of new car chemicals and leather fill my nostrils as he climbs into the driver's side and slides a pair of aviator sunglasses onto his face.

"You can just toss that in the back," he says, referring to the length of material in my hand. I assume it must belong to a dog.

I throw it on the seat behind me and send a quick text to Stefan to let him know where I am, and tell him not to worry. We fasten our seatbelts, the engine roars to life, and we drive out of the compound.

Once we're on the road, I give him the address to my parents' house. Sinking into the stitched leather seat, my tummy rumbles, and I'm grateful for my parents' weekly invitations to Sunday lunch. That, and their impressively wide snack selection. Today will also be the first time I'll see my sister since she left rehab.

Memories of the past year resurface, and my stomach flips thinking about the last time I saw Kiki in her own environment.

"E.S.T.P," he says, catching me off guard.

I'm not sure if I hear him right, but if I did, I haven't a clue what he's talking about.

"What's that?"

"My personality type. It means; extroverted, sensing, thinking, perceiving."

"I mean, I was going to say asshole. But okay, Maverick," I say, teasing his choice of eyewear.

"May also be wrongly perceived as cocky, smartass narcissists," he says, treating me to an eyeful of those dimples.

"So, what's mine?"

"I'm still trying to figure you out."

My eyes meet my reflection, but even through those mirrored shades, I can feel the intensity of his gaze. It's only for a moment—and probably a little longer than deemed safe—but it's enough to feel the heat rise through my body and spread across my cheeks. After a beat, he turns his attention back to the road. "So why do you hate Audi drivers so much?"

"I've been knocked off my bike...three times," I say. He glances towards me with raised eyebrows. "Two of the cars responsible were Audis."

"You have every right to be mad at us then," he says.

"Anyway, I don't *hate* the people who drive them. But they all seem to have a certain...attitude. A superiority complex. Plus, they're not exactly the car that springs to mind when I think "climate-friendly.""

"Oh, you're one of those eco warriors. Now it makes sense."

"So what? I care about the planet, as everybody should. I was always taught to leave things how I found them. The same applies to all aspects of life." I find myself getting heated. I might not go around hugging trees, but that doesn't mean I'm in favour of cutting them down. Quite the opposite in fact.

"Is that why you work at Ivy Rose? Their ethos is really impressive."

"It is. I would never want to work for some big shot CEO who thinks it's okay to test on animals and use unsustainable materials. I try to do my bit for humanity. The pay could be better, but—"

"You stay true to yourself. I like that."

His smile quickens my pulse. Am I staying true to myself? It was only last night that I made a vow not to sleep around, and now I'm in some guy's car, secretly hoping for something to happen. I'm the world's biggest fraud.

"What else?" he asks, fishing for more information while I adjust the volume dial to an even number.

"I have a thing about odd numbers," I say, ironically.

"They turn you on?"

"They freak me out. If the dial isn't even, I get it in my head that something bad will happen."

I feel ridiculous for saying it out loud.

"That's...different."

"We all have our little quirks. What's yours?"

"I'm really into giving lifts to strangers. I like to show off my driving skills."

"I'm impressed," I say, with more than a hint of sarcasm.

"Not yet. But you will be."

He glances at me and smiles. In actual fact, I *am* impressed, and pleasantly amused. To avoid any incoming awkwardness, I tear my gaze away and turn up the dial to its original volume.

"I love this song," I say, mouthing the words to Monty James' new release. Danny cranks up the volume a couple more times, making a point to keep it even, and sings along while his fingers drum the steering wheel. His pitch and tone proves that he's no Frank Sinatra, but his singing voice is far from terrible.

"Did you hear Monty's playing a secret gig at Quiet Waters next weekend?" he says.

"No way, are you kidding? We tried to get tickets for his last gig, but it sold out so quick. It was impossible."

I swipe across my phone screen and frantically type, "Monty James Quiet Waters," into the search bar. After a few moments of tapping, I find what I'm looking for.

"Sold out," I say, throwing my phone into my lap.

"It was worth a try."

Danny asks about my family, and without going into too much detail, I mention that my parents are still together and that my sister, Kiki, is recovering from an illness. Once again, he seems genuinely interested in what I have to say. Either that, or he has great acting skills. Once I'm finished, he shares his parents' expectations of him to be the next Clapton or Chopin.

"When I was little, they threw my brother and I into guitar and piano lessons, and, luckily for them, I instantly fell in love with music. My brother? Not so much. We were in secondary school when we formed The Wandering Dragons. My brother was the singer before he gave it all up and Ollie joined."

"You wanted to impress all the teenyboppers?"

"We wanted to be the next Oasis," he laughs. "But we always knew it wasn't a viable career choice. Music was and always will be my passion, but it won't ever be a steady form of income.

"After I graduated Uni, I launched my business in wealth management. It works for me. I still get to do what I love, and what I like."

"That's kind of beautiful," I say, half-joking, half-sad.

In a way, I feel sorry for him. Sorry that he had to grow up with what seems like pushy parents, and I'm grateful that my own have always been beyond supportive of my own life choices.

"I'm sorry for the way I behaved at the gym. It was childish," I say.

Apologies have never been my strong point, but I owe it to him to at least try.

"Like I said, I don't offend easily. For what it's worth, I'm sorry, too. I have a habit of digging myself a hole when I'm intimidated by a beautiful woman."

My mouth falls open, and I struggle to speak. I don't know whether to thank him, or jump out of the moving vehicle. Luckily, I don't have to make that decision. When his cheeks turn a pale shade of pink, and his laugh breaks the silence, I follow suit. It's refreshing to know that I'm not the only one who noticed how cringe-worthy those words sounded.

"I'm sorry, I didn't mean for that to sound so cheesy. I'm not a melt. Promise."

"You almost gave me the ick," I say, still laughing.

"I thought I could win you over with my charm."

"You'll need to work harder than that."

"I intend to," he says, sobering.

His prospective intentions are intriguing to say the least, but it's probably best to change the subject, before Summer gets me into trouble.

"So, you have a dog?" I ask, assuming the reason for the belt in the backseat.

"No, that's my kink," he deadpans.

Oh.

"Oh."

When my gaze accidentally lands on Danny's crotch, I instantly look away, but my cheeks flush beet red.

"I'm joking. You're not the only sarcastic person in this car."

"There's someone else in here?" I ask, lowering my voice. He shoots me a sardonic smile.

Relief sweeps over me. But I'm curious to know where that conversation would have led had he been serious.

"Hey, I'm not here to judge," I say, raising my hands in defence. "If that's what you're into, own it."

"Actually, I can't say I've ever tried it. Have you?"

Silence sucks all the air out of my lungs and my pulse quickens as I prepare an answer in my head. I do a pretty good job of talking the talk, but I've never felt the need to be honest and open with a potential conquest before. This is different. *Danny*'s different. I can feel it.

I shake my head.

"No, I've never trusted anyone enough to be vulnerable like that. The thought of letting go of myself completely..."

...it scares me.

I can't bring myself to finish the sentence, and he doesn't push me to continue. How can I admit to an almost-stranger that I'm scared to be vulnerable? That I've made it twenty-six years living by my own rules, dancing to the beat of my own drum, putting up walls that aren't made to be knocked down. If I can live like that, I'll always be in control.

We travel the rest of the journey in silence, and when he pulls up outside my parents' detached house, a part of me wishes that he would drive around the block a few more times, enough for me to bask in the safe and comfortable silence, with nothing but the quiet hum of the engine and him for company. But if Stefan's so-called fate would have it, we'll run into each other again.

"I hope your sister is okay," Danny says, with a kind and genuine smile.

"Thank you."

I return the gesture as my palm hovers over the door handle. Usually, I can't get away from men fast enough, but with him, I'm hesitant to leave. He definitely isn't the monster I had initially perceived him to be, and part of me wants to find out all there is to know about Danny Pearce.

Walking up my parents' driveway, I can still hear the hum of the engine behind me. A moment later, Danny calls out the window.

"Her name is Penny."

I turn around and meet his gaze. "Who?"

"My dog. I'm sure she'd love to meet you one day."

A wide, sexy smile spreads across his face, giving those perfect dimples a final shot of glory before the engine roars, and he gives one final Maverick salute goodbye.

Chapter Six

❤

MY SENSES ARE INSTANTLY comforted by the smell of roast chicken the moment I enter my parent's house. I follow the warming scent through to the kitchen and slide open the patio doors leading to the garden where my parents tend to their vegetable patch, and take a wild guess that it's where I'll find them.

I'm the image of my mother, Alessandra. We both have the same slim, petite frame, dark brown eyes and fiery nature. My mother is a force to be reckoned with. She commands every room she walks into, but we haven't always got along. I call her Don DeLuca, because she is fiercely protective of her family, and she's never afraid to put people in their place. But underneath her tough exterior, she's sweet, and loving, and the best mother a child could ask for.

My dad, Costanzo, looks like he could be an extra in a mafia movie. His almost black hair is peppered with flecks of white, that classic older Italian gentleman look, and he owes his year-round tan to working overtime in his pristine garden; his pride and joy. He's a man of few words, but he's gentle and hardworking, and I'm pretty sure he doesn't mind being bossed around by a beautiful woman eighteen years his junior. He likes to live the quiet life, but my mum never lets him get too comfortable.

Once my parents notice my arrival, Mum slips off her gardening gloves, tucks a loose strand of hair behind her ear and pulls me into the jasmine scented safety of her embrace.

"You've lost weight," she says, holding me at arm's length.

"Mum, can you not—" I know she means well, but I don't take it as a compliment. Throwaway comments like that are partly responsible for my sister's illness.

Mum turns around and calls to my dad, "For goodness sake, Costanzo. Come and say hello to your daughter."

If there's one thing she seems to love as much as Kiki and I, it's giving my poor dad a hard time.

"You know ma, one day that's going to get you into trouble."

"He knows I'm messing with him," she says, with a wide grin. "Shh…he's coming."

Dad removes his gardening gloves, and, just as my mother had, pulls me into a brief, stiff hug.

"Where's Kiki?" I ask.

"She's having her lunch," mum says.

My expression falls.

Kiki had been a dancer since she could walk. Three years ago, she started getting serious about her training. None of the family knew it at the time, but her teacher had suggested she lose weight to help her perform better. She hid her tiny frame under oversized jumpers, and used homework deadlines as an excuse to eat her meals in her bedroom, which she would take to school the following day and discard on the grounds. Her work suffered, as did her dancing, and eventually, she became too weak to walk. Before anybody realised what was happening, it was too late, and she was hospitalised with anorexia nervosa.

"She isn't eating with us?"

"She isn't ready, sweetheart."

"Is it really a good idea to let her eat on her own?" I say, lowering my voice.

My dad sighs.

"Have a little faith," he says. "If we don't trust her, this won't work. She needs her freedom back."

Faith has nothing to do with it.

When Kiki was a toddler, and I was in my mid-teens, I had already started to lose faith in my parents when I realised they weren't as wonderful and wholesome as I'd originally thought.

"She's thirteen. She's still a child. I'm sorry," I say, lowering my voice. "I know we all want what's best for her, but how do you know she's not hiding her food again?"

"We don't," mum says, rubbing my arm. "But like your father said...have a little faith."

Dad glances at his watch.

"Give her ten more minutes," he says, "then you can go up and see her."

"I'll put the kettle on," mum says, with a warm smile.

Ten minutes and a strong cup of tea later, I stand on the threshold of my sister's bedroom. The last time I saw her in her own room, sitting cross-legged on her own bed, is a memory I'd rather forget.

I choke back tears to memories of tantrums, grey skin, jutting bones and the scent of ammonia. The image of her now is a far cry from the shell of the girl she was half a year ago.

The past six months have been hard on everybody, and the only time I was able to see her was in a clinical setting at our weekly family therapy sessions.

I shake the thought away, plaster on a smile and make a choice to focus on the positives; the immense joy it brings me to see her finally wearing clothes that don't swamp her tiny frame, the subtle pinkness in her cheeks, and the half-eaten plate of food in front of her.

"Hey, Kiki Bear," I say, entering the room.

Kiki greets me with the widest grin I've seen in years. Although still seemingly fragile, she looks marginally healthier than she did a week ago. Tiny changes haven't gone unnoticed. Her skin is plumper, and her complexion a little brighter, although she's still pale. Setting the plate aside, Kiki jumps off the bed and into my arms.

"I've missed you," I say, breathing in the scent of her.

The baby powder-like smell—a side-effect of the disease that I've grown accustomed to—has finally been replaced by her natural scent. Kiki's hair hasn't fully grown back to the lush, thick mane she had before, but I know these things take time to regulate. Basking in the sight of her genuine smile, I hold her at arm's length. My heart is the happiest it's been in a long time when I notice the newfound sparkle in her eyes.

"You look so beautiful," I say.

Kiki smiles while blinking back tears, and we share a knowing look that claims silent victory to her illness. She's back home, and safe in my presence. I know it's against the treatment plan to talk about appearance, but I can't help myself. Seeing her now brings back the fondest memories of the first time I held her thirteen years ago. With her soft, round cheeks and huge brown saucers for eyes, I remember thinking that she was the most beautiful thing I had ever seen, and she still is.

"So, how was it?" I ask, after we make ourselves comfortable on the bed.

I try to ignore the half-eaten plate of food, but it proves difficult. The last thing I want to do is make a big deal out of it. I remember my dad's words.

If we don't trust her, this won't work.

Kiki casts her eyes down, and plays with a loose thread on her duvet.

"Good."

"Just good? You are such a teenager."

"I don't know what to say," she says, gingerly.

I know it will take time for Kiki's confidence to return, but it's heart breaking to witness the change in her personality.

"Did you make friends? What kinds of activities did you do? How was the f—"

I bite my tongue, hoping Kiki hadn't realised what I was about to say.

"The food? It's okay, we can talk about it. It was actually really good. It was healthy, and nutrient-rich, and they catered to my allergies. They didn't force us to eat, but we were supervised."

"I'm so proud of you, I know it can't have been easy," I say, placing my hand on top of hers.

I follow her gaze to the plate.

"There was so much to do. I think they must do that to keep our minds busy. We had a choice of group therapy or one-to-one sessions. We did art classes, crafts, yoga. There was one girl, she reminded me of you, actually. She taught me how to draw a perfect cat-eye. See."

Kiki closes her eyes and proceeds to show me her winged eyeliner.

"That's amazing—much better than mine."

She's beaming.

"And yoga? That's great. How did you find it? Did it help?"

Kiki nods.

"So, what are the next steps?"

"I'm still an outpatient, so I have to see a dietician and go to a support group or have therapy once a week."

"That's really positive, right? How do you feel about going back to school?"

"I'm supposed to be starting back in September. There's so much to catch up on, so I'm feeling a little anxious about it all, but my teachers have been amazing. They've sent me everything I need to be getting on with."

"You'll be great. Just take your time, and don't forget to be kind to yourself. I'm always here if you want me to take you through a meditation or yoga practice. It will really help with your anxiety."

"You sound like mum," Kiki says, rolling her eyes.

"The audacity," I say, feigning shock. I grab a cushion and throw it towards my sister. "Anyway, I'll leave you to finish your lunch. I love you."

I rise from the bed, and start towards the door.

"Wait, Phi. Would you sit with me?"

Tears well in my eyes, and my attempt to blink them back proves futile.

"You don't need to prove anything to me."

"I know, but I want to."

We sit side by side, talking about nothing in particular and laughing like we used to until Kiki finishes every last morsel from her plate. It's a slow process, and a tiny amount by anyone's standards, but she's eaten all of it.

"I'm so proud of you," I say, embracing Kiki in a hug. I never want to let go. "I'll see you soon."

Chapter Seven

♥

ON THIS SAME SUMMER evening, I manage to fall
down the proverbial rabbit hole of the Myers-Briggs
type personality indicator while laying in bed, and I spend
far too much time debating with my internal Summer as to
whether I should slide into Danny's DMs with the results.

I draft countless messages, and delete every single one. He
probably isn't interested, anyway. After a lot of second-
guessing, I go for it, opting for something short and simple.

Sophia: Straddling the line between INFP and ENFP.

Again, I mull one kiss at the end, two, or none. In the
end I opt for one. I sign a kiss at the end of every text I send;
why should it be any different for him?

My finger hovers over the little blue arrow icon. For
something that shouldn't matter, I sure am overanalysing the
shit out of it. I hit send, and a little while later, my phone
chimes with his response.

Danny: You can't be both. Pick one.

Sophia: It's not that simple.

Danny: Go with the one that feels most natural to you.

After further research and deliberation, I make a decision,
figuring that most likely, I'm an introvert. Correction:

Sophia is an introvert; Summer is an extrovert.

Sophia: INFP.

Danny: Good girl.

Sophia: I'm not a dog.

Danny: Shit, I'm sorry. Slip of the finger.

My mind wanders to the times in recent memory when I've admired his hands, and I can't help but imagine those fingers slipping somewhere else. Heat rises through my body, turning my cheeks crimson.

Danny: Fun fact: human personalities can always be attributed to that of our canine counterparts.

Smartass.

Three grey dots continue to bounce on the screen.

Danny: Stop rolling your eyes.

Sophia: I'm not.

I am.

Danny: According to Professor Google, the Cavalier King Charles matches the INFP personality type.

Sophia: I can't believe you just likened me to a dog.

Danny: I happen to have a soft spot for Cavs.

A lazy smile spreads across my face.

Sophia: Why?

Danny: My first pet, Trudi, was a Cav. She thought she was a Rottweiler, but that was all part of her charm. She was so happy and sweet, but so stubborn. They're a good breed, though. And they love to be in a lap.

My mind flashes back to the place my eyes landed in his car. To those dimples and his golden-green gaze. To those hands wrapped around the steering wheel.

Three grey dots bounce on the screen, driving me wild with anticipation. Is he thinking the same things?

Danny: Do you like to be in a lap, Miss DeLuca?

Butterflies swarm my tummy with a resounding yes. Images run through my mind at lightning speed. Strong hands lock around my waist. Hips grind in the driver's seat of his obnoxious car. Fire and hunger in my eyes reflect in mirrored shades.

I lose all control.

The last one cuts the fantasy short, and my mind flashes back further to all the fuckboys I've loved before. Whether I like it or not, I'm clearly determined to spoil Summer's fun.

Sophia: So, what breed are you?

It takes a moment for the grey dots to reappear across the screen, and for a moment, I think I've blown it.

Danny: Dalmatian.

If anything, I'm a little disappointed that he didn't pull me up on my obvious swerve of his thirsty statement.

Sophia: Cute.

Danny: They are extremely intelligent. Not to mention their unmatched good looks.

Sophia: Okay, now *I'm rolling my eyes.*

I don't have to ask to know they're a dominant breed, and I find myself wondering about dog personalities, a subject I never thought would intrigue me. Don't get me wrong, I love animals, but I've never owned a pet. My parents never allowed it, and in all honesty, the responsibility scares me.

I think carefully about my wording for the next message, debating whether to even ask, but I have to know.

Sophia: Can I ask you something?

Nausea settles in the pit of my stomach as I continue to type.

Sophia: You said you used to be married. What happened?

In an attempt to offset the nausea, I sit upright, but it worsens. A moment passes before my phone chimes, and the thought crosses my mind that if I hadn't blown it before, I have now. With my eyes closed, I focus on my breath, grounding myself before I pick up my phone again for his answer.

Danny: I'm separated.

Sophia: Why were you wearing a wedding ring the night we met?

Danny: It's a deterrent.

Sophia: What?

Danny: Something that is intended to discourage someone from doing something.

Sophia: I know what a deterrent is, smartass. So you wear a fake wedding ring?

Danny: I would say that it's supposed to prevent unwanted attention, but would you believe how many people don't give a shit if you're married? The truth is, I wear it to remind myself that I'm still legally married. I don't want to mess anything up, and I won't put my career on the line for the sake of a weak moment. We've been separated for almost two years now. It's almost done.

Sophia: Why not just get a divorce straightaway?

Danny: Nobody was technically at fault. There were no grounds for divorce, so the best option was be to separate for two years, then go from there.

I question the part where he said nobody was technically at fault. What does that even mean? There must be more to the story, but I barely know him, and the last thing I want is to make him uncomfortable if he isn't willing to share.

Danny: Anyway, enough about that life-sucking chapter. Positive vibes only.

I'm grateful for the light sarcasm, and for his honesty. It takes a lot for some people to open up, I of all people know.

Sophia: Spoken like a true millennial. For the record, I didn't mean to pry.

Danny: It's fine, really.

I sense a slight shift in his energy, which leads to overthinking, but I manage to pull myself out of it. I've done enough work on myself to know that my overanalysing is an internal childhood issue.

Danny: Anyway, I need to get some sleep. Busy day tomorrow, as always. Goodnight, Summer.

Sophia: Night, Daniel.

I smile to myself, half expecting a satirical telling off for using his full name, but when the blue tick appears to indicate the message has been read, no more grey dots bounce on the page.

I feel strangely sad about it.

"You want the good news or the bad news?" Lauren asks when I'm called into work early the following Friday. The boxed blonde has always been pretty relaxed, so naturally my stomach is tied up in knots.

"Well, the bad news is: Auréale have bought Ivy Rose Organics," Lauren says. "Which is also, evidently, the good news."

My heart pinches. Auréale are a large pharmaceutical company, with zero ethical stance or morals. A quick google search would tell that to anybody who cared, and they aren't the type of brand I aspire to work for.

In my mind, everything I've worked for, everything I believe in, comes crashing down, and I can't fathom the reason why Ivy Rose's owner would sell her soul to the devil. What does this mean for my future? Most likely, I'm going to have to continue working at Ivy Rose for the next couple of years, at least until I'm established enough to make a career out of teaching.

"The benefits are amazing, think of all the discounts."

Lauren's face lights up like a child's on Christmas morning, and mine drops like I've opened the most disappointing gift.

"I've booked you on a two day Social Media and Influencer Marketing course in London so you can what they're all about. How exciting is that?"

I already do a pretty solid job of managing the social media for the store, as well as juggling the job I'm actually paid to do. Don't get me wrong, I love being in a customer-facing role. I can't imagine any other job being as socially rewarding as the one I'm in, but the excitement of going on a course to improve something I enjoy is somewhat tempered by the disappointment of knowing that it's run by Auréale.

"I was thinking about setting a few hours aside once a week so you could film some content? How does that sound?" She twists her engagement ring and smooths her long hair over her shoulder. Okay, maybe that isn't so bad. It will be refreshing to get away for a couple of days and venture outside of my comfort zone. Maybe some time away from Brighton is exactly what I need.

"That actually sounds like a breath of fresh air." I glance around the store. "But we don't have any equipment. Or the space."

"The company will fund the equipment, and in regards to space, I was thinking that we could set up a permanent station on the shop floor. We'll work alongside our marketing department, and film the tutorials based on their trend predictions. It will be so much easier with a larger team on board."

I force a smile. Maybe if I can see past my morals, it could work. "That's a great idea. When is the course?"

"July 12th and 13th."

Less than two weeks away.

"Sophia, I know I don't say it often, but I think you'd be perfect for this. Sometimes I think your talent is wasted here, and I think that this could really help you thrive and give you something to be proud of."

I don't know what to say. Instead, I utter a simple thank you, but it's hard to ignore the ache in my heart.

"Oh and this came, by the way." Lauren hands me a white envelope with *Sophia* scribbled on the front. Relishing in the little buzz I always get from receiving unexpected mail, I tear it open and pull out four tickets to Monty James' sold out secret gig. I check the inside of the envelope to see if I've missed anything, and pull out a note which says:

Impressed?

I know exactly who sent them, and I don't care how Danny got those tickets, but my positive opinion of him has just multiplied tenfold. Slowly, I'm starting to warm to that obnoxious smartass, whether I like it or not.

Chapter Eight

♥

J UST SHY OF TWENTY-FOUR hours later, I bask in the buzzing, pre-show atmosphere of Quiet Waters where Monty James is due to headline.

"Ryan's not coming," James says, raising his voice over the music coming through the PA system.

"Why?" I ask.

"Training, or something."

"That sounds like an excuse. Basketball season is over, right?"

James shrugs. "Whatever, I'm texting April," he says.

"Don't," I say.

"You can't let the ticket go to waste, and you can't stop speaking to each other forever over a tiny misunderstanding."

"Wrong. She's been ignoring my messages all week. The ball is in her court."

"You two need to sort out this high school drama," Stefan says, cutting in.

"Fine, ask her. But I'm not apologising again for something that never happened. I don't see why I'm the one being punished while Ryan gets off scot-free. I didn't *invite* him into my bed."

It's true, I didn't. But I still have this niggling feeling of guilt in my chest. I never meant to hurt April.

"Stop being such a baby," James says, retrieving his phone. While the bartender sets down our drinks, he types out a quick message, then slips it back into his pocket. I take a long pull of my gin and tonic, savouring the cool botanicals coating my throat, and tap my card against the machine before we make our way through the bar into the main room.

Quiet Waters is an intimate beachfront venue housed inside a classic Victorian building. It's home to heavy hitting indie acts and superstar DJs, as well as household names road-testing new material. Rows of pillars run alongside the right-hand wall, creating a perfect space to lean on, rest drinks or climb up to jump out onto the mattress of people below, if one were that way inclined—though my crowd surfing days are dead and gone. In terms of clarity of view, it's lacking, but we manage to squeeze in next to the sound desk along the back left-hand-side. The other alternative is more spacious, but its location in an alcove by the bathroom is unappealing. Naturally, we veto that option.

It isn't long before the first warm-up act, an Americana-style cover band, start their set. Early noughties throwbacks spark nostalgia, instantly lifting my defiant mood, and I catch myself glancing around the room while I vibe with the music.

"Who are you looking for?" Stefan shouts.

"No one."

"Look, there's Danny," he says, pointing behind me.

In an instant I'm following Stefan's finger, and falling into his trap. Danny isn't there. Man, how desperate do I look right now?

"Dickhead."

"I knew it," he says. "You like him."

"Do not."

I hate when Stefan's right, which seems to be more often than I am. If I refuse to admit my feelings for Danny to myself, I sure as hell won't admit them to Stefan.

When the first band approaches the end of their set, I sneak a second look around, and realise James has slipped away from us. A few moments later he returns in an arm link with a sombre-looking April.

"Can we talk?" April asks, cocking her head towards the side door.

I down the rest of my drink, and set the empty glass beside a pillar. Outside, the sun is low, and the breeze coming from the ocean switches the air from scorching and uncomfortable to balmy and bearable.

Across the road, people play volleyball to a stunning backdrop of deep red clouds and a violet sky. I lead the way through puffs of vanilla-scented vapour and cigarette smoke, towards a quiet corner. My defensive stance takes hold as I fold my arms across my chest. I need to be ready for anything April throws my way.

"I'm so sorry, Phi."

Well, this is unexpected, and surprisingly easy. I breathe a sigh of relief, dropping my shoulders and loosening the grip around myself.

"I'm sorry, too. I don't know why I didn't say anything to begin with. I feel terrible. Yes, Ryan stayed over, but I swear nothing happened. I came back from seeing Alex, and he was asleep on our couch. He woke up, and told me that Chrissy broke up with him, and he told me about you two. He was really upset." I take a breath. "And he asked if he could stay in my bed because he's a fucking giant. That's all."

The silence is almost too much to bear.

"If I knew that Ryan staying over was going to be an issue and cause a rift between us, I would have flat out refused," I add.

"You don't know how relieved I am to hear you say that. I had no idea I even had real feelings for Ryan. When I found out that the two of you had...something inside me snapped. I hate that I went off on you like that, and that it's taken me a week to finally apologise.

"You've been there for me through everything, Phi. Stuck up for me when I needed someone strong in my corner, you've given me your shoulder countless times because of countless guys...and that's how I repay you. I don't even know how to begin to tell you how sorry I am."

I open my mouth to speak, but no words come out.

"I was jealous, and insecure, and I know that doesn't justify the way I acted..."

"Come here."

I extend my arms to my fallen friend. I know exactly how it feels to have irrational levels of insecurity, and those little voices in my head that tell me I'm not good enough. Years of bullying and being teased will do that to a person. April locks into my embrace, and although she's at least a few inches taller than me, she feels small in my arms, like a child that needs protecting.

"Internalising your feelings doesn't stop you from getting hurt," I say.

At this point, I'm quite proud of my own wisdom.

"Says you."

I hold her at arm's length.

"What is that supposed to mean?"

"Oh come on, don't pretend you don't want Danny's D."

I shoot April a pointed look. Is it that obvious? "Indie guys aren't my type, and even if they were, I don't get the impression he's into me. Not in that way, anyway."

"Trust me, he likes you."

"In what fucking world?"

"Why else would he have got you these tickets?"

"He either feels sorry for me, or wants to fuck me. Or both."

"Well, in that case, you should be thanking me," April says, a playful smirk spreading across her face. "But seriously, you're the sweetest person I know, and you're hot AF, especially in that outfit."

I smile, flicking my gaze over the Nirvana t-shirt dress and chunky trainers I'm wearing. It's my go-to cute, casual, don't-fuck-with-me ensemble, but I have minor reservations about wearing another band's merch to a Monty James concert.

"Come on, let's go inside."

April buys a round of drinks, and I keep a hand over my glass as we slide amongst the crowd back to the sound desk, finally settling beside Stefan and James. The first warm-up act has just finished their set, and we're waiting on the next band to show up.

"I see you two made up," James says, with a look of approval.

"We said it wouldn't take long," Stefan smirks.

"You two are so smug, it's nauseating. Maybe I should find some new friends." I say.

Stefan rolls his eyes.

"Like those four worldies up there?" he asks.

I follow his gaze towards the stage, take a sip of my gin and tonic, and almost spit it right back out when I see Danny up there.

Holy shit.

Is there any outfit in the world that this guy can't rock? How can he make the most ordinary black Henley look so damn good? It has to be witchcraft. Indie boys are fast becoming my new favourite thing to fantasise about, and I immediately retract the throwaway statement I voiced outside with April. Skinny jeans and rolled up sleeves will become my masturbatory affirmation.

Sure, he doesn't have Alex's bright blue eyes, or Luke's tall stature, or Ryan's bulging biceps, Stefan's thick curls, or James' pretty boy looks, but his energy—his whole demeanour—is magnetic. Up on that stage, he's nothing like the cocky prick I met just over a week ago, and that carefree half smile spread across his face exudes quiet confidence, and is completely infectious.

The music starts, and Danny and his Wandering Dragons are bathed in bright lights against a starry backdrop. My heart races as I watch him, and I'm a little disappointed that I miss the chance to catch his gaze.

They kick off with a playful and upbeat opener, creating the atmosphere for their set list, and I'm safe to ogle to my heart's content without my friends' judgement.

As Danny plays, I'm mesmerised by the effortless way his fingers slide along the fretboard. He has this easy way about him which is, dare I say, so incredibly sexy. Warmth fills my belly, and I find myself fantasising about his hands on my body. I imagine what those fingers and his years of experience could do to me. I press my thighs together in an attempt to offset the ache between my legs, but it proves pointless. I've worked myself into some sort of frenzy over those perfect hands and that smile. My god, that smile. Too late now, my underwear is already soaked to the point of no return. I could touch myself here so easily that nobody would know. I could look right into his eyes and imagine those fingers making circles on my clit, and no one, not even Danny, would ever know.

I shake the thought away after I seriously consider excusing myself so that I can at least ease the pressure in a grimy toilet cubicle. What has gotten into me? Before my thoughts have a chance to manifest, the song ends, and the lead singer, who introduces himself as Ollie, addresses the audience.

He wears a neat, blonde pompadour haircut and a nose ring, and has a tiger's face tattooed on his forearm. With natural charisma, he speaks about music and relays anecdotes like he's talking to old friends. He seems sweet, and a lot younger than the other band members.

Ollie introduces the rest of the band, and when Danny greets the crowd with a nod and a half wave, he momentarily caches my eye. Or at least I think he does. His smile widens, but I manage to convince myself that it isn't because of me. There's no way he can see past those lights, right? Warmth and want stirs deep in my belly, and I will him to notice me, but he looks away before I can return the smile.

We pass the time dancing and drinking in what little space they have to The Wandering Dragons' upbeat, easy songs, and the set comes to a close in a rowdy, energetic finale, leaving me pumped full of adrenaline and raring to go for Monty James to take the stage.

"What did you think?" Stefan asks.

"Surprisingly good, actually," I say.

Stefan eyes up my empty glass. "Would you like another?"

I shake my head. "No thanks, I'm good. A couple more and I'll be anyone's."

"Is that right?" Danny says, approaching us.

Words fail me.

Chapter Nine

♥

"YOU GUYS WERE AWESOME," Stefan says, pulling Danny into a hug.

"Thanks, man. Appreciate it," Danny says.

"You were okay," I deadpan, folding my arms across my chest.

"Gee, did it hurt to say that? Nice top, by the way. Have you even heard of Nirvana?"

"It's a dress. And yes, I know who Kurt Cobain is."

He doesn't need to know that I can't name any song of theirs other than Smells Like Teen Spirit and Come As You Are, but vintage band tees have always been a wardrobe staple for me, regardless of whether I'm their number one fan, and I don't need to justify my sense of style to anyone.

"I wondered where the rest of your outfit was," he says, treating me to those gloriously sexy dimples.

I meet his gaze, and a slow smile spreads across my face. Butterflies swarm my belly, and a familiar warmth spreads deeper throughout my body.

"You want a drink?"

"I think I've peaked, but thanks. Anyway, I should be buying you a drink for scoring these tickets."

"Can't, I'm driving," Danny says, raising a glass of reddish-brown liquid and taking a sip. When he licks his lips, my nipples pinch, and I'm overcome with the urge to lick the cola off them. "But if you really want to thank me, I wouldn't say no to breakfast."

Oh.

"Oh. I'm not really a morning person," is all I can say before an image of waking up next to him creeps into my mind, but I swat it away when I register the confusion etched on his face. Is breakfast fuckboy code for something else?

"No, I mean—"

"Guys, I'm cock-blocking," James says, approaching us.

Yes, you are. I snatch my gaze away from Danny's bright hazel eyes.

"Look at those two," my roommate continues.

He jerks his head towards April and Ollie standing at the bar. They both sport huge, matching grins while my redheaded friend pets the huge tiger on his forearm. I've always admired my bestie's ability to make quick work of hot men.

James turns his attention towards Danny and offers his hand.

"You're Danny, right? You guys were awesome. I'm James."

Danny shakes his hand and modestly thanks him. The lights dim, eventually fading to black, and the music starts again. The whole crowd roar as Monty James struts onto the stage bathed in bright lights and a black leather jacket. Danny takes up residence beside me, while the audience gathers in front of us, leaving no space unoccupied.

"Can you see?" he asks, his warm breath sending a sheet of goosebumps across my skin.

I struggle to find a clear opening, but every now and then I catch a glimpse of the stage.

"Here," he says.

Gently, he places a hand on the small of my back, guiding me into a small space in front of him. I want to lean into the warmth of his palm, to step back just a little to feel him behind me.

"Better?"

I close my eyes to savour his touch before turning around to thank him.

"No worries."

Dimples indent his cheeks as he returns the smile, and I spin back around. I'm dizzy, and my heart is racing. I can't decide if it's a delayed side effect of the alcohol, or a Danny side effect, but I could easily get used to this feeling. The only downside is that his proximity resurfaces every ache I'd tried to bury when he was up on that stage.

My only hope to avoid going completely overboard with want for Danny Pearce is to focus on the music; the beams of light oscillating between us and the stage; the sensation in my body as the bass ripples through the floor and diffuses at my feet.

I try to focus on anything but the ghost of his breath in my hair, teasing trails down my neck. I lose balance, swaying with no rhythm as his body heat radiates onto mine, and I hope to God this feeling goes both ways. If not, I might die.

Monty addresses the crowd, snapping me out of my stupor. Much like Ollie had done previously, he relays anecdotes and speaks about his music, although his demeanour errs on the side of cockiness over confidence. He introduces his band, thanks the audience, and shares more self-indulgence, but there is no denying his talent.

The band continue their upbeat energy over the next few songs, and the crowd rambunctiously bounce along to hit after hit. But I can't ignore the all-consuming pulsing and throbbing taking over my entire body, especially when there's no way of avoiding Danny's addictive Riviera scent.

Without a glance behind, I finally gather the courage to test the waters. I've never made the first move with anyone before, and I like it that way. I'm terrified, but if there was ever a time to take agency over my life, facing the fear of rejection in favour of something better, fighting the voices in my head that tell me I'm not good enough, this is it.

If I don't try, I won't know.

The biggest chart topper sends the floorboards pulsating and shaking. I step back a little, inching closer into Danny's personal space. He doesn't move. I consider it progress, and a green light to carry on.

A moment later, warm fingers graze the back of my hand. My heart is racing. That little bit of contact tells me all I need to know. Blistering heat, want and electricity races through my veins, but it's cut short as an overzealous partygoer crashes into me, sending beer flying through the air.

When ice cold liquid hits my skin, I fall back, colliding with Danny's rock-solid body. His hands slide onto my shoulders, catching me, and I shoot the perpetrator a sour look as I try to catch my breath, which would be a hell of a lot easier if I didn't have Danny's arms wrapped around me.

"I'm fine, thanks for asking," I shout, but they don't hear me. I turn to face Danny. "I'm so sorry."

"Don't be."

If I'm being honest, I'm not sorry at all. The ice-cold liquid on my shirt is a blessing in disguise, serving as my own personal cold shower.

"I can get him kicked out if you want?"

Those dimples undo me again. There's a fire and a vulnerability behind his eyes that I haven't seen before. I shake my head. "No, it's okay. You've done enough."

My gaze travels downwards. First, I notice the empty glass, then the huge wet stain on his shirt.

"Are you okay? You're soaked."

He looks at his chest and shrugs. "It'll dry."

He eyes my dress, which is arguably more wet than his shirt. "I think I have a spare t-shirt in the car. You want it?"

Would it be weird to say yes? My better judgement politely declines the offer. "As much as I'd love to see you take the shirt off your back for little old me, I think I'll pass."

"You snooze, you lose, princess. Care to join me, anyway?"

"Sure."

"Okay, hold on a sec."

He approaches Ollie—who has taken up residence beside April—and leans into his ear. In the darkness and over the music, I can't hear nor lip read. Ollie takes the lanyard from around his neck, and hands it to his bandmate, then I follow Danny towards the exit.

Outside, it's dark and cloudy, and the waning crescent moon is barely visible. Despite the drop in temperature, the weather is still warm. I shiver as my damp dress clings to my chest and thighs. In hindsight, my proverbial cold shower is what I needed to keep my Danny fantasies in check. I don't need another fuckboy to distract me from my goals.

"Here, put this on," Danny says, handing me the lanyard.

I inspect it, then place it around my neck. "What's this?"

"Backstage pass. You don't want to miss the epic finale." He pauses, then points across the road. "My car's just over there."

"You picked a good spot for people watching," I say, referring to the empty volleyball courts as we cross the quiet street.

He clicks the key and opens the boot, then pulls a tennis shirt from his gym bag. "Are you sure you don't want my spare?" he asks, offering it to me.

I consider wearing it for a moment, but then I question whether I'd be able to contain myself if his shirt carried that delectable scent. "I doubt that would cover my butt."

Danny leans across to openly check out my ass. "Hmm, that could be distracting. Although you're doing a pretty good job of it in that dress.

My cheeks flush, and I'm mad at myself for secretly liking his obvious display of perversion. His fingers find the hem of his shirt, and as he lifts it, I catch myself staring at the lean contour of his abs, and the happy trail extending to the waistband of his jeans. When he stops, so do I.

"Can a guy get some privacy?"

"Says the guy who was checking me out less than a minute ago?"

"I'm only messing." He tosses me the keys. "Here, go wild."

Sinking into the leather passenger seat of the Audi, I sneak a glance at the wing mirror. Everything is telling me not to look, but curiosity gets the better of me. One little peek couldn't hurt, right?

He peels off his shirt, balls it up, and tosses it into the boot, a strange move for someone who outwardly seems so uptight and straight-laced. Maybe Danny has his own alter ego.

Taut abs, strong shoulders and a lean, athletic torso are a welcoming, albeit unexpected, sight. I'm pleasantly surprised. He's completely cut and his physique is nothing like I'd imagined.

Okay, maybe I shouldn't be looking. It's self-sabotage at it's finest. But I wouldn't have been satisfied with the small glimpse of skin which was thrust upon me. I have every right to live out one of my perverted fantasies.

Leaning over to the driver's side, I start the engine, and turn up the radio to distract myself from the glorious view.

As I wait, I fiddle with the controls and crank up the heating in an attempt to dry out my dress.

"Are you cold? Want me to warm your seat up?" he asks, climbing into the driver's side.

I shake my head, then glance around the interior. "You know, this car's kind of grown on me."

"See? It's not all bad." He sobers. "How's your sister doing?"

"Better than I expected, if I'm honest."

"That's good. It helps to be positive." He smiles warmly, holding my gaze. My tummy rumbles, and I instinctively place a hand there. "So, how about that breakfast?"

I glance at the time on the dashboard. "Now?"

He nods.

"It's 10pm," I say.

"I see no issue here. I promise not to order a bowl of corn flakes," he smirks.

I smirk right back. "Breakfast cereal is a superior night time snack, everybody knows that."

"I don't disagree."

My smile mirrors his.

"I need to go and grab my guitar first. You want to wait here?"

"And miss the epic finale? Not a chance."

I wait in the wing, with a perfectly unobstructed view of the stage, while Danny collects his guitar from the dressing room.

"This last song is about the common fear of opening up to someone." Monty says, addressing his audience for what I assume to be the final time. "Our basic human instinct is to protect ourselves. But when you find the right person, none of it matters. Because that person will open you up and find their way into your heart. The most important thing in the world is love. Human contact. Connection. Who would we be without it?"

For a moment, he seems to forget where he is. But he quickly snaps out of it. "So, on that note, please welcome back my good friend, Imani Brown."

The crowd roars as Monty switches his guitar, and welcomes Imani, the lead singer of the first band, back to the stage. She has that kind of all-encompassing beauty, with dark, flawless skin, a megawatt smile and a powerful, yet serene, presence.

"I hope we can do this song justice for you guys," Monty adds, before launching into the opening bars of James Bay and Julia Michaels' Peer Pressure.

Their chemistry is off the scale electric, and they're a match made in vocal heaven, rousing the atmosphere with heart-wrenching emotion. Watching them perform so intimately feels voyeuristic, but I'm completely captivated, and admittedly, a little jealous.

"Are you ready to go?" Danny says, approaching me from behind.

"Wait a minute, I think they're almost finished."

"I kind of wanted to sneak away."

"Why?"

"Because he might steal you away, and then I won't get my breakfast."

I throw my head back and force a laugh. "I guarantee that's not the case. Have you seen her? She's a freaking goddess."

"Have you seen you?" he rasps.

Judging by the awkward clearing of his throat, giving compliments isn't in his repertoire, and in my mind, I'm not sure how to feel about receiving one, but the heat rushing through my body at lightning speed is a pretty solid indicator. Heart racing, I turn to face him.

"What has that got to do with anything? Are you jealous?"

"Maybe a little. But don't tell anyone. I have a reputation to uphold."

"Oh yeah? What reputation is that?" I ask, folding my arms across my chest, a deliberate attempt to create space between us.

He leans closer, breaking through my boundaries. "Well, there's my academic prowess, my unmatched confidence and great banter. Oh...and my sharp wit."

"Not to mention your delightful modesty," I say, with a smirk. "Anyway, how do you know he's my type? He is, for the record."

The song comes to a close, and Monty, Imani and the band join us in the wing, leaving the audience bathed in electric ambience and satisfaction from a spirited climax. Danny retreats, leaving me unsatisfied and unfulfilled from my anti-climax. He smiles at a sweat-drenched Monty, who clocks him as he sips a bottle of water.

"Danny, mate," he says, offering himself for a bro-hug as the crowd chant, anxiously awaiting their encore.

"You guys were great," he says.

Monty takes a step back and casts his gaze over me. "Thanks, man. I only caught the end of your set, but I'm loving your new sound. Who's this?" Monty asks, his eyes never leaving my face.

"This is my friend, Summer," Danny says. "She's a fan."

Star struck, I greet Monty with a bashful smile, which eases when he offers one of sincerity.

"Good seeing you guys. I've got to go, but no doubt I'll see you at the next family gathering."

He takes another sip of water, then bounces back onto the stage for the encore.

I turn to face Danny.

"You're related?"

"Not for long. He's Belle's cousin."

I look at him blankly, as if that name means anything to me.

"My soon-to-be-ex-wife."

"He doesn't know you're not together?"

"We don't see him very often."

Danny's reasons for calling me Summer, and for practically running away before Monty spotted us, is now abundantly clear.

"So what you really meant before was that you didn't want him to see us together?"

"Sort of. I'm sorry I didn't say anything."

I'm not silly. I know how I look. How people judge and perceive me. Heck, I've even been guilty of slut-shaming myself in the past, before I realised that I don't actually give a fuck about other people's opinions. But it's made me hard, and I was wrong to think that Danny sees me as anything but Summer, party girl extraordinaire, always up for a laugh and a good time, nothing more, nothing less.

"It's okay, let's just go."

"You don't want to stay until the end?"

Casting my gaze towards the stage, I linger, captivated once again by Monty's effortless vocals and boundless energy. I send a quick text to Stefan, then turn to face Danny.

"No, let's get out of here."

Chapter Ten

♥

DANNY LEAVES HIS GUITAR in the car, and I lead the way along a row of Victorian arches which houses a multitude of beachfront cafes, until we approach Barney's Bistro. Ever popular with tourists and night owls, the late-night eatery has become world famous over the last twenty years or so. It's cheap and by no means classy, but it's open for 24 hours, and has an extensive menu for hungry partygoers.

Danny holds the door open, while I peruse the menu displayed on the outside wall.

"Not here," I say.

"It's the only place that's open."

"No it's not. Come on."

He follows me up a set of stairs which leads onto the busy main road, and we cross over to reach the main part of town. We swerve groups of tanked-up twenty-somethings to a back street lined with laid out cardboard and sleeping bags, until we're the only ones left.

"So, what's the plan now you've had your claim to fame?" I ask.

"What do you mean, exactly?"

"You're not going to use the fact that you have a famous ex-cousin-in-law to your advantage?"

"Not everybody wants to be famous. We earned that gig, Monty had nothing to do with it," he says, pausing as we approach an incline. "Okay, maybe he had a little bit of input. We had our chance to make it, but it didn't work out."

"What happened?"

"I mean, it's a sob story that will put the saddest X Factor contestant to shame. You sure you want to hear it?"

"Yep. I'm a sucker for a tearjerker."

He takes a deep breath and adopts a dramatic narrative voice.

"Picture it. 2010. Mumford and Sons, and Biffy Clyro dominated the charts. Muse headlined Glastonbury that year, and The Wandering Dragons were set to be the next big thing. Victory was in our reach. We could smell it, taste it. But fuck this façade," he continues, in his normal voice. "We were playing a lot of gigs around the UK. Every weekend we were in a different county. It was fun, but my parents hated it. I barely ever saw them.

"One of our gigs was at Newcastle Uni. We heard about scouts coming to see us, and the pressure got too much for Ollie. We were all young, but he was a teenager. To think we could be mainstream was pretty overwhelming, but it really affected him."

He pauses, his breath hitching as we reach the brow of the hill. "My dad's best friend, Ray, owns the studios we rehearse at. He's like a second dad to all of us. He lost his son to mental illness, and he didn't want that for any of us. After a lot of talking, we came to the conclusion that nothing was worth sacrificing for the price of fame. I'm the closest thing Ollie has to a brother. It was my duty to protect him."

My mind immediately races to Kiki.

"You know how it is."

"I'm so sorry, Danny."

"It's okay. Life's too short to have regrets. We still love making music, but there's less pressure to now."

"Why music?"

"Why yoga?"

"I asked you first."

We share a slow, deliberate smile.

"Music is like an anchor. It's a feeling, a surrender. Music has the ability to capture, bind and free you all at the same time. It's healing." He clears his throat. "At least, it is to me."

"Good answer," I say, not being able to contain my smile.

Douchebag Danny is actually the furthest thing from the asshole I thought he was, and I'm glad, because I'm about to let him in on a little secret. "Wait here, I'll be right back."

With that, I disappear into an alleyway, leaving him stranded on the dark, deserted street until I emerge holding a takeaway pizza box, a wad of napkins and a small, rectangular deli box.

"I thought I'd been ditched for someone better looking," he says, eyeing up the boxes. "Do you need a hand?"

"Sure," I say, handing him the smaller box. "But no peeking."

"I had no idea there was a pizza place around here."

"That's because it's a well-kept secret amongst us second gen immigrants."

"Are you sure you didn't just go round the corner to magic one up?"

"I can only do that on a full moon," I deadpan.

He looks up, and I follow his gaze to the dark, cloudy sky.

We make our way back to the beach, finding a flat surface to sit by the volleyball courts, and I lay the pizza box down on the pebbles and flip the lid. Danny, in turn, lays the smaller box in front of us.

"So, what's for breakfast?" he asks.

"Spinach, prosciutto, caramelised onions, wild mushrooms, eggs and rocket on a sourdough base."

"Sounds delicious. It was a pretty bold move of you to assume I like pizza."

"Who doesn't like pizza?"

"Spoken like a true Italian."

I shoot him a pointed look. "We can't be friends if you don't like pizza."

"We're friends now, are we? I had no idea you felt that way."

"Don't flatter yourself."

Danny picks up a slice, and after taking a bite, his eyes grow wide and his mouth curls into a satisfied smile. "Mmm, that's too good," he says, barely breathing between bites. He pauses to swallow the last mouthful. "So, I'm curious. Why the alter ego?"

"Buffy was taken," I say, taking a bite of my own.

Danny shoots me a pointed look, and I roll my eyes. There's no denying that this man has seen through my facade from day one.

"I grew up watching angsty teen dramas about American rich kids. I always envied that carefree California girl lifestyle. Summer's my favourite season, and it just happens to be my favourite slayer's surname, and my favourite O.C. character."

"A Summer trifecta," he muses. "You know, a privileged lifestyle isn't all it's cracked up to be."

"Says the rich person who surrounds themselves with equally rich people," I deadpan. "So anyway, a few years ago, I was out with my friends, and this guy kept following me around. He wouldn't leave me alone until he knew my name. I got freaked out, panicked, and Summer was officially born."

Danny's eyes darken.

"Did he try something?"

"No, nothing like that. But he scared me. I thought if I just told him my name he'd leave me alone, but he didn't. He slipped something in my drink. I don't remember anything, but Ryan said he found me barely conscious, slumped against a wall. I guess he scared him off.

"I thought that was the end of it, but he stalked me on social media. I had to get the police involved, and now I have a restraining order against him. It was really stressful for all of us. We didn't know it at the time, but that's when Kiki's illness took hold. At first, she started excusing herself to eat in her room, but really she was hiding her food. Eventually, she was hospitalised with anorexia. I felt so responsible. All the signs were there, but somehow, I was so wrapped up in my own shit that I didn't notice how thin she had gotten. I should have known."

"I'm sorry that happened to you, but you can't blame yourself."

"It's hard not to. I feel like I have to constantly put on a brave face for Kiki's sake. I feel so guilty for letting her down."

"It's not your fault. The psychology of eating disorders is so complex. You can't feel guilty for something out of your control."

"That's the thing. If I hadn't been so wrapped up in my own issues, I would have realised that Kiki was hurting herself. That's what hurts the most."

He places a hand on top of mine, pain etched on his face. "I'm sorry this happened to you, and your family."

"Thank you." I let out a breath. "Sorry, I got carried away. You're surprisingly easy to talk to. Maybe because you're old and wise, huh?" I let out a small, pathetic laugh.

"Less of the old, thank you." Danny's smile is infectious. I'm glad he's here. "So, effectively, Summer is a shield."

"I guess so. Like my protection."

"Protection from what?"

I don't answer, because every answer in my head sounds ridiculous. What have I always run from? Men, feelings, commitment, love, myself. The list is endless. He doesn't ask again, and for that I'm grateful. In the quiet, we tuck into another slice of pizza while a backdrop of waves crash against the shore in the distance.

"Does that happen a lot? Guys harassing you?" he finally asks, breaking the silence.

"All the time."

"On behalf of all men, I apologise."

"You shouldn't have to."

"Nobody should have to go through what you did, and still do. But it explains a hell of a lot about your reasons for having your guard up."

"Sometimes it's easier to play the role people want you to," I muse, remembering his first, extremely vocalised impression of me.

"Why do you think so little of yourself?"

What an odd thing to ask. I'm taken aback, and although I hate to admit it, hurt.

"Excuse me? I've practically bared my fucking soul and you—"

He shakes his head.

"No. What I mean is, why do you think you would have to play a role for anybody? Because from where I'm standing, the you I know is pretty damn remarkable, and I would love to know who you really are."

I debate whether to continue. Nobody, aside from my parents, has bothered to ask or care how I was after that night, but I won't let what happened define me.

"Oh." I pause. "I guess I've always felt like a bit of an alien. I've always questioned my purpose, always been a foreigner, never truly belonged. After the incident, I hit a really low point. I felt guilty for craving that validation because it led me to lose my power, and at a time in my life when I questioned who I was, and how people perceived me, yoga and meditation was the only thing that was there for me."

"Is that why you decided to become a yoga teacher?"

I shoot him a questioning look.

"I overheard you and your friends talking at Lilura."

"I want to help people like me, and people like Kiki. I want to give teenagers something to identify with, to give them an outlet. Teach them that yoga isn't just about the poses they see on Instagram. It's about lifestyle, and mind-set. It's about compassion, and boundaries, and kindness to self and others." My mouth goes dry. "I'm not used to doing all this talking. You're the only person I've met recently that has asked so many questions of me."

"What does that say about everyone else?"

I'm not sure, but it speaks volumes for the kind of person he's showing himself to be.

Fuck the pact I made with myself. Life is about living. I need to stop running and embrace my opportunities while I still have them.

His gaze falls to my mouth, and I remember his words from earlier.

Life's too short to have regrets.

I allow myself to be in the moment, to be pulled in by his gravity. I drop my gaze to his lips and inch closer, but before I have a chance to seize the opportunity, a car alarm sounds, and jolts us back to reality.

Once we're over the initial embarrassment, we share an awkward laugh, and I put a band aid on my wounded ego by telling myself this isn't meant to be. There's no going back now. We both know what was about to happen, and that can't be erased.

"So, tell me about you," I say, in an attempt to gracefully change the subject. I'm grateful for the darkness hiding the flush in my cheeks.

"What do you want to know?"

"Where do you stand with pineapple on pizza?"

"Fruit doesn't belong on pizza. What are your thoughts?"

"I mean, I don't hate it." I shrug at his look.

"You call yourself Italian? You should be ashamed."

I laugh just as my phone chimes with a text.

Stefan: Heading home. Everything okay?

Sophia: All good. Won't be long.

He replies with a winking face emoji, and I roll my eyes. I can feel Danny's gaze on me as I place my phone face down on the pebbles, then I turn to face him. In my peripheral, a light flares over the sea, followed by a loud and drawn-out, subsiding roll.

"It's just Stefan checking up on me."

"He seems like a good guy."

"He is. I'm lucky to have him."

"He's lucky to have you, too." He mirrors my smile. "So, what's in this box?" he asks, picking up the smaller one.

He opens it and looks inside.

"Pasticcini. Breakfast pastries."

"They look amazing."

"They are. I got you a mixture."

"Are you having some?" he asks, offering the box. I shake my head. I would stuff my face with those bad boys if I had the chance, but I need to show a little willpower.

"Don't tempt me. It's my way of showing my gratitude...for the tickets."

When I lean across his lap to reel off the names in my less-than-perfect Italian accent, I try not to notice our proximity.

"Cannoncini, cannoli, bignè, sfogliatelle, babà, and fruit tart."

"Is there no Italian word for fruit tart?" he smirks.

"Probably, but I don't know it."

My hand grazes the top of his thigh, and I swear I can feel him lean into my gravity. A quick sequence of fantasies flashes through my mind. There's something about the ocean, the sound of the waves, the smell of the air and the salty sea spray. It's so incredibly freeing. Now is the golden opportunity for him to make a move. But he doesn't.

Suddenly, a drop of water bounces off a cone of puff pastry, and he snaps the box shut.

"Shit. I think it's about to hammer it down. Shall we head back?"

"Sure," I say, but my mind tells me different. I would happily stay in a downpour with him.

Boxes balanced, we head towards his car, picking up speed as soft, thick droplets start to fall. He places the boxes in the backseat, and once we're safe inside and in the comfort of the leather interior, he turns on the engine and I give him my home address. Closing my eyes, I shiver as my damp skin welcomes the first blast of warm air.

"So much for changing your shirt," I say. "That's what you get for calling me entitled."

"Karma is indeed a bitch. I'm sorry I said that. I wasn't having a great night."

"I'm pretty sure you've redeemed yourself." I flash him a smile. "So, when's your next gig?"

I hope I don't make it too obvious that I have every intention of seeing him again. But then again, there's no harm in going after what I want.

"Monday."

"That soon?"

"Technically our rehearsal day. You should come along to the studio if you're not busy."

Busy? Moi?

"What time?"

"Five-thirty."

"I have yoga at six."

"So come after, we'll still be there. That is, if you want to. You can bring Stefan and James if you like. And I'm sure

Ollie would love to see April again."

Great. Nothing screams strictly platonic like bring your two gay housemates and your best friend.

"Actually, that sounds good."

"Maybe I'll bore you with my life story."

The fact that he feels comfortable enough to tell me things speaks volumes. I smile, and I can just about make out his dimples in the dark.

Chapter Eleven

♥

"WELL, WELL, WELL, LITTLE one." James says, as I walk through to the living room. "How was your impromptu date?"

"It wasn't a date. We were hungry, and I wanted to thank him for the tickets."

"Oh my," he says, clutching at imaginary pearls. "Look at you embracing your hot girl summer."

"He's not my type."

"You don't have a type," Stefan scoffs. "Ryan and Alex are polar opposites."

"Physically," James adds.

"What about me?" Stefan asks.

"I fancied you for like a day in middle school, Stefan," I say. "Anyway, I liked your accent."

"You felt sorry for me because I wore glasses and couldn't control my curls."

"I liked you because you had a kind heart."

I perch on the arm of the sofa, swinging my little legs around to rest my feet on Stefan's thighs.

"You still do, and even if I did like Danny, he's still married."

"He's separated. It's not the same."

"It still makes it complicated," I muse. "So get this...Monty James is his wife's cousin."

Their mouths fall open.

"Wow, well if she's half as hot as he is, she must be a supermodel."

"Thanks for that," I say, dying a little inside.

Whatever spark I had left burning through me as a result of my evening with Danny, Stefan's comment had singlehandedly extinguished it.

James gives me a sympathetic smile, then pats Stefan's leg.

"I'm going to bed. Goodnight, gorgeous."

Stefan glances at his watch, and rises to follow his husband. It's not late, but I'm dealing with a married couple who are old beyond their years.

Once I'm alone, I slump down onto the couch. My clothes are still damp, but the sofa has soaked up the warmth from Stefan and James' body heat. Sinking down into the worn fabric, I pull out my phone, check my Instagram notifications and re-read my last DM conversation with Danny.

I sit with it for a few moments, contemplating, thinking about him. Replaying the night's events over and over in my head while I study the avatar on his Twitter profile. In the photo, his hair is at least a shade darker, and the lines around his eyes aren't as prominent as they are now. There's no light, no warmth or happiness behind his eyes. I feel sad for the person he used to be. I try to convince myself to go to bed, but Stefan's words resonate in my head, and curiosity gets the better of me. I open up Facebook like the stalker that I am now becoming.

My search for Danny Pearce, Daniel Pearce and Belle Pearce returns zero results, but I don't quit. I have to know who I'm up against.

I pull up Monty's Instagram, and after a few moments of scrolling, I click on a post of him sandwiched between two impossibly beautiful and similar looking women. The caption is a gushing tribute to his cousins, Isabelle and Amira James. Wearing a figure-hugging black dress, Belle's glossy dark hair falls like a silk veil over her shoulder, and her bronze skin and long, lean legs make her look like a Victoria's secret model. I scoff. Of course, she lives up to her namesake.

A lump forms in my throat as I fall deeper into the proverbial rabbit-hole of Isabelle James, until sleep beckons, and finally, I give up the fight.

By the time Monday rolls around, Stefan had spent twenty-four hours in an endless cycle of fever, vomiting and nausea. Sweat dampens his pale, sallow skin, which is strangely devoid of its usual orange hue.

Before I leave for work, I bring him a glass of cold water and set it on the bedside table, then feel his forehead with the back of my hand.

"I think it's flu," he croaks.

"It's probably just a summer cold. Can I make you a smoothie? Green juice?"

He screws up his face and shakes his head.

"Wow, you must be feeling bad."

"I feel like I'm living in Satan's armpit."

"That was a visual I didn't need," I deadpan. "Have you called your boss?"

"Can you do it? It's so painful to move."

"Do I look like your mother?"

"Can you text her then?"

He forces a smile. I can probably count on one hand the amount of times I've said no to this man, and this will not be one of them. I feel far too much pity for him.

"Please?"

Swiping his phone from the bedside table, I point the screen towards his face, but it displays a *no match* message.

"It's not working. What's your code?"

"My phone doesn't even recognise me? How bad do I look?"

I side-eye him. "You really want me to answer that?"

"No." He nods towards his phone. "It's James' birthday."

"How sweet," I say, with a hint of sarcasm.

After getting the green light to access his device, I send a WhatsApp message to his boss. A notification chimes almost instantly, but it isn't from his boss.

Ryan: How do I tell Phi?

Before the temptation to read it takes over, I click off the screen and return the phone to Stefan's bedside. Ryan will tell me whatever it is when he's ready. I have to respect their privacy.

"Do you need anything before I go to work?"

"Just your unconditional love."

"You already have that. When will James be home?"

"Around six."

"Okay, call me if you need anything. Get some rest. I love you."

"Love you too."

I blow him a kiss, wave goodbye, and wash the hell out of my hands.

After yoga, I journey inland to a part of town I've never been before, a forty-minute cycle ride to be exact, if Google Maps can be trusted. It takes me thirty-four minutes of weaving through drive-home traffic and uphill sprints in air heavy with humidity until I finally round a corner, slipping away from the main road onto an industrial estate which houses a row of converted Victorian warehouses.

Evidently, Stefan didn't feel any better by the end of the day. James didn't want to leave him, and April had plans, so that left me to join The Wandering Dragon's rehearsal on my own.

By the time I arrive, my scalp is itchy from the damp braid tugging on my roots, and a healthy dose of sweat has gathered on my top lip. I don't need a mirror to know that I'm dripping from head to toe, and a complete mess.

Ollie is loading equipment into a white SUV with two other band members as I pull up, he spots me and waves me over as I approach the unit. When I dismount my bike, I remove my helmet, and wipe what I can of my perspiration away.

"Hey, sorry I'm late," I say, trying to catch my breath.

"No worries. We're actually heading off now, but Danny's still in there." Ollie jerks his head towards the entrance, then back again. "He snapped a string. You can take your bike inside."

I thank him, and say goodbye. Once the SUV is down the road and out of sight, I pull my phone from my backpack, and check my reflection with the front facing camera. To say I have a healthy glow is an understatement.

I wait a moment for the redness in my cheeks to soften to a pale pink, and I take out my braids, shaking them out to a beachy wave. Taking a long swig of water, I apply some lip balm and pop a mint in my mouth, then I enter the pin code Danny has given me into the door security system and wait for the buzz to indicate authorised entry.

I keep telling myself the shakiness in my hands and the nausea are due to a lack of food, but it doesn't explain the reason for my racing heart.

I'm not used to feeling nervous, and I don't like it. Actually, I loathe that the sheer *thought* of Danny is having this much control over my body and emotions. I want to turn back.

Summer, the avoider of feelings, tells me it's a bad idea, but Sophia—and that little piece of me that begs to be told I'm enough, the little piece of me that has hope—wins, and I push the door open.

Inside, the studio is larger, and surprisingly cosier, than expected. The walls are lined with vintage instruments, amplifiers, noisemakers, modulators and synthesisers. It looks lived-in, but clean, with exposed brick walls, floor to ceiling windows, and industrial lighting hanging from wooden beams on the high ceiling.

A worn black leather sofa and matching ottoman sit on a large patterned rug, which covers the light oak flooring. A raised platform is set up with a Pearl drum kit, two Fender telecasters, a precision bass, and a couple of microphones on stands.

I see Danny perched on a stool on the platform, guitar in hand, with a vacant smile spread across his face. He looks comfortable and content.

"Hey," he says, softly.

My heart skips a beat when I hear his voice.

"I won't be a minute."

After carefully leaning my bike against the wall, I drop my bag and helmet beside the door, jolting as it slams shut behind me. Walking towards him, I kneel on the floor by the edge of the stage while he alternates between playing notes and twisting tuning keys on a maple-coloured Gibson Les Paul. After a few moments, he sets the guitar on a stand next to him.

"Isn't there an easier way to do that these days?" I ask.

"There's apps and electronic tuners, but I like doing it this way. It's more authentic."

"Or you're just a technophobe?"

"I don't trust it as much as my own ears."

"I wouldn't trust your hearing if I were you," I smirk.

He flashes his dimples.

"I'm sorry I missed your rehearsal."

"You didn't."

"But everyone's just left."

"I know." He glances at his watch. "I booked extra time on the room, so we're good for another half hour or so. I like to hang out here once they've gone."

"I didn't peg you for a closet introvert."

He shrugs, and the corners of his mouth curl into a smile. "I straddle the line from time to time."

Heat floods my cheeks and my nipples pinch when I'm treated to those perfect dimples. The way his smile reaches his eyes is arguably the most distracting thing. I want to pocket that image forever. He's beautiful.

"Ouch," Danny says, wincing as his hand shoots to the top of his forearm. The dreamy vision of him turns into dust.

"What is it?" I ask.

"An old tennis injury. It's been gradually getting worse the last few weeks."

"Mind if I have a look?"

"Sure."

He props the guitar on a stand, and joins me on the floor, mirroring my position. "This is comfy. Maybe I should do yoga."

"It's a good stress reliever. I mean, I'm not half the bitch I used to be."

"And here I was willing to bet money that you were, in fact, one hundred percent *that* bitch."

"I'm surprised you've even heard that song," I deadpan. I am offended, delighted and surprised in equal measure.

"Sorry, I couldn't help myself. Keep going."

I grab a cushion from the couch and lay it on Danny's lap. "Rest your forearm on this," I say.

Once he's ready, I start to massage the inside of his forearm.

"Remember how you described the way you feel about music?"

He nods.

"That's how I feel about yoga."

My fingertips settle into the crease below his bicep, and using my thumb, I gently knead either side, noticing every vein, every tendon, every dark hair raised, the warming of his skin each time I touch somewhere new. It feels so good to be skin-to-skin with him.

"Everything about it, the freeness of flowing through the sound of soft music. The smells. Bergamot, lavender. Sweat. The sea of dreamy bodies of all shapes and sizes bending, flexing, and breathing as one. Working through their personal issues. Healing. Sometimes I get distracted by the beauty of it all. It's magic and power and everything in between."

Dragging my fingertips down his forearms, I interlock our fingers, palm to palm, and try my best to avoid eye contact. But the weight of his gaze is strong, and I can't deny myself any longer. Softly, I glance up through my lashes. His eyes completely captivate me, and I stumble on my words.

"I think you'd really like it."

I guide his arm towards me in a full extension, then make circles with our wrists.

"It sounds tempting, but I can't guarantee I won't get distracted by you in those yoga pants," he smirks.

Heat spreads across my cheeks, and buries its way into my body. Shifting to my side, I suck in my bottom lip.

"Here I was thinking you were a nice boy."

"I think we're past the pleasantries. Don't you?"

He holds my gaze for a moment too long before I let go of his hand. "So, this is effectively your hiding place?"

He smirks a little at my change of subject, but answers the question. "I suppose. There's something about being in this room. It's familiar. It's...home."

Danny mirrors my actions as I reach out, stretching my arms forward with my fingers interlocked. I've always found the physical practice of yoga to be extremely sensual, and I can sense his eyes on me as I take my final pose with my arms raised above my head.

The silence between us is comfortable. Danny makes me feel safe. There's never any rush to speak, or move. With him, I no longer feel like I have to hide behind Summer. I can just be.

"How do you feel?" I ask.

"Like a new man." He rises from the floor. "Now that I'm cured..." he says, walking back to the raised platform and grabbing his guitar from the stand.

"...Are you ready for your private show, Miss DeLuca? I figured since we missed the encore on Saturday, you deserve to have your own."

He lifts the strap over his head and proceeds to tune the telecaster by ear. Slow hands begin to play, instantly transporting me back to the night of the gig. His breath in my hair, the beach, his car, his sexy but subtle Riviera fragrance. I can smell it now. Our almost kiss...

Long fingers move with grace along the fretboard, and my heart threatens to burst through my chest at the sound of his voice breaking through the instrumental. Fine lines deepen around his eyes as he closes them, a surrender to emotion with every brush of the metal. This is the sexiest and most beautiful thing I've ever seen. To see him come undone to the music, to completely surrender, it undoes me as well.

With each repetition a new and subtle variation is born. His eyes remain closed, creating the perfect opportunity to study his face, and I swear I can almost see the music coursing through the veins of his exposed forearms, the way those little muscles flex every time he changes chords drives me wild. In twenty seconds, I've become the girl who goes gaga over musicians.

My scalp tingles, slowly spreading to my spine, legs, arms. The span of my fingers, the tips of my toes, and the warmth flooding my body sends me into a blissful, almost meditative state. He's my own tailor-made ASMR experience.

Gaze softened, I press a palm between my legs, rocking my hips against it to relieve the building pressure. I imagine myself in his hands. Deft fingers sliding across my neck, moving down my body, tracing my curves with slow hands and a delicate, yet confident, touch.

Heavy-lidded, I visualise the roughness of his palms on bare, soft skin, swaying back and forth to the easy rhythm in an attempt to dull the ache between my legs. I want to draw out this feeling for as long as possible until the song is over and beyond. I want his eyes on every inch of my body, his mouth on mine, and his hands pressed between my thighs.

Music and breath thunder in my ears as Danny plays harder. Tipping my head back, I close my eyes, letting my senses take me on a journey. Every movement he makes, every chord change, every slight alteration in pitch and tone sends my pulse racing as subtle wisps of citrus and white florals perfume the air. I rock harder against my palm, a crescendo carrying me to the edge as my toes curl, my body jerks and I cry out.

My voice echoes into the open space, cutting through silence and shaking me into reality. The ringing pressure in my ears doesn't subside, nor does my struggle for a full inhale. Opening my eyes, I regain focus. Danny's gaze is dark, like a deep, mossy amber, compared to his usual honeyed-olive hue, and his expression completely unreadable. One thing is certain, we are both utterly speechless.

I will him to say something. I would take anything over this unbearable silence. I count my in-breaths while I wait for him to speak, but I soon realise he isn't going to. My phone chimes, pulling me away from the most awkward and confusing moment of my life.

"Um...I should get that."

I scramble for my backpack, dropping my phone on the floor as soon as I pick it up. Danny has his back to me, hands in his pockets. When I check the missed call, his hands are in his hair. Calling April back would be my get-out-of-shame-jail-free card, but I can't leave the studio with this hanging in the air.

Again, I wait for him to speak, but I'm too afraid to look at him. In my peripheral, I can hear him moving around, and I figure that he's either just as embarrassed as I am, or he's completely mortified, and has no idea how to tell me to leave without being rude.

After moments of silence, I accept defeat on the assumption that his silence is his form of rejection. Without a word, I braid my hair and fasten it, then buckle on my helmet. I've already made myself seem desperate, I may as well add to the humiliation by looking like a complete dork as well as some kind of nympho.

Danny has made it pretty clear—he doesn't want me, regardless of the earlier signs to the contrary. My heart races even harder than before at the realisation, because I actually care about the way he perceives me. I've never had to deal with unrequited feelings before, but I'm starting to realise that I like him, and I have no idea what to say or how to feel.

It takes two attempts of trying to simultaneously hold the door open and drag my sorry ass along with my bike outside before he rushes to hold it for me, and my common goal to save face proves futile the moment he holds my gaze.

"Sophia."

"I have to go," I say.

My name hangs heavy in the air, and I refuse to give him the time or traction to voice a rejection. Eyes on the ground,

I mount my bike, and don't look back.

Chapter Twelve

♥

*C*AN WE TALK ABOUT *what happened?*
    After spending the longest forty minutes of my life cycling home, Danny's is the last name I want to see flash across my screen. I ignore the message and return April's call.

"Hey, so I found out the reason why Ryan has been MIA." April says. "He's back with Chrissy. Hold on, I'm putting you on speaker."

A pause, followed by a slight rustling.

"So, anyway, Stefan sent me this cryptic message earlier. I called him, and he must have been in some sort of drug-induced haze, he said that Chrissy knows everything. She knows I was the one he cheated with. That isn't even the best bit. When I called Ryan, he said he can't be friends with us anymore, that one of Chrissy's terms was to, and I quote, cut us off."

"Are you fucking serious right now?"

"He wants to tell you himself, so don't tell him I said anything,"

My stomach coils, and anger wells in my chest. "After everything? I can't believe he could be so spineless. Fuck.

111

Are you okay?"

"I will be. Are you?"

"I'm not sure, I need some time to process. I guess I'll just wait for him to contact me."

What a typical Ryan move to do things on his own terms without any thought of who he's hurting in the process.

"Let's arrange a night out for when you're back from your course. Just us girls."

"Sounds perfect."

I hang up, reeling from our conversation. I can't deny that this has been a long time coming. Ryan stomped on my heart all those years ago, and it never fully healed. I realise I've never truly forgiven him for cheating on me, and I conclude that he's partly responsible for the way I act with men. Two silent rejections and my flurry of emotions is enough to deal with for one day. Now it's time to rest.

I hit the gym straight after work the following day. After sleeping on my feelings about Ryan, and using the time to gain some insight, I'm still ready to confront him in the least diplomatic way possible, especially as I've been expecting to hear from him all day, and all I've gotten is radio silence.

After working up a sweat on the Stairmaster, I hop off and move over to the weights. Across the room by the water machine, I spot Stefan. His tight curls are twisted into a tidy bun, and he wears loose fitting shorts and a matching vest the same colour as his pale blue eyes.

"Feeling better?" I ask, startling him.

He almost drops his water bottle when he turns to face me. "Much better. I think it was a bug. You're here early."

"I was hoping I'd catch you, seeing as I didn't this morning. I thought you might be working."

"I finished my shift half an hour ago. He just got here, too," he says, jerking his head towards the weights area.

Ryan is sitting on a bench scrolling through his phone. As far as I know, he hasn't seen me.

"Has he told you? About Chrissy?" I know Stefan well enough to know that his poker face sucks. If he has any idea what I'm talking about, he has a pretty good way of hiding it. But it's unlikely. His brows knit together like he's trying to remember something while I take a long pull on my drink, then I top up my bottle. "Come on," I say, dragging him by the forearm.

Ryan looks up from his phone as we approach.

"Hey, Phi."

"Don't," I say.

"April called you, didn't she?" Ryan asks, looking over his shoulder.

"What's going on?" Stefan asks, looking between the two of us, concern etched on his face. He must have been so out of it yesterday that he didn't read Ryan's messages, and probably doesn't remember speaking to April.

"Were you going to tell us? Or were you just going to leave it up to April?" I ask. "Because I'm sure Stefan and I would love to know why you're throwing away over ten years of friendship over *her*."

"So what if I am. I specifically told April not to say anything because I was going to come round and tell all three of you tonight. Phi, the way you and April are towards Chrissy means it's never going to work. The constant bullying, the—"

"Excuse me? Who's the bully in all of this?"

"I know she and April didn't get on in school, but she's changed."

"People don't change."

"No, but they grow," Stefan chimes in.

"Whose side are you on?" I ask.

"It's not about taking sides," Ryan says. "Stop being so fucking childish."

There's that word again. Childish. Seems to me that's all I'll ever be. An entitled, sophomoric child, just like Danny said the night we met.

"Clearly not, you've obviously made up your mind."

"Do you honestly think this has been an easy decision? What do you think I've been doing all week? No amount of rehearsing this conversation in my head was going to make it easier. This is hard for me, too." Ryan buries his head in his hands, then looks up at me with watery eyes. I can feel his pain, because this is just as hard for me. Because it's crystal clear that now is the time to let our friendship go. "I don't understand why you can't just be happy for me."

"Because she doesn't deserve you," I spit, then pause in an attempt to regain some sort of composure. "Do you realise how hurtful this decision is?"

My question is met with silence, but I own my decision to be completely honest and open with him while I still can. "I don't know why I gave you a second chance. You know how badly you hurt me all those years ago, why didn't I realise you'd do it again and again? Always thinking with your dick, always bringing out the worst in people. I don't know what's worse, your selfishness or my weakness. I should have called you out ages ago, but I didn't, because I thought you might change."

And because I owe you for saving me from *him.*

I'm so angry, I can barely see. I blink back a tear, and glance to the ceiling.

"I thought I'd give you the benefit of the doubt. But you're just like everyone else—a disappointment. This was your last chance to redeem yourself, and you betrayed the only people who have ever given a shit about you. Never come near me, or talk to me, ever again."

Tears well in my eyes when I walk away, my pride allowing me to compose myself long enough to walk out of the building. I'm confident neither of them will follow me. They know me well enough to know I don't want them to.

Crouched on the concrete, my heart races as I fumble with my bike lock. Once it's set free, I jump on and ride away, as thick, hot tears roll down my cheeks.

After making several pit-stops to dry my eyes, I'm finally home. Once I get through the door I fill a pint glass with water, down half and grab a banana. All that crying and adrenaline has got me dehydrated and craving sugar.

I creep past the living room, hoping that James is too engrossed in whatever trashy show he's currently bingeing on Netflix, but he doesn't miss a beat.

"Baby, what's happened?" he asks, clearly registering the mess that stands in front of him.

I can't care less about what I look like right now. "I'm okay, I just needed to eat something."

"You expect me to believe that you've been crying because you're...hungry?"

"It wouldn't be the first time. I'm sure Stefan will fill you in when he gets home."

James shoots me a pointed look, and in turn, I roll my eyes. Sighing, I make myself comfortable beside him, tucking my legs underneath me and hugging a cushion to my chest. I tell him everything that happened, starting with the phone call from April.

"Oh love. I had no idea." He gives me the pity eyes I hate.

"It's not even that he's back with her. It's the fact that he's thrown away our friendship and used April in the process."

"I'm sure he'll come around."

"I'm not even sure I want him to."

James pauses. "Want to get drunk and order pizza. My treat?"

"That's just going to make me feel even more shit. I didn't even get to work out. Thank you though. Men are pricks."

He pulls me towards him and kisses my hair.

"Not you, though."

"I know, baby."

Before I retreat upstairs, I gather up the banana skin and empty glass, then turn to James one last time.

"Do you think I'm a bully?"

"Don't be ridiculous. Sometimes you're a bitch, but you're *that* bitch. You know what you want, and you go for it."

The TV claims his attention, and my stomach growls, but no amount of food will fill this emptiness.

A little while later, I'm freshly showered and dressed, and have re-joined James in the living room along with Stefan.

"Are you okay?" Stefan asks.

"I will be. I'm just heading to Alex's. I need to blow off some steam."

I contemplate reaching out to Danny, but I'm not ready to face him yet.

"I can take you through some breath work?"

"Thanks, but I've tried that already. A Nidra won't work this time. I just need some space, okay?"

"I know I'm not your favourite person right now, but I love you. Be safe."

"I will. I love you, too."

When I approach Alex's apartment complex, I dismount my bike and lock it up outside. I haven't had a call or reply back since my earlier text, and I'm starting to think it's a risky move to show up unannounced, especially given our last conversation. But this itch won't scratch itself, and my own hands won't provide the relief I crave. I need the intimacy of another person's skin on mine. I need to forget the shit show that is my life right now, and I need to visit my good friend, external validation, to help me get there.

I bypass Lilura, and go straight to his apartment. Luke opens the door wearing nothing but a pair of grey sweat shorts and a raised eyebrow.

My eyes widen as I give him a quick once-over, hoping that he doesn't notice.

Thanks to his gym selfies on Instagram, his thick-set, muscular physique is no secret, but I can't help but marvel at his hard work every time I catch him with his shirt off. I'm starting to realise that I most definitely am a pervert.

"Hey. What are you doing here?" he asks.

"Is Alex here?" I ask, sliding past him.

I don't care if I seem rude, now is not the time for pleasantries.

"Come in," he mutters under his breath.

I drop my helmet and backpack by the door, and head into the living room.

"Peroni?"

"I'd love one."

Only the best.

He fetches the drinks while I kick off my shoes and make myself comfortable on the sofa. When he returns, he hands me a bottle, and sits beside me. Leaning against the armrest with my legs tucked beneath me, I take a sip, instantly relaxing as the first drop of icy liquid hits the back of my throat.

"Alex is gone."

"What do you mean, gone?"

"He moved back to London."

I sit there awhile, silent and shocked. "Wow."

How many more times can I stand to be let down?

"I'm sorry, I thought you knew."

"I mean, I know we were having fun, but I thought he might have had the decency to say goodbye."

"I think it was pretty sudden. I'm not excusing his behaviour, but he booked a huge modelling campaign, and couldn't turn it down. He wasn't supposed to stay here permanently, anyway. I'm sure he'll be back for graduation."

"Well, I won't be waiting around."

"Come on. I don't think that's fair. I think he really liked you."

"Oh, don't give me that bullshit, Luke. Even if I felt like that—which, for the record, I don't and never did—I could never trust him. He was constantly screwing around."

"I could see it was different with you."

I throw my head back and scoff. "That's adorable. I'm obviously not enough to stay for, though, right? Not even to say goodbye to. I'm never enough."

"I think you are."

In the eerie silence, his gaze falls to my lips. He inches closer, and in a hasty decision, I kiss him. It isn't long before my nails claw his skin, tearing at the tension, anger and frustration that has built up over the last few days, sating my desire for human contact.

Straddling his thick, muscular thighs, I pull my top over my head, and find his mouth again. His kiss is hungry, and that passion exactly what I need, just not his.

Gripping his strong, wide shoulders, I push my body into his, grinding against his hardness as he grabs my hips. Running my hands along his smooth pecs, I throw my head back and let him explore my body with his mouth.

Soft moans escape my lips, and my body responds in all the right ways under his touch, but my mind is elsewhere.

"Are you sure you want this?" he asks, between heavy breaths.

No. I want Danny.

I don't answer. Instead, I throw myself into another kiss and try to push the thought to the back of my mind, but every time I do, it comes charging forward stronger than before. The irritating little voice in my head keeps insisting that I'm done with feeling nothing. That I'm done with feeling lonely and empty. But I'm not ready to admit to what my heart is trying to tell me.

"Sophia? I need a yes or a no."

Luke's words trigger something inside me, giving me the push I need to stop this from escalating any further.

"I'm sorry," I say, climbing off his lap and admitting defeat. "I can't."

I bury my head in my hands, and when I finally emerge, he's clutching my shirt to his chest.

"You don't have to apologise. I could sense something was off. We can talk about it, if you'd like?"

His dark eyes are warm, soft, and full of pity.

"Fuck. What the hell is wrong with me?"

"Real talk? I think it would have been a mistake." He pauses, running a hand through his perfectly mussed hair. "This must be what breaking bro code feels like."

"Anyone would think the two of us together would be fire, right? But it just feels all kinds of wrong."

"Some things aren't meant to be."

"Amen to that. Thank you for not being an absolute dick about this." Although the bar is set dangerously low, he has singlehandedly restored my faith in men. Maybe I'm being hasty about how I left things with Danny, but I want to let things simmer before I reach out to him. I'm not ready to bare my feelings. I have a heart to protect.

"Contrary to popular opinion, I'm a real neat guy," he says.

His terrible attempt at an accent sounds like an American taking the piss out of a Brit who's trying to do an American accent.

"But seriously, you know how Italian women are. I grew up in a family full of matriarchs, and even if Alex—or anyone for that matter—doesn't respect you, know that I do."

I smile. This is the most unlikely friendship, but I'm here for it.

"Who knew you were a secret cinnamon roll?"

"I don't know what that means, but I'll take it. Cinnamon rolls are sweet and gooey, and they taste fucking delicious. Plus, there are plenty of girls on Insta who keep my ego topped up," he smirks.

I huff a quick laugh. "Sure...what happened with that girl you were seeing, anyway?"

He shrugs. "Didn't work out."

"Oh?"

"I accidentally said your name when I was...well, you know."

I go to sympathise with him but then my tummy rumbles and I blush. "I'm going to head off. I'm starving, and I'll take an educated guess that you have no food. So, I'll leave you to your adoring Insta fans," I say.

"Well, you could've had a sausage."

"A chipolata won't fill me up."

"That was uncalled for. How do you know I'm not hiding a salami under here?" Luke gestures to the slight outline in his shorts. Smirking, I side-eye him.

"I'm sure a mini chorizo is more accurate."

"Charming. Here I was, about to suggest Mexican takeout."

"Well, I'm here now, we may as well get some tacos. No chorizo for me."

Chapter Thirteen

♥

THE FOLLOWING MONDAY, I drag myself onto a train to London for my course. This past week I've done a pretty solid job of keeping myself distracted with course preparation, but in the quiet moments my thoughts have strayed to Danny.

After the non-situation with Luke, I made a decision to dedicate the first half hour of my day to meditate, so I could make sense of my thoughts, and be with my feelings, my body and my breath in stillness. It weighs on me that I might actually be falling for someone who doesn't feel the same, and it scares the shit out of me.

After checking in with the receptionist at Auréale, I help myself to a coffee from the machine and take a seat on a sofa in the waiting area. Sipping the silky warm roast, I scroll Instagram, liking posts without bothering to read the captions. Once I have my fill of memes and inspirational posts, I pick up a magazine from the table and thumb through the celebrity-filled pages.

"Hi, is anyone sitting here?"

A young woman with large, expressive brown eyes gestures to the adjoining arm chair. For a moment, I can't speak—the girl is stunning. Teal hair cascades in long waves over her shoulders, and intricate tattoos in shades of baby blue, lavender and rose adorn her arms and chest. She looks like a mermaid. Once I pick my jaw off the floor, I manage a nod.

"I'm Ellie," she says, taking a seat in the armchair.

"Sophia," I say, offering a smile.

"Are you here for the Social Media course, too?" Ellie asks. I nod.

"What are you reading?"

"Oh, just the latest toxic celebrity bullshit. You know what? I used to enjoy reading these things, but I don't even know why I picked it up. You want it? I'm pretty much done." It isn't just the magazine; I'm done with a vast amount of the pretentious things I used to love. I close it and hand it to Ellie, who proceeds to flick through the pages.

"I just like the puzzles."

I smile, absorbing Ellie's bright, contagious energy. Sipping my coffee, I quietly watch her fawn over the questions, while a handful of people enter the room, helping themselves to drinks and sitting down on separate tables so that they can peruse their phones in peace. Ellie signals the end of the quiz with a flick of her pen.

"That was impressive," I say.

"What can I say? I have no life." Ellie lets out a high-pitched chuckle, which would sound annoying coming from anyone's else's mouth, but on her it's charming.

"I don't believe that for a second. You're like what? Eighteen?"

"Nineteen. Honestly, I'm a bit of a recluse. I have social anxiety, so that keeps me in a lot."

"I'm sorry. You seem so confident."

"That's what everybody says. Sometimes it's hard, but I'm lucky to have a job I love. When I'm at work, it's like a switch flips. I can be anyone I want to be. The shop floor is my stage," she says, dramatically.

"That's great. So you've really found your calling? That's amazing to have that so early on in life. Your parents must be really supportive."

"Actually, I live with my grandparents. My mum died when I was small, and well, my dad isn't really that interested."

"Oh, I'm so sorry to hear that."

Ellie shrugs. "It's okay. Life isn't supposed to be easy."

The last statement grips my heart. My dad is a man of few words, but I know his heart is in the right place, and at least he's still around. I feel sorry for his tough Catholic upbringing, and part of me resents the effect that it's had on my own.

I've never met someone who's lost a parent so young, and I struggle to imagine a life without mine being so supportive. The thought enforces the reality that life is cruel.

Although my father has never told me he loves me, or is proud of me, I know that he is. In the grand scheme of things, it's trivial, but sometimes the little girl inside needs to hear it. I make a mental note to call my parents and check in on Kiki once I get to the hotel.

A few more people shuffle into the room and sit down, and they scroll their phones as if technology is the most interesting thing in the world. A sudden wave of loneliness washes over me. I wish it was easier to engage in a group conversation with a bunch of strangers instead of being stuck in our own social media silos. Halfway through my cup of coffee, a man with perfectly groomed facial hair gives a quick head count and addresses the room.

"Good morning everybody. If you'd like to follow me, please," he says.

The clatter of chairs pushing back and bags slinging on shoulders is a welcome sound in comparison to the incessant tapping of phone screens a few moments ago.

"Can I sit with you?" Ellie asks me, as the man leads us down a long, bright corridor.

"Sure." I smile. But I feel as though no amount of smiles can compensate for the sheer amount of sympathy I have, and the overwhelming urge to protect her, which is strange considering we've just met. But she seems delicate, and a little naïve, and mostly, she reminds me of Kiki.

We follow the man into a large room which is set up with a large round table and chairs in the centre. In the corner is a selection of camera equipment, lights, fabrics, foam boards, and a computer monitor. At the front of the room stands a beautiful Black woman sporting a scarlet lip and short, natural curls. With a warm smile, she greets each of us as we walk in and find somewhere to sit. The interactive whiteboard behind her displays the words, "Social Media & Influencer Marketing," and the name, "Zahra Davis," along with social media logos and handles of the same name. Once the group is seated, she introduces herself.

"Welcome, everybody." The softness in her voice matches her smile, and her whole demeanour has an ethereal quality.

"Welcome to Auréale. My name is Zahra, and I am the Head of Social Media and Marketing. This is Romesh, my assistant," she says, gesturing to the man who guided us into the room. "I'd like to take a moment to congratulate you all, and welcome you to our company. This is an extremely prestigious course, and we have a lot to cover in the next two days, but I promise that you are all more than capable of keeping up. You wouldn't be here otherwise. Don't be embarrassed to ask questions. There is a lot of equipment we will be discussing, and a lot of terminology you probably haven't come across before."

As she explains, Romesh hands out branded notepads and freshly sharpened pencils.

"This morning we will cover a little bit of theory, with a focus on setting up your space."

She points to the corner of the room where the equipment is piled up.

"As you can see over there, we have a limited selection of equipment. These props are purely there so that I can show you the type of equipment we use when creating our videos. This will include an introduction to lighting, backdrops, bounce boards, sound, and optimal use of your camera.

"After our morning break, we'll move on to some practical sessions. You will work in groups and all have a go at setting up your own workspace and utilising that space to its upmost efficiency. Lunch will be around 1pm, then we will have more theory this afternoon focusing on content and themes, ready for a whole day of filming and editing tomorrow. We will have a short afternoon break, then aim to finish at 5pm."

I can sense an impending headache. Zahra turns to Romesh, and asks if she's missed anything. He ponders for a moment, then shakes his head, and she turns her attention back to the class.

"Any questions?" The room is silent while she waits a few more seconds. "Good. Let's get started, shall we?"

Ivy Rose has booked the same budget-friendly hotel for every member of staff attending the workshop. I've stayed in this type of hotel before. The rooms are basic, but comfortable and equipped with the essentials, and the food is adequate. I invite Ellie to join me in the evening to order room service and watch a cheesy movie—a hobby we learn we both have a penchant for.

After I lay out my handbag and small suitcase on the bed, I wander around the tiny room, checking out the bathroom, cupboards and wardrobe space while I wait for my sister to answer her phone.

"Hey, Kiki Bear. How are you doing?" I ask, when she answers.

"Fine."

I always worry when someone tells me they're fine, but especially when it's Kiki. The last thing I want is for her to go into herself and stop trusting me like she has done in the past. "Fine like the acronym or fine like you're okay but you'd rather I leave you alone?"

"Erm...both?"

Oh no, please don't let it be happening again. "What's up?" I ask, trying to keep my voice level and calm.

"I'm just feeling a bit anxious about going back to school."

There it is, at least she's being honest. I breathe a sigh of relief.

"Have you been doing your five senses like I showed you?"

"It doesn't always work."

I'm too far away to help her, but the least I can do is try. This will be the ultimate test for the both of us—if I can help her from afar, it's a huge win. I rack my brains. "Maybe a bit of movement will help. Where are you?"

"Sitting on my bed."

That's good. "Okay, try sitting on your shins, with your hips resting back on your heels." I pause. "Now, bring your chest forward onto your thighs and rest your head on the pillow with your arms by your side. Try to relax, and take ten deep breaths."

Child's pose always works for me, it's my fail-safe ticket to calmness. I take deep breaths alongside her and place the phone on loudspeaker on the bed while I sift through my clothes, finding a cardigan and wrapping it around me. Hidden underneath, I notice a small, cotton tote bag containing two cans of ready mixed gin and tonic, a family sized bar of chocolate, and a small organza pouch. Before I have a chance to look inside, I'm distracted by a knock at the door. I throw the pouch down on the bed, and invite Ellie in.

When my new friend enters the room, I signal to my phone conversation with Kiki, and Ellie quietly perches on the bed, setting down a wooden box carved with moons and stars.

I excuse myself, finishing up my conversation with an infinitely calmer version of Kiki in the bathroom, and I can relax knowing that the exercise worked before I join Ellie on the bed.

"What's that?" Ellie asks, turning her attention to the organza bag.

"I don't know. I was just about to look."

She picks up the bag, opens the drawstring, and pulls out a small crystal pendant. It's a beautiful, sunshine yellow with raw edges, and comes with a handwritten note which says,

A little something for good luck. Have a fab time. We love you.

I instantly know it's from Stefan and James. I smile at their lovely gesture.

"It's citrine," Ellie says. "Your health, wealth and happiness crystal."

"You're into all that stuff, too?" I ask. Ellie nods. "You and Stefan would get on so well."

"Who's Stefan?"

"My housemate, the one who—" I gesture at the crystal.

"You're lucky to have a friend who cares so much," Ellie says, smiling.

I crack a can open and hand it to Ellie. Then I open the second one, take a long pull, and move my attention to the mystery box she brought with her.

"What's in there?"

Ellie takes a sip and sets the can on the bedside table. "Tarot cards. I thought it would be fun, you know, to get to know each other. But you probably think I'm a big weirdo now."

"Not at all. That sounds like fun."

Ellie looks up at me with wide eyes. "I'm not very good. I'm still learning."

"That's okay, I'll be your guinea pig."

Although I generally err on the side of sceptical, tarot has always intrigued me. I place my drink next to Ellie's and clear the bed, then put my clothes away while Ellie arranges the cards into four piles.

"Ready?" Ellie asks.

We both sit cross-legged on the bed facing one another, with the cards laid out between us. Ellie utters a verbal disclaimer statement, which sounds like an informal version of a police officer reading the Right to Silence.

"Now, I want you to choose a pile. Meditate on them if you need to, but don't think about it too much. Just go with your gut."

I soften my gaze and take a few deep breaths as I focus on the cards. After the situation with Danny, I've now deemed my intuition broken and untrustworthy. Without further thought, I pick the second pile from the left, then bring my hands down to rest on my thighs. Ellie discards the other cards and lay out my choice in a row with the cards facing up.

"Okay, so the first card I have for you is The Moon. Something new is taking form. The Moon reflects new possibility rising from your subconscious to fill the space you have created within your internal work. It also shows me that you're very sensitive. Your ability to pick up energy from others and experience what they're feeling, can be extremely draining on your own energy. You know when people are mad at you, and you have huge amounts of empathy, which is a natural spiritual gift, but it can be good or bad depending on how you look at it.

"I feel like in the past you may have come on too strong with friendships and relationships, and that's maybe caused people to back off a little. I also feel that you're quite vulnerable, and not very good at hiding your emotions or faking feelings. The Moon represents your fears and illusions, and often appears in a reading when you are projecting your fear based on past experiences into your present and future. I just need to add that the Moon also hides things, so others might like to make assumptions based on the way you act or look, perhaps. This is telling you to let go and trust your intuition."

I think back to my first meeting with Danny.

You're an entitled, sophomoric child who measures her worth from Instagram likes.

Does he still see me that way? Is that the reason why he doesn't want me?

I know I've blown it, but I still hold on to the tiniest bit of hope that he doesn't feel that way about me anymore. I hate to admit it, but I don't want him to see me the way everybody else does.

"Next we have The Fool and Six of Pentacles. The Fool represents new beginnings and taking a leap of faith. It could be linked to your Six of Pentacles card, which is about helping others and giving back. Acts of charity and donation. I can see you making a living from a spiritual practice, something like teaching yoga, or making crystal jewellery. Something goal-orientated where you can help others in the community to reach their own dreams and aspirations."

There's no way Ellie could know about the teaching course, but it's reassuring to know that I'm taking the right steps for my career.

"One of the great qualities you have is that you are a very real, raw, and down to earth person."

Ellie takes a deep breath, and points to the next card. It shows a woman bound and blindfolded. "Eight of Swords. I feel like recently you've been through quite a tough emotional journey, but you're learning how to intellectually handle your emotions instead of behaving recklessly to deal with them, which is something that you may have done in the past. We often punish ourselves before others can, but now is the time to take off the blind fold and cut those ties that bind you to limiting thoughts and victim mentality. Now is the time to leave your past behind you and walk away."

I think about my near-miss with Luke. At the time, I didn't see it for what it was, but now, with the truth laid out bare in front of me, I can't ignore it. I'm not all about makeup and selfies, or getting drunk and going home with whatever fuckboy prize has my name on his tongue. How long can I honestly keep up the facade?

I'm growing apart from the girl people perceive me to be. The girl I've suppressed for fear of never amounting to anything, or being good enough, is awakening. Sophia and Summer are two completely different people, and Ellie is slowly helping me realise that.

"Finally, we have Ten of Cups. Your happily ever after card. We both know what that means." She gives me a knowing smile, and before I have a chance to overanalyse that one, she's shuffling another deck.

"Do you mind if I use my Oracle cards, too? I like to use them to reinforce what the tarot reading has shown," she says.

"Sure," I say, and pick another pile.

She lays five more cards out in front of us. "Sagittarius reveals your purity. You are sweet and pure hearted, and more sensitive than you like to admit. I sense that you've been going through and dealing with some family issues recently."

I nod, careful not to give away too much. I think about Kiki, and a lump forms in my throat, but I manage to swallow it down and keep the tears at bay.

"Do you need a minute?"

"I'm fine," I say.

Fine like the acronym.

Ellie reluctantly continues. "Okay, so moving onto the personality aspect of the cards. Taurus and The Bombshell. It's probably likely that your path will lead you onto something to do with beauty or physical exercise, which may or may not take you away from Ivy Rose. I just need to add that Taurus and Sagittarius are not good at self control. You have a habit of leading with your emotions, kind of flitting from one extreme to the other. But I can also see you going through a lot of personal growth."

She points to another card. "Mars. You act on impulse, and have a free-flowing attitude. You pretty much do what you want."

"I feel attacked," I say, smirking.

I lean across to take a pull on my drink, and Ellie does the same, then we focus on the cards once again.

"Last one—Spirituality. You have an incredibly healing energy. Whether it be physically or emotionally, I can see you healing others. I feel like this card echoes the Six of Pentacles from earlier. Your calling is in teaching or travelling or doing something spiritual within your life. Living against the norm, like a spiritual, nomad lifestyle. I truly believe that's where you will find your happiness."

Ellie takes another sip of her drink, and I down the rest of mine, pleasantly surprised at the accuracy of the reading. Maybe there's reason to believe in tarot, after all.

"Any questions?"

How do I stop myself catching feelings? I shake my head.

"How did I do?"

"Pretty much nailed it."

"Really?"

Ellie jumps up like an excited puppy. She's so adorable.

"You were so born to do this," I say, reassuringly.

Room service arrives, and we gorge ourselves on prosecco and tapas while we become acquainted. I talk about Kiki, Alex and Ryan, but I keep Danny to myself. Ellie talks about her family, and work, and how learning tarot with her mum's cards helps her feel closer to her.

In one evening we bond like two old friends reuniting. We talk into the early hours, and once Ellie leaves, the crisp white linen beckons me to sleep.

The following day, the group is split into teams. In separate studios, we're shown how to set up the equipment, record and edit videos, and showcase them to the class. The entire day, my head pounds, and my muscles ache. Worst of all, when it's my turn to take on the influencer role, my hands don't stop shaking.

I'm disappointed in myself for drinking too much last night, and for ruining my chances of making a decent first video—one I can actually use for Ivy Rose's YouTube channel. Something I can be proud of. By the end of it, I'm drained and exhausted, and I can't wait to go home.

Before Ellie and I part ways, we exchange numbers and social media handles, and promise to keep in touch. I love London, but it makes me feel dirty, and I can't wait to be home by the sea again and in a steaming hot shower. Popping in my earbuds, I listen to The Wandering Dragons on Spotify, and let my thoughts drift to Danny.

I let myself think about his hands, and the way he holds his guitar, the way his fingers move, so deft and effortless; the vein that pops from his bare forearm every time his fingers change position. I think about his hazel eyes, and his permanent five o'clock shadow. How I felt being alone with him in that room, and how badly I wanted him to stop playing his guitar and touch me instead. Then my mind wanders to the humiliation I felt in the moments leading up to my departure, and the way my name rolled off his tongue when he said it for the final time.

Maybe a change of scenery is what I need. A spiritual, nomadic lifestyle like Ellie suggested. I'm single, and Kiki's getting better. Does anyone really need me anymore?

Maybe the universe dangled Danny in front of me as some kind of test. I could bypass my teacher training in Brighton and go further afield. Greece, maybe? Or perhaps even India? It would mean learning from the best of the best. But a quick Google search tells me that the expense of doing that is far out of reach, and it pulls me back to the drawing board.

Chapter Fourteen

"SOMETHING'S DIFFERENT," I SAY, taking a sip of Prosecco.

April says nothing, but the quiet curl of her lip makes it obvious that she's hiding something.

I shoot her a pointed look. "Who is he?"

"Nobody," April says, drawing out the word.

I raise my eyebrows, and she turns away from the mirror to face me.

"I didn't want to say anything yet, because I don't want to jinx it, but I've been chatting to Ollie." Her emerald eyes brighten a thousand watts when she says his name.

My stomach is in knots. "Danny's Ollie?"

"How many Ollies do you know?" April says. Her gaze returns to the mirror as she swipes a blusher brush from her makeup bag on the floor.

"When did this happen?"

"Right after the gig. You disappeared with Danny, so we went out for a few drinks. He made sure I got home safe. Nothing happened. I don't think he's like that, anyway." Her expression falls a little. It would be unnoticeable to the untrained eye, but I know her well enough to know when something's niggling her.

"So, you like him?"

"I think so. He's lovely. And gorgeous. I just find it odd that he *isn't* like that. I haven't even had a dick pic. All we've done is flirt."

Wow, an actual decent human being. I can't contain my sarcasm. "Could it be? No...that maybe he's just a bit more mature than other guys our age? He obviously likes you, I could see it at the gig. He couldn't stop looking at you."

"Really?" She brightens up again. "He does make me laugh." Her phone chimes. As soon as she reads the message, a megawatt smile spreads across her face. "He said they're out tonight. They might come and meet us."

My stomach lurches again at the thought of seeing Danny for the first time since the incident. April sets down her phone and carries on with her makeup.

"Anyway, what about you and Danny?"

"Technically he's off limits. I googled it."

"But you'd go there if he wasn't?"

"Well, he's not, so I don't know why we're even talking about it."

My thoughts flash back to the studio as I draw wings on my eyeliner. I try to shake the image of him out of my head, but it's pointless. The self-inflicted distraction causes my hand to jerk, throwing my makeup application off course.

"Shit, I fucked it up."

I fuck everything up.

"Your liner? It's fine, nothing a cotton bud can't fix." April says, fishing one out of her makeup bag. She hands it to me. "What's wrong? Are you nervous about seeing Danny?"

"I like him, and it took me to the point of almost fucking Luke to realise."

April's mouth flies open.

"I'm done with casual sex. It isn't enough anymore. I'm not going to go ahead and say that Danny makes me feel special, but—"

"—but he does," April says softly, giving me a knowing smile.

"He's what I want," I muse. "Fuck, when did I turn so mushy? I mean, it could never work. He's so much older, and—"

"Since when did age mean anything? Isn't your dad like twenty years older than your mum?"

"Eighteen, but that's not the point. I'm not my mum."

"Harrison and Calista have been together for over twenty years, so have Michael and Catherine, and Ellen and Portia. Need any more examples?"

"The common denominator in those relationships are money and lifestyle."

April shoots me a condescending look.

"Danny is out of my league. He's well educated, well travelled, and judging by Belle's Instagram, they run in similar crowds. I don't even know where I would fit in to his lifestyle."

"People divorce for a reason. It's almost over, right?"

I shrug and take a long pull on my drink.

"He told me it was."

"So, what are you scared of?"

"What if he decides that, after all this time, he wants to be with her?"

A weight settles in the pit of my stomach, and a wave of nausea hits. Normality for me is being let down, so now that I have the potential to have something good and real, and genuine, it baffles me. I've been let down so many times before that it almost feels normal, like I don't deserve my happily ever after because of the way I've treated people. Maybe Ryan was right; maybe I *am* a bully.

"When does that ever happen? I love you, and I mean this in the nicest possible way, but stop overanalysing, it's annoying as fuck." April snaps her blusher compact closed and picks up a tube of mascara. "What does she look like, anyway?"

"Like she models Savage Fenty lingerie."

"Well, even if she looks like the queen Rihanna herself, they're not together anymore. If you need some reassurance, just talk to him."

I fix my eyeliner while I rehearse conversation starters with a version of Danny in my head. It won't be easy, but growth means trying, and that, I have to do. He needs to know how I feel.

Lilura is packed wall to wall with bodies. In a pre-drinks buzz, we make a beeline for the bar, and order a couple of Sambuca shots. I savour the sweet, burning aniseed as it slides down my throat and turns to fire on my tongue.

April holds my hand while we weave through the crowd and slip onto the dancefloor, letting the good vibes flow as the atmosphere chokes with the traffic of bodies and the smog of sweat.

I can't lie, since the night my drink was spiked, nights on the town have been tainted, and it's taken a long time for me to feel safe again, but I know April will always look out for me.

Nothing makes me feel more free than when I'm lost in the music, dancing to my own rhythm, with my best friends by my side. I'm never going to let what happened define me. I'm just a little more careful with my drinks, and with my friends' drinks.

A while later, April heads to the bathroom while I queue up at the bar. Ahead of the crowd, I spot a familiar forearm tattoo, and there's no mistaking the striking tiger image which belongs to Ollie. Beside him, Danny leans on the bar with his back turned, and I catch a glimpse of his profile as he laughs at something Ollie says.

His outfit, a white shirt tucked into taupe chinos, hugs his athletic physique in all the right places, I swear my heart stops for an entire second at the sight of his lean, muscular forearms peeking out from rolled up sleeves. My pulse races when his bright smile unleashes those perfect dimples, and I find myself thinking that, although it's all kinds of cheesy, I want to be his reason for smiling.

Shamelessly, I admire him from my secret viewing point, confirming that butts in beige trousers are fast becoming my favourite thing in the world. As far as I'm aware, he has no idea that I'm behind them, and I have no intention of making myself known. I slip into the crowd, making a swift exit towards the upstairs bar.

After knocking back two more shots of Sambuca, warmth from the alcohol beats and pulses through my veins, and I calm. All the seats are taken, so I lean against the glass balcony, and scan the crowd below in search of April, and it isn't long before I spot that fiery red hair brushed up against a tiger tattoo.

With no sign of Danny, I scan the room again, bypassing Mr Unpopular sitting at the bar with his bottle of champagne and a veil of misery on his face. I smile at my earliest memory of Danny, his words from that night haunting me.

Loneliness is dangerous.

I know it. I fear it. But rejection and injured pride is an entirely new concept for me, and I hold him solely responsible. I'm well aware of the way I look, the way people perceive me, the type of men I attract, and I'm okay with having that reputation, because it means that nobody comes too close for comfort.

I never have to reveal myself.

I can be whoever I want.

"So this is where you've been hiding," Danny says, dampening the noise in my head.

Before I turn, I close my eyes, taking a moment to breathe and extinguish my thoughts. "I'm not hiding, you are."

I cringe at my choice of words, but Danny's smile is soothing, and it's the perfect visual to accompany Dua Lipa's Break My Heart. Even the DJ is mocking me right now.

"Well you found me, then," he says, raising his hands in mock surrender. He leans over the balcony and cocks his head towards Lonely Man, then turns to face me. "Spying on our friend, are we? I mean, I'd go keep him company, but somehow I don't think I'm his type."

"Not blonde enough," I muse, trying to sound serious. "What are you doing here, Danny?"

In my head, I sound assertive, but out loud, it's a little more than a whine. I hate it.

"Having a drink."

I deadpan.

"Oh, right. You mean up here...with you?"

Folding my arms across my chest, I tilt my head and raise an eyebrow.

"I wanted to see you. I hate how we left things, and I wanted to say I'm sorry for the way I acted."

"You don't need to apologise. I'm the one who..." I trail off.

I don't have the nerve to admit what I did, even though he was there in plain sight watching me.

"There's no shame in what you did, Sophia."

My name sounds like velvet sliding off his tongue.

He leans in a little. Fuck, he smells good. Sharp citrus and muted florals engage my senses, transporting me to balmy summer evenings on the Italian Riviera, and the smallest hint of whiskey on his breath intoxicates me further. Hazel eyes lock with mine as blood and alcohol fuse together, rushing through my body at lightning speed. My breath quickens.

"I didn't say it before, but I'm saying it now, and I'll say it again. I thoroughly enjoyed watching you come apart for me."

Fuck. His confession renders me speechless. Every line and conversation I have drawn up in my head somehow vanishes from my memory. Nobody makes me nervous like he does, but when I gauge the darkness in his eyes, and the outline in his chinos, I realise how much his own words affect him, too.

"I'm sorry for assuming that you wanted anything from me just because you're nice to me. But that's what I'm used to."

His expression softens. "What do you mean?"

"Most people I meet just want something from me. In the words of Ariana; they see it, they like it, they want it, they get it." My eyes fall to the floor. "And then they leave."

"Do you think I'm like that?"

"I don't know. Are you?" I don't know what to say or think or do. I'm not used to being open with people outside of my circle about my so-called reputation. But I've been open with him before—about Kiki, about me—and it feels strangely right to just say what I'm thinking.

"You don't need to feel ashamed about anything that's happened in your life. I can see the good in you, but I know you don't."

Tilting my chin with feather light fingertips, he searches my eyes. I think he might kiss me, but he lets go and composes himself. "Sorry, I'm a bit drunk."

"It's okay."

It's not.

My heart sinks, and I try my best to hide it with a closed-lipped smile.

"Maybe we should find the others," Danny says.

An awkward moment passes before I respond. "Sure, I'll meet you there. I need to go to the bathroom first."

It's a blatant lie, but I need the solitude, even if it means standing in a mile-long queue and breaking the proverbial seal. I contemplate sneaking off and going home, but first I need to make sure that April is okay.

I'm far from being drunk, but my vision is hazy as I lead the way downstairs. Holding onto the banister for support, my head swims with thoughts of not being enough, and in my stupor, I misjudge my footing.

I trip, slide and land on my butt a few steps from the bottom. Heat turns my cheeks beetroot, and I don't know whether to laugh or cry. There's no way I can style this out, but I'm grateful that years of squats has finally paid off; my butt sure knows how to cushion a fall.

"Are you okay?" Danny asks, taking a seat on the bottom step.

I appreciate the concern etched across his face when he looks up at me, but when I look deeper, the sparkle in his eyes indicate his desire to stifle a laugh.

I make an incoherent sound as I bury my face in my hands, and the heat from my skin burns my palms. The music drowns out my surroundings, and I will the ground to swallow me up. After a while, when I realise that it won't happen, I bring myself back into the room, and my eyes focus on Danny. I know I said I wanted to be the reason for his smile, but he is full-on hysterical laughing at me right now.

"It's not funny," I say, trying my hardest to pout. But in the end, I can't contain my laughter.

"I'm sorry." He holds out his hand for me to take and pulls me up to standing. "I am. Really. But you should have seen you." He's quiet for a second, and I can see how hard he's trying not to laugh. It's adorable. He catches my gaze, and the lines around his eyes crease into laughter again. God, I wish he'd kiss me. I can't help but echo his infectious sound, until our bubble of giggles and awkwardness pops.

"What is it with you two disappearing together?"

My eyes dart to April, who stands with her hands on her hips and an eyebrow raised as high as her hairline. I can't contain myself; I feel like a naughty school child being told off by the principal. Ollie comes up behind April and wraps his arms around her waist, and she visibly relaxes.

"Hope you're not doing anything you shouldn't be doing," Ollie says, wagging his finger at us.

"We're not," I say sweetly.

I don't know if Ollie's close to Belle, or even if he knows her at all. But I have to assume that his moral compass is squeaky clean, and I have to be careful.

"I, um, fell down the stairs." Heat flashes across my cheeks again when the words come out.

"Oh shit. Are you okay?" Ollie and April ask in perfect harmony.

Their connection is clearly undeniable. I nod. "I'm fine."

"Are you coming to dance?" Ollie asks.

Danny looks to me for an answer, and a hint of a smile plays on his lips. Suddenly I'm not so sure about going home.

"Sure, but I need the bathroom first. I'll meet you guys on the dancefloor."

"I need to go too, after all that laughing." Danny says.

"Overshare much?" I smirk, taking the lead.

Chapter Fifteen

ONCE THE BATHROOM BREAKS are over, I meet Danny outside the ladies' restroom. Leaning against the wall with his arms loosely crossed, a suggestive smile breaks across his face when I approach him. Beside us, a roped off staircase leads down into what I assume is a stock room cellar.

"Come here," he says, unhooking the rope and gesturing into the darkness.

I shoot him an inquisitive look.

"Just go with it."

He walks into the dark enclosure, then steps aside to allow me to enter. Reluctantly, I follow him, and he leans behind me to clip the rope back onto the metal post.

I stand at the top of the stairs, looking down. The darkness and the unknown sends a wave of fear crashing into me, quickening my pulse as my subconscious brings back fragments of *his* dirty hands on me and the stench of alcohol on *his* breath.

I fight to hold back tears.

Danny's here. You're safe.

"What are we doing here?" I ask.

"Don't look back in anger, DeLuca. Take back your power," he says, finally. The ghost of his breath in my hair sends a sheet of goosebumps across my skin, and as I turn to meet his dark green gaze, I am naked, weak and completely surrendered.

"What?"

"Change the narrative. Give into the fear and take back your power."

Suddenly, it all makes sense. He isn't using my past as a weapon against me. This entire time, he's been fighting for me. With me. And now he's giving me the push I need to change the narrative and take back my power in the place I felt powerless. The reasons why he held back at the beach and in the studio finally become clear. He needs me to take the lead, to be in control. He's giving me the chance to make a new memory, one that's light in the darkness.

His face edges closer, and butterflies swarm in my belly, fluttering up through my chest. I swallow them down, pushing them deep into my stomach. The warmth of his breath dances across my lips and I close my eyes, savouring the closeness I crave from him. It's all I can think about.

Next thing I know, I'm kissing him, and everything about this moment, about his lips on mine, is sweet, and soft, and incredibly perfect. In this moment, we're back in our bubble —without the laughter and the awkwardness—and the whole world dissolves around me.

"I'm sorry," he says, pulling away, his lingering breath a heady scent of mint and single malt. "I shouldn't have—"

"Stopped?" I ask, smiling against his mouth.

Now I know how kissing him feels, I can't be without it.

"I mean...I should have asked."

With wide eyes, I break contact, and suck my bottom lip. "Want to try again?"

He gives a gentle nod. "Sophia DeLuca...may I kiss you?"

I close the gap, parting my mouth, willingly offering myself to him, back to those lips that are more cushioned than I could have ever imagined. Nobody has ever bothered to ask before, and I find it so incredibly sexy.

With a tender touch, he cups my cheek, and wraps his other hand behind my neck, pulling me towards him, deepening our connection. His teasing tongue slides amongst mine, and I mirror his slow, deliberate movements as he unravels me. I've never cared for the taste of whisky, but on him, it's exquisite.

Heat spreads between my legs as my heart threatens to pound through my sternum. I lay a hand on his chest, and I swear I can feel his heart beating just as hard. This is all too much and not enough at the same time.

I'm aching, itching for his closeness, but I tell myself to go slow, be patient. For once in my life, this has the potential to be something real. Wrapping my arms around his waist, I melt into his lean, muscular physique, backing him against the wall.

Disclosure's Latch lends itself to my ears, while our bodies fuse together in this force field, like the famous lovers of Pompeii. My entire body feels like I've been injected with some kind of life-altering drug, sending me into a higher sense of self. I don't want this to end, not when everything about kissing him feels so natural. Because when his lips are on mine and he's kissing me like no one's ever kissed me before, I'm finally seeing what I refused to see in him.

"Hey. You're not supposed to be back here."

Gasping, dizzy and breathless, I turn to see who's responsible for popping our perfect bubble. A surly woman carrying a crate of glassware stands behind the rope, and I remember where I am.

We apologise, taking a moment to compose ourselves, and climb underneath the rope, leaving the woman baring her teeth.

"Again with the disappearing act. You guys took forever," April says, as we approach our friends.

"You know how the queue gets," I say.

I can't bring myself to look April in the eye. Instead, my gaze meets Danny's, and we share a smirk. Dormant butterflies awake.

"Umm, anyway, I was going to get us all a drink." I manage to tear my gaze away long enough to convince myself that I need a moment alone to process what has just happened, but really, I want to leave right now with Danny.

I want him in my bed, all night long until the sun comes up. I want to make him breakfast, and spend the entire day nursing hangovers, laughing and crying in equal measure at some ridiculously cheesy romantic comedy. I want to share funny and sad stories, and everything in between, and feast on our favourite foods. I want to make new memories.

The funny thing about alcohol is that it acts like a truth serum. Because the sad reality is that Danny still belongs to someone else, and even when that's fully over, does he really want to jump into another relationship?

He halts me by the arm as I head towards the bar, and those long fingers wrapped around my skin are enough to send electricity shooting through my veins again.

"I'll come with you," he says.

Does he have any idea what he does to me?

Leading the way, I squeeze into a space at the front. It isn't overly busy, but busy enough that our bodies are touching. Our forced proximity makes my skin tingle all over, and I'm brought back to the moments before.

In an attempt to free myself from sensory overload, I lean on the bar away from Danny, certain that if I stay put, I'll explode, and I fear I won't be able to keep my hands to myself.

Catching the attention of the bartender, I order a bottle of prosecco and four glasses. I notice Danny sneak a glance over his shoulder before his hand grazes mine, and it takes a moment for me to realise that he has claimed it.

Entwining our fingers, his thumb makes small circles on my knuckle. It's a fairly normal, non-sexual thing to do, but I'm so turned on right now. How can one tiny, insignificant movement feel so good?

That small movement sends my imagination into overdrive, as I picture his hand pressed between my legs, his thumb making circles on my clit. Fire rushes to every part of me, and it's as if that movement on my knuckle is a direct link to every nerve in my body that's responsible for turning me on. Again, I'm dizzy with want. I am this close to guiding his hand underneath my dress and letting him feel just how much I want him. I would totally get arrested for indecent exposure for this guy.

The bartender claims Danny's attention, snapping me out of my stupor. He continues to hold my hand until the drinks take precedence, and that signals the end of our physical contact for the night, with little more than stolen glances and wishful thinking until it's time to leave. He doesn't need to tell me that we have to be careful because of legalities. The fact that he's still technically married is a grey area, and I like to live in black and white.

When the night ends, we make our way to the taxi rank and say goodbye. I know it's for the best. A one-night stand with him will satisfy my cravings, but at the same time, I want to be more for him than that because—although I don't like to admit it—he's so much more than just another one-night stand to me.

A sinking feeling sits deep in my gut when we say goodbye, and when we leave in separate cabs, a DM chimes on my phone almost at once after the car door closes.

Danny: Monday.

Chapter Sixteen

♥

A SUNNY, CLEAR-SKIED MONDAY morning rolls around, and to say I'm looking forward to the day ahead more than usual is an understatement. This will definitely go down in Sophia history as one of the least Mondayest of Mondays I've experienced in my lifetime. I love my walk to work, but the thought of seeing Danny again puts an extra spring in my step as I try to contain my excitement. When I round the corner to the high street, my good mood is short-lived and I'm frozen by the woman before me.

Beautiful, flawless Belle. She suits her name perfectly. In reality, she looks every inch the goddess she is in her photos, and the little girl who's hand she's holding bears the same ethereal, sun-kissed skin and perfectly formed features with long, flowing, dark locks.

My throat tightens. By comparison, I'm a dollar store version of Belle. They stop outside a bookstore while I watch, frozen in awe and admiration, the same bookstore that's only a few doors down from Ivy Rose Organics.

Once I snap back to reality, I glance at my watch. With four minutes to get to work, I know I don't have a choice but to walk straight past them. Avoiding eye contact, I rush past, and as I do, I catch the heady scent of elegant florals and money, leaving a pleasant smell in my nose, and a vile, bitter taste in my mouth.

When I get in, I slam the door shut behind me without thinking. Lauren jolts, causing her mascara to smear. She turns around and waves the fibrous wand in the air.

"Do you mind?"

"Not really," I say, heading straight past her towards the bathroom.

I don't know how to feel, but all I know is I need to let my emotions run riot. Whether that means crying, screaming, or breaking something. Before I have a chance to plan my next move, Lauren stops me in my tracks.

"Okay, what is with the attitude? Talk to me."

"Fine," I say, perching on a stool by the makeup station. I hook my block heel onto the metal footrest, and as I swing myself sideways and glimpse my reflection, I'm reminded of all the ways I'm not Belle.

I take a deep breath, and start to reel off the story from the beginning, right from the first time I met Danny at Lilura, the wedding band confusion, and all the moments leading up to our kiss on Saturday night, right up to seeing Belle and the little girl a few moments ago.

Luckily, Mondays are quiet, and are usually reserved for filming content. The lack of customers allows me to be completely open and honest, and deal with my feelings in a healthy way instead of my usual feat of resorting to reckless behaviour.

"When Michael and I first met, he was technically married," Lauren says.

Most of the time, Lauren is a closed book. She's never delved into her relationship with her fiancé.

"He and his wife had been living separate lives for a long time. But they carried on as they were, both unhappy and going through the motions, neither of them having the guts to say anything.

She pauses to straighten her engagement ring.

"I thought it was a one-way street, a crush, but I wished for us so badly, and I was completely shocked when he told me he'd left her. I mean, nothing ever happened between us until it was all finalised. Even then, I had to constantly fight a battle in my head. I kept thinking that maybe I was just a rebound. I never felt like I was the marrying type, and if you're not, that's totally okay. I thought that maybe he would just get bored of me and go back to her."

She pauses.

"Look, I'm not saying it was easy—it wasn't—but he was worth the wait."

I smile. "I just don't know how I'm supposed to know what I want when I'm used to skipping the feelings part and going straight to sex. What if I'm chasing something I *think* I want?"

A moment passes, and I take a breath. "When I was on that course, I met this girl, Ellie. She read my tarot, and the cards basically said that I'll find my true happiness living a free spirited lifestyle. With Danny, I feel that freedom, like I can completely be myself around him. I've never felt a connection like that. Never had someone in my corner like that. I mean, it's different to how lust feels. Infatuation, perhaps? I really can't explain it."

"So, what's the problem?"

"I can't help feeling like I'm out of my league. I don't have any expensive hobbies or go to fancy restaurants. I've never even been outside of Europe." I pause. "Belle, she's otherworldly gorgeous, and she's obviously super smart. She has a great job, and she seems like she's a great mum..."

"You don't even know if that little girl is theirs. She could have been babysitting. Trust me, being the wicked stepmother isn't something I ever thought I'd have to do, but I love the twins, and of course they have their moments, but I'm pretty sure that they love me too.

"It doesn't have to be difficult, and you can't make huge life decisions based on a deck of cards. We create our own happiness, and if things are meant to be, they'll work out. You just have to want them enough, and believe that you deserve it. Life's too short for regrets. Be bold. There's no shame in going after the things you want."

"Thanks, Lauren."

Of course my boss is right. Now I can only hope that I'm wrong about the little girl. There's no denying that children complicate things, and I still don't know where I stand with Danny, let alone entertain the idea of being the wicked stepmother. After a five minute crisis meditation in the staff toilets, I'm ready to do what I do best—create a kickass tutorial.

I feel ridiculous for wearing a full face of makeup to yoga practice, but I wouldn't have had time to reapply before meeting Danny at the studio, and although I don't want to admit it, seeing Belle in the flesh has knocked my confidence. I need my game face on.

When I arrive at Unit 5B, I raise my hand to knock, but the melody playing on the other side inspires me to stop. I let myself in, closing the door softly behind me. Danny is sitting on the couch, guitar in hand with his eyes closed.

I slip off my backpack, and set my helmet down on the floor. Leaning against the door, I watch him play a sweet, soft melody. The tune is familiar, and it only takes me a few bars to recognise it as Peer Pressure—the James Bay cover that Monty and Imani sang at the concert. This version of him, raw, emotional, serious, and soft, is refreshing to see, and I can't help but smile.

He opens his eyes, and the music trails off, reaching a natural end as a slow smile spreads across his face, deepening his dimples and the lines around his eyes.

"Hey," he says.

"Sorry, I should have knocked."

Leaning across the arm of the couch, he switches off the amp and unplugs his guitar, resting it against the sofa. Rising, he walks towards me, twirling a plectrum between his fingers, stopping inches from my face.

"There's something I've been meaning to ask you," he says.

The butterflies awaken and I say nothing. I don't know what he's about to ask, and I'm not sure I want to.

"Do you like to watch? Or be watched?"

Under the weight of his gaze, I cast my eyes down, and attempt to swallow the lump that's forming in my throat. I wasn't expecting that, even after knowing the way he feels now. It's a pretty bold thing to say. Warmth spreads through my body, and I throw my focus on his hands, watching the way the pick rotates between his nimble fingers. It's calming. Grounding.

Looking up through my lashes, my eyes meet his honey green gaze. I want to reach out to touch his face. To run my fingers along his jawline and pull him towards me.

"Is there an option three?" I ask.

He shakes his head with a Marlon Brando smirk I could easily become obsessed with.

"No."

"Then both, I suppose."

I look him square in the eye when I say it. Inside, I congratulate myself for maintaining a cool, calm demeanour, and in an attempt at being offhand, I look away, and wander towards the stage. Inside, I am the furthest thing from calmness.

I can sense him watching my every move as I run my fingers across the well-worn plastic of the snare drum. Stalling, I take the time to inspect every bump and ridge, before I step off the stage and approach the guitar-lined wall.

"Does this work?" I ask, pausing to admire a shiny black and gold Gibson Les Paul.

Within seconds, he's beside me, and that scent of his completely captivates me while he carefully unhooks the vintage guitar from the bracket. He makes his way to the couch, sets the Les Paul against it and props the other one on a stand. Plugging it in, he leans across the leather arm and switches on the amp again.

"What shall I play?" he asks.

I assume he's talking about song choice, but when I approach him, I ignore the question, and prise the plectrum from his hands.

Be bold.

I can hear Lauren's well-meaning wise words in my head.

This is my attempt at being bold.

"Other than me," I say, twirling the pick between my fingers.

I kneel in front of him with my legs tucked beneath me.

"I want to watch you play...whatever your heart wants."

With a steady gaze, his eyes darken.

"And I want you to watch me."

His gaze is pure, dark, addictive poison. If I could bottle the way he's undressing me with his eyes, I would. I want more, and still, that would never be enough.

I've never felt so empowered in all my life. To have the freedom to ask for what I want, and to know I won't be shamed for it.

Still, I can't shake that question that's been drumming around in my mind all day long. "I need to know something first. Is anybody going to get hurt?"

I know I could have asked him outright about the little girl who was with Belle earlier, but I want to avoid mentioning either of them at all costs. If he felt any guilt whatsoever, he would stop this.

He pauses, shakes his head and says, "no," then he proceeds to tune the guitar.

It's a good enough answer. Just like Lauren had said, there's no shame in going after what I want.

Once the sound is pitch perfect, he picks up the melody once again. I rotate the plectrum, watching his fingers move along the fretboard, and with that visual in my mind, I close my eyes. Pressing it between my lips, I swirl my tongue around the tapered end, and slide it over my bottom lip, down my chin and neck, to the dip above my collarbone, leaving a glistening trail.

To the rhythm of his sound, I drag the pick south, and gently press the sharp end into the skin between my breasts. Opening my eyes, I glance at the superficial mark it leaves, then I meet Danny's dark green gaze. I suck in my bottom lip, and the savage way he looks at me fuels my body with heat and want.

I've never wanted anybody so badly. Sure, lust and I are good friends, but this insatiable need, this infatuation with him I have is taking everything I have. Every part of me wants him, and wants him to have me in every way. Every nerve, every beat of my heart, every inch of skin and every hitched breath I take. This is all for him, and I give it to him freely.

It takes all my willpower to slow down, but the desire to tease him overrides my need for quick relief. I shift my position, rocking my centre back and forth on the heel of my foot to ease the pressure building inside of me.

I flick my tongue over the sharp edge of the plectrum to get it wet and press it against the fabric covering my nipples. They pinch under the pressure, and I'm grateful that the layer of cotton covering them is thin enough for me to feel them brush and harden against the plastic tool. Heat pools between my legs, and my breath quickens.

I use the sharper edge to switch up the sensation, making small circles on one nipple, then repeating the process on the other. When the rocking brings me close to the edge, I slide it down to my navel and into my yoga pants.

Raising my ass off the ground, I widen my knees, and steady myself. My heart races with the anticipation of what I'm about to do. A tiny dose of anxiety threatens to change my mind, but I have to keep telling myself that this time is different than the first time we were in this room. I'm in control now.

I look to Danny for reassurance, and the darkness in his gaze gives me the green light I need to continue.

With the plectrum held between my thumb and forefinger, I flatten the cool plastic against my clit and press down, making small circles. My breath hitches, and my low, guttural moan is drowned out by the sound of the guitar. Closing my eyes, I lose myself in the music, losing all self-control. And I don't care who hears my moans.

My middle finger slips inside easily, and I mirror his rhythm. The tempo changes, becoming faster as he plays harder, and the music grows louder. I'm a puppet he controls through the strings of his guitar, but the way my body responds to the music has never made me feel so free. My ring finger slips inside, and by this point I'm gasping for release, but it's not the pressure I need. In one swift movement, I discard the plectrum onto the floor, and push my hand into my yoga pants once again, alternating my fingers between my clit and fucking myself. I'm torn, because I never want this feeling to end, yet I'm so close to complete bliss and satisfaction that I can't stop myself. I bring myself closer, until I'm moaning and gasping for air, and my entire body charges and shakes.

Within seconds, I'm free falling off the edge, and my body goes rigid before my legs give way. The backs of my thighs collapse to meet my calves once again, leaving my entire body warm and flushed from the top of my head to the tips of my toes.

The room falls silent apart from the sound of my heavy breathing, and a lazy smile spreads across my face.

"Mmm...I needed that," I say, slowly opening my eyes. I'm on such a high.

Danny pulls his guitar strap over his head and sets it aside, and my gaze falls to the hard outline threatening to burst through his chinos.

"You need a hand with that?"

His line of vision follows mine. "I can't."

Just like that, I'm back on the ground. His answer—the one I'm so desperate not to hear—sounds full of regret, and he buries his face in his hands as a swarm of wasps infiltrate my belly, leaving me nauseous and feeling completely rejected. Again.

"You can't, or you don't want to?"

Another image of Belle flashes through my mind. I know the little girl isn't his daughter, but all I'm hearing is that this man is quite clearly still in love with his wife. How did I not see it before? How could I be so naïve to think that someone like him could be interested in someone like me?

My legs are still weak, but I manage to rise and walk towards the door without resembling Bambi.

"Where are you going?"

"Home." I thread my arms through my backpack straps and pick up my helmet. I raise my hand to let myself out, but he moves fast, stopping me with his palm flat against the door. I turn to face him, arms folded across my chest.

"Tell me Danny...what do *you* want? Because all of this seems like some sort of game to you. A game I have no interest in playing."

"I want you to stay."

"That's not good enough," I say. I'm exasperated.

With a clenched jaw, he screws his eyes closed and leans his forehead against the door. I wish I could take the pounding in my heart as a sign for the way I should respond, but I'm unsure as to whether I want to kiss him or slap him.

Moments pass, but I watch him long enough to notice his jaw soften, and his breath slow, and when his eyes finally open, his expression takes on the same one he has when he plays his guitar—raw, emotional, serious, and soft. But he ceases to look me in the eye.

"I woke up this morning, and yesterday, and the day before—and every fucking day since I met you—thinking about you."

"Then why don't you want me?" It comes out so quiet, so meek, and I hate myself for it, but it captures his attention. Finally, he faces me. Mirroring his stance, I lean sideways against the door.

"Is that what you think?" He draws in a breath, taking his time to exhale. "I feel so much guilt. What I want doesn't matter. Until that piece of paper is in my hand saying that I don't belong to somebody else, I just can't."

"You had no issue kissing me in Lilura."

"I got caught up in the moment. I just think we need to be careful, that's all. Things with Belle...they're complicated."

Thoughts swarm my mind, but the most potent one, the one I still can't shake, is that he's still in love with her.

"Well then, I guess there's no point in me staying."

"Don't go. Please."

"I'm not here to entertain you, Danny. Let me go."

I don't want him to, but right now I have no choice but to admit defeat.

He backs away from the door, and I pull the handle. I avoid eye contact, but I can sense his eyes on me.

Hesitating, I pull it towards me, the heaviness a perfect metaphor to the weight bearing down on my chest.

Please, beg me to stay.

"Fuck it. I want you."

Chapter Seventeen

♥

HIS HANDS PRACTICALLY FLY to my face, and in one swift movement he has me slammed against the wall, his lips against mine, kissing me like I'm the only thing that can sate his hunger.

If this is how it feels to be wanted, I won't settle for anything less ever again.

I melt under his touch, encompassed by his warmth and the sweeping scent of citrus and white florals as the low sun beats through the windows, bathing us in warmth and golden light.

I shrug off my backpack, and it falls to the floor with my helmet. His palm slides down my back, and he pauses when his fingers reach the hem of my top. My breath hitches, and my lips tingle, begging to be touched again.

Inching up the soft cotton, he uses both hands to pull it over my head, then he kisses me again with his hands in my hair, free flowing between my neck and collarbone, before exploring my mouth once again. Butterflies swarm my belly, and heat spreads between my legs as he gently caresses my tongue with his. I tighten my arms around him, and I can feel his mouth curl into a smile.

A soft bite on my lower lip signals a time out.

"Don't stop," I moan, wanting more.

He moves his mouth down my chest, and my breath hitches as he pulls down the top of my sports bra and takes my nipple in his mouth. I moan a little louder, and he gently tugs it between his teeth. Warmth floods my insides as I grip his hair.

"Is this okay?" he asks, between heavy breaths, meeting my gaze for approval.

I nod.

"I need a yes."

"Yes."

"Fuck, you're so beautiful." Never have I ever been called beautiful, and it sounds glorious coming from his mouth.

He repeats the motion on my other breast, slowly trailing down to my navel, and pausing to catch his breath. I remove my sports bra and kick off my trainers. Light, soft kisses trail down towards the waistband of my yoga pants. He pulls them, along with my underwear, slowly over the curve of my ass, then down over my thighs and calves, and I step out of them.

It doesn't bother me in the slightest that he's still fully clothed, because him in a crisp, white shirt with the sleeves rolled up turns me on just as much as if he were naked. He could wear a potato sack and still be one million percent fuckable.

He nestles his head between my legs, and the anticipation kills me. I raise my arms above my head, using the weight of the door to steady myself. He kisses the inside of each thigh, leaving teasing wet trails on my skin as he moves closer to my centre, which burns from the heat of his breath. The instant his mouth makes contact, I let out an involuntary moan, arching my back as my whole body tingles.

Slow and meticulous, he caresses me with his whole mouth, sliding his tongue over my clit as he slips in a finger.

His five o'clock shadow grazing against my bare skin heightens every sensation, and I fight every urge to pull him towards me and grind my hips against his face.

"Fuck," I breathe, my hands in his hair.

He glances up, arresting me with those hazel eyes and perfect dimples, while he pumps his finger and buries his mouth on me, upping the tempo to compliment my breathing.

This. This is how I've always wanted to be looked at. With undeniably raw, savage lust. This is what I've been missing my entire life.

With his other hand, he grabs the back of my thigh, lifts it, and hooks it over his shoulder. I buckle, dripping beads of nectar as his confident tongue explores deeper.

Pushing my hands into his hair, I grip his scalp, pulling at the thick dark strands. Writhing against him, he laps up my liquid, and my body gives in to the mounting pressure, forcing my legs to weaken. My entire body pulses and floods with warmth.

Sweet relief engulfs me. I pause, taking a moment for my heart to slow, and I focus on deep, measured breaths, while he carefully unhooks my leg, and kisses my knee.

Satisfied, and completely at his surrender, I slide down to the ground, tucking my legs beneath me. He kneels beside me, and brushes his lips against mine in the softest and most delicate way, but it's enough to taste my sweetness on him— a taste I could easily get used to.

"That was...incredible," I finally say.

I can't find a better word to describe the insatiable feeling, but it doesn't stop me feeling hungry for more, or for wanting to climb on the roof and shout out every delicious detail of Danny's perfect mouth.

I eye the bulge in his chinos once more, and for a slight second, I hesitate. I can't face being rejected again, not after the first time I mentioned it. But curiosity gets the better of me.

"Why didn't you want me to take care of you before?" I feel the floor for my clothes and slide them back on. "Believe it or not, some girls actually like giving. I'm some girls…just so we're clear."

"It's not that I don't want you to." He pauses. "Fuck, I want you…more than anything. But until I have the piece of paper in my hand telling me that my marriage is completely over, I don't feel like I can give in to you. If I put a foot wrong, I'll lose everything. I don't trust her."

"I can fully appreciate that it's a grey area, but you're separated. Can you honestly tell me this doesn't feel right?"

Please tell me I'm not alone in this.

"Everything about us feels right," he says, and I relax.

"Then why does it matter so much? I'm pretty certain after almost two years, she can accept that you've moved on."

My statement is met with silence.

"Do you have kids? Is that it?"

"No, we don't."

A huge wave of relief sweeps over me. Oh, thank goodness.

"Do you still love her? Am I just here for a distraction so you can use me? Fulfil some sort of fantasy for sexual gratification and go back to your perfect life?"

"That's absolutely not it."

"Then what is it?"

More silence.

"She's a bully," he sighs, burying his head in his hands.

An unwelcome pain twists in my gut, and I feel an overwhelming urge to protect him. I wasn't expecting it, especially as *bully* triggers all those emotions that hit when Ryan used it describe me.

"You know people say you can't see a bad situation when you're in it, but once you step back, everything becomes clear?"

"From the outside, we gave everybody this illusion that we were the perfect couple. Powerful. Unbreakable. But that couldn't have been further from the truth. After we got married, Belle's parents loaned me the start-up I needed to set up my business. My parents wanted to help, but they couldn't because all their money was tied up in property. I paid them back in full as soon as I could, with interest, but it still wasn't good enough. She would always find a way to bring it up in conversation. Now I realise it was a way to belittle me."

I shift, folding my legs behind me.

"I started noticing a change when she became partner at her firm. The more she rose to the top, the more she treated me like I was beneath her. Like she resented me for being a lower earner, or something. She started to spend a lot of time away from home. Court cases in London, that sort of thing. We barely said two words to each other, and when we did, it was the same tired, pretentious bullshit. All in the name of keeping up with her social circle. Don't get me wrong, I'm so incredibly grateful we could afford to live a life of luxury, but for me it's just as important to have quality down time at home.

"I'm not saying I never loved her, or that she wasn't my everything once upon a time. But power changed her. Status changed her. I'm not saying I was the perfect husband, either. Nobody's fucking perfect. But I didn't throw away my old friends when newer, richer, shinier ones came along. Sometimes once upon a time doesn't end in happily ever after," he muses.

"I'm so sorry, I had no idea." I say, placing a hand on his forearm.

"Over the years, I could feel my confidence gradually being chipped away, bit by bit. She made me feel ashamed for the way I was, and for the things I wanted to explore sexually. I thought there was something wrong with me, so I kept them hidden. But since you bared your fucking soul to me, as you put it, I can't stop thinking about it. About you."

"I know it sounds corny, but one day I opened my eyes, and everything started to make sense. Why she never came to any of our gigs. Why she had never been supportive of the band. Once we hashed things out and agreed to separate, I realised that she was ashamed of me, and she resented me for borrowing the money from her parents. My mind started replaying snippets of things she had said in the past. She always used to say that music was a waste of time because it's not a real career. All I wanted was for her to support us, because it made me happy. Do you remember when I told you about Ollie?"

I nod, and Danny swallows a lump in his throat.

"That wasn't the whole story. I went to her for advice—I mean, she's a solicitor, it's her job. I didn't know what else to do, I was so scared he was going to harm himself. She managed to convince me that there was no other way than to turn down the contract. It took years for me to realise that I'd been manipulated. I could have paid for Ollie's private care; I could have helped him."

"You did help him. I mean, I don't know him well, but April seems to really like him. He probably has you to thank for that. You can't throw money at something and expect all your problems to be solved, it doesn't work like that," I say.

"Some things do work like that."

I shoot him a pointed look. Seems I never tire of teasing his middle-class lifestyle.

"So why separate when you had grounds for divorce."

"When I told her I wanted out, she managed to convince me otherwise. Apparently, that's called gas lighting. Who knew? I'm actually pretty ill-informed for a smart guy. God forbid I tarnish her reputation, or drag her precious name through the mud. Ultimately, that's the reason we decided to separate. By the time I changed my mind, and realised what she was doing, what she had been doing all along, we were too far into the separation. It's too late to file for a divorce; we only have a few weeks left."

"I can't believe someone would do that to someone."

Despite Ryan and Chrissy's opinions of me, I can hand on heart vow that I would *never* do that to someone.

"You totally had me fooled," I say.

"Why is that?"

"You're so charming, and confident...borderline cocky, actually. I would never have guessed that you were a soft, squishy, sweet Dalmatian puppy."

"Well, that was instantly emasculating," he smirks. "And now you know that it's all a defence mechanism...kind of like your alter-ego, Summer."

He flashes a smile, and my heart melts. I have this innate urge to protect him from all the Belles and Chrissys of the world.

"I didn't say it like it's a bad thing. But nobody deserves to be treated that way. She doesn't know how lucky she is. Was." I offer a smile, and the way he looks at me makes me want to curl up into him and against his chest. So I do.

The air hangs heavy as silence fills the room. I don't know what to say next, if anything. I'm terrified of potentially ruining the moment. I'm terrified of being anywhere but here.

"Can I ask you something?" Danny asks. "Why me? I mean, you could have anyone you want."

"Because you're everything I'm not."

He sobers, and I flash a weak smile while my brain screams at me to change the subject.

"And the fact that you're almost due your bus pass is a pretty big turn on, not to mention the dad bod."

"If you want to see me naked, all you have to do is ask."

"I did...twice."

There's no chance in hell I'm going to mention the fact that his confidence is enthralling, and his unprompted show of vulnerability makes me want to take care of him. That he has the ability to make me feel completely at home and out of my comfort zone all at the same time.

And I definitely won't tell Danny that I'm falling hard for him, because feelings are sacred, and they don't come around often enough for me to give them away freely, not until I'm one hundred percent certain that they're reciprocated.

I shift my body onto my opposite leg at the exact moment the door gives way behind us and we jolt backwards. Reality hits in the form of four young bewildered faces staring down at us. Saved by the band.

"Same time next week, DeLuca?" Danny asks, his hopeful eyes a softer shade of honeyed green.

Smiling, I push the plectrum into his hand, and render him speechless.

"Can't wait."

Chapter Eighteen

♥

TWO DAYS LATER, I sip an iced rose latte on my lunch break, while a coffeehouse cover of The Cranberries' Linger plays on the speakers at The Ethical Coffee Co.

"I know it's going to be a lot of work, but I'm excited." I fork my salad. "Once I finish my two hundred hours, I can start my teacher training for youth yoga and mindfulness."

"That's wonderful, min älskling," Stefan says.

Spending time with Danny has somehow launched my brain into business mode. I pride myself on staying true to my values, and Ivy Rose Organics' new Auréale status has given me the push that I need to pursue a different path. With my long-term goal in mind, and inspired by Kiki's love of hip-hop music, I've spent hours trawling YouTube and TikTok, and researching fun, child and teen friendly yoga aesthetics on Pinterest.

My plan is to video journal my teacher training journey and, using my newly-acquired social media management skills, build up a following from there.

"How did Lauren take it?"

"I haven't told her yet. She already agreed to let me have the two weekends off a month that I needed to study. I can't leave until I'm qualified, anyway. I need the money."

"If you need help with the rent, we can work something out."

"No, it's fine. I'm pretty positive I can do it. I just won't be able to go out as often...but it's no big deal."

"Oh?"

"Why is that so hard to believe?"

"Because you're a party girl."

"Fact. But I'm willing to sacrifice my party girl status to make this work."

Smiling, he reaches for my hand across the table, holds it, and says, "I'm really fucking proud of you."

The comment turns my insides to mush, and I'm overcome with emotion. Shark week must be looming.

"So, does this have anything to do with Danny, by any chance? And don't you downplay it. I can tell when you're lying."

My smile broadens. "I really like him."

"But?"

"You said it yourself—I'm a party girl. What if he thinks this is all just a bit of fun? I know the kind of vibe I give off."

I stare at the warped pink coffee art, but I can feel Stefan pinning me with those deep blue eyes. "What's really in your heart?" he asks, he can see right through me.

"This whole thing with Belle...it's complicated. I'm glad Danny finally opened up to me, which I know can't have been easy for him, but I can't seem to let go of the tiny bit of fear that still has a hold on me."

"Honey, we all have self-doubt sometimes, it's what makes us human. How boring would life be if we didn't take a leap of faith once in a while? You are Sophia fucking DeLuca. Who are you?"

I sigh. "Sophia fucking DeLuca," I say, quietly.

"That's right bish, and don't you forget it."

"It's just...I feel different with him. Like it could actually *be* something. It's not even about sex. I mean, don't get me wrong, I'm intrigued to find out what it would be like if the way he kisses is anything to go by."

My skin flushes a similar shade to my latte, and a wide smile creeps across my face. I haven't divulged to Stefan the exact location of where Danny's lips had been, and I don't need to.

"But I have to respect his boundaries."

"There's a Swedish proverb my mother always says: 'those who wish to sing always find a song.'"

I smile at the beauty of his words, and he glances at his watch.

"If you want to make this work, you'll find a way. Anyway, I have to go to work. Make sure you eat your salad; it's starting to look like a saggy ballbag."

I grimace, and push the plate away. Stefan pecks my cheek and squeezes my shoulder. "I just want to see you happy, it's all I've ever wanted for you. Don't you think you deserve it?"

A beat later, he's gone, leaving me with the remnants of my sad, uninspiring salad and his question replaying in my head. My phone chimes, snapping me away from my thoughts.

Mum never calls this early in the day.

"Mum? Is everything okay?" I ask, a little concerned. She usually saves calling me until the evening, right before she catches up on the soaps.

"It's Kiki. I don't know what to do. Every time I try to talk to her, she lashes out. She's hysterical."

I can tell from her muffled voice that she's been crying. My heart breaks at the sound of my mother's words. I loathe that the woman who's always been there for my sister and I sounds so helpless, when she's always been so strong.

I'm not sure I can go through this again.

The pounding of my heart drowns out the background noise of the coffee shop. I know I have to step up and be the strong one this time. Kiki's diagnosis almost ruined our family the first time round, and I'll do everything in my power to prevent it from happening again.

"It's okay, Mum. Take deep breaths."

The advice is just as relevant for myself to keep from freaking the fuck out. I eye my latte, and suddenly it no longer seems appealing. My mind races with flashbacks to the first time Kiki was admitted. Her screams and the thud she made when she threw herself on the floor of the landing, a sound I'll never forget. Taking a deep breath, I muster some strength, grabbing my purse before exiting the building.

"Try to keep calm. I need to go back to work and pick up my bike, but I'll be there as soon as I can. Have you called anyone at the clinic?"

"We've just come from there. I'll tell you about it when you get here. Sophia, try not to worry. We need you here in one piece."

"Okay, I'll be there soon. I love you."

"I love you, too."

When I arrive, the house is quiet. Too quiet.

"Where is she?" I ask, when I enter the lounge in my parent's house.

Both my mum and dad are sitting on opposite couches. I pull them both into a hug, but stares are vacant and their bodies rigid as they watch a blank TV screen. Seeing the fear on their faces again breaks my heart.

"She's upstairs in her room," my dad says, not making eye contact.

Old feelings resurface, and I feel small, like he can't bear to look at me. Like somehow this is my fault, and Kiki is the only sibling he really cares about. I swat the thought away. My dad loves me and my sister needs me.

"What happened at the clinic?"

"They want to take her in again," mum says, softly. "She won't talk to us, but she might talk to you."

Upstairs, I hover in the doorway of my sister's bedroom while Kiki sits cross-legged on her bed and scrolls her phone, dry tears making a trail along her flushed cheeks.

"Hey, Kiki Bear."

There's no answer or acknowledgment, but I still offer a smile. Over the years, I've become a pro at hiding my concern, because I know it doesn't ease anyone's anxieties in a difficult situation. I've always been calmer than my mum, so, naturally it makes it easier to communicate with my sister. But I have to be tactful. When she was in the worst grips of her illness, Kiki took advantage of my laid-back demeanour, and that's when she became an expert at hiding things. I know it wasn't her, not really, but it makes me cautious even now.

"How are you doing?"

"Fine," Kiki mumbles.

I perch on the edge of the bed. "What did they say at the clinic?"

Kiki carefully places her phone beside her. She's always been a gentle child—always favoured insects and animals to humans—she likes to look after things. I know that she lashes out through fear and frustration, not because she doesn't want to cooperate. "They said I've dropped too much weight." She screws her eyes shut, and a tear escapes. "They didn't say how much, but I've fallen below the first centile. I've tried so hard, I really have."

Her breath hitches, and as tears roll down her cheeks thick and fast, I fight to hold back my own. I hand her a box of tissues from the nightstand, and pull her into a side hug. "I feel like such a failure. Mum doesn't believe me, and Dad doesn't even care."

"Never think you're a failure. You are so strong. You can beat this."

Kiki sobs louder into my shoulder.

"Look, we know the first eighteen months of recovery is the hardest. You know there's going to be highs and lows, but you have a family who love you and fully support you...that's a lot more than what some people have. And I know Dad can be a bit quiet when it comes to dealing with emotions, but he does care, I promise you. He just finds it hard to say it out loud."

If only I would take my own advice.

Kiki hugs her knees into her chest and folds her tiny arms around them. "I'm so tired. Tired of being told what to do...how to be. I'm tired of all the talking. I just want to breathe."

"So, let's breathe."

I manage to convince Kiki to try Nadi Shodhana—a yogic breath control practice I use to help ease anxiety and promote mind and body relaxation. We sit cross-legged on opposite ends of the bed, with our left hands resting on our left knees.

"Close your eyes, relax your brows, and lift your right hand towards your nose," I say. "Now, place your index finger and middle finger in the space between your eyebrows. This is your third eye. You can look up at this anytime you start to lose focus."

I demonstrate as I call out each step, with Kiki following my voice guidance.

"Take a deep breath. In through the nose, and exhale completely out through the mouth. Then use your thumb to close the right nostril, and inhale through the left.

"Now, close the left nostril with your ring finger, and exhale through the right nostril. Inhale here through the right side, then block the right side and open the left nostril. Exhale through the left side. This is one cycle. We'll keep this going for five minutes. Remember to look up at your third eye if you lose focus."

After the first cycle, I notice the small changes in Kiki's body language. The slight drop in her shoulders and the slow rise and fall of her chest as she delves into deep relaxation.

Before the five-minute timer is up, the doorbell chimes. Hushed voices follow, pulling Kiki from her practice. A moment later, there's a knock on the door.

"Come in," I say, after receiving a green light nod from my sister.

Mum and Dad follow close behind Kiki's therapist, Rebecca, who I recognise from our family therapy sessions. Rebecca is kind, gentle and softly spoken, and I'm fond of her. Most importantly, I trust her.

"Hi, Kiki. Do you mind if we have a chat?"

Kiki nods, and shifts to a more comfortable sitting position. I give Rebecca a smile as we switch places, then I join my parents in the hallway.

In the half hour that we wait, my dad's incessant fingernail-biting habit and my mum's stress cleaning coping strategy has me on edge, almost to the point of needing to practice another Nadi Shodhana. When Rebecca emerges and meets us in the downstairs hallway, I'm grateful for the reprieve.

"As you know, Kiki's weight has dipped dangerously low again, so we need to take her back to the unit to run some tests. She's happy to stay overnight until we have her results, but she's insistent that she wants to continue her care at home. How do you feel about that?"

"If you think that's for the best," mum says.

"I think so." Rebecca gives her a reassuring smile, and glances up the stairs. "She's just packing some things. Take your time. I'll meet you there."

Ten minutes after Rebecca leaves, Kiki comes downstairs with an overnight bag, and my dad loads it into the car.

"I'll come visit tomorrow," I say, giving my sister a hug. "I love you."

"I love you, too."

Chapter Nineteen

♥

B Y THE TIME I leave my parent's house, it's mid-afternoon. Nearby to my old primary school, I weave through busy stop and start traffic, hitting the bike's brakes at a set of red traffic lights as two little girls hold hands and skip across the road. The smaller of the two bears a similar resemblance to Kiki when she was around five or six years old, and I can't help but smile at the distant memory of picking my sister up from school when I was a teen.

Back then, I thought I was so grown up. Our thirteen year age gap and my aesthetic maturity meant that I could just about pass for being Kiki's mum, and we would die laughing from all the filthy looks we received from the teen mum shame brigade. Will life ever be that carefree again?

A lump catches in my throat, and I will myself not to cry —to wait until I'm home, at least. The last thing I want is for this hideous disease to take over my sister again.

My body defies me, and thick tears fall down my face. I know the situation with Kiki's illness could be worse, but I can't argue with statistics. I know that anorexia has the highest mortality rate of any mental illness. I know that only 46 percent of anorexia patients fully recover, and that Kiki will most likely be battling with herself for the rest of her life.

Through my veil of tears, I pull out of the junction, and am met with a loud screech. Tyres scream when a black SUV suddenly comes into view and bumps the side of my front wheel, throwing me into the road. I don't have time to thank my sharp reflexes or past experiences of falling, but I'm lucky my body knows exactly what to do. My hip and butt absorbs most of the impact, but I can't stop myself landing partly on my shoulder.

"Are you okay?"

The woman in the SUV parks up on the curb, and rushes to my side. When I try to move, my muscles feel tight and dry, like they've shrivelled up on impact to protect me. Luckily, I feel no physical pain.

"I think so."

It hurts to speak. My throat is scratchy to the point of painful, like it's lodged with fragments of glass.

"I'm so sorry. I didn't see you." The woman helps me up and I walk my bike towards the curb. "Can I call someone for you?"

I can hear the woman speaking but her voice is muffled, and my vision is out of focus, like I'm underwater. In an attempt to find calm among the chaos, I close my eyes and take deep breaths to ground myself. When I'm ready, I open my eyes and get reacquainted with my surroundings.

One final deep breath serves to dislodge the shards in my throat. I rise to the surface and finally feel the moisture of my tears as they roll down my cheeks. Pain sears through my hip and shoulder, and I know now that my body will bruise like a bitch.

The woman's words finally register in my brain. My first thought is my parents, but there's no way I can call them. Kiki needs them more. Most people I know work on a

Wednesday. I try Stefan and James, but neither of them pick up. April answers on the third ring.

My throat hurts like I've been chewing on gravel, and my voice doesn't even sound like it belongs to me, but I manage to briefly explain what happened and send my location.

Before the driver leaves, she passes on her insurance details and makes sure I'm okay. The woman has two young children in the car, so I don't expect her to stay, not that I need her to, anyway. I remove my helmet and perch on a low wall by the scene while I wait for April.

I'm pretty certain that I haven't hit my head, but when a white SUV pulls up alongside a grey Audi, I have to question my reality. Within moments, Danny is in front of me, cupping my face in his hands. I must be mildly concussed.

"Are you okay?" he asks, his eyes tight with worry as he searches mine. "You're cold."

He rushes towards his car as April flees to my side. I touch my cheek where Danny's hand had been moments ago.

"Are you hurt?" April asks, pulling me into a hug. "I didn't know what to do. I was so worried, I couldn't drive, so I called Ollie." I follow her gaze to the white SUV. "We'll take your bike."

"And I'm taking you to hospital," Danny says, reappearing again. "Here, put this on." He wraps a hoodie that smells like him around my shoulders, and opens the Audi's passenger door. I hug the fabric closer to my skin and breathe in that Riviera scent.

"Hospital?"

"You need to go to Accident and Emergency."

Disorientated, I climb in, and say goodbye to April through the open window while Ollie loads my bicycle onto the rack of the SUV. New car scent and leather triggers my senses, and I realise the interior of this Audi isn't the one I'm used to.

"You got a new car," I say, as Danny climbs into the driver's side. It's more of an observation than a question. I don't expect an answer.

"I figured it was time for an electric upgrade. Be a little kinder to the environment."

"Mr Bougie," I say, half teasing, half not knowing what the fuck I'm talking about.

It's probably the trauma speaking, but there is no end to the ways this man can impress me. He pulls his seatbelt across his body, and I follow his lead, pausing to rub my left shoulder to ease the ache. He passes me a bottle of water.

"Here, drink this. Small sips, you might be in shock."

The engine roars to life, and he drives away from the curb onto the road. I gulp some water, and my throat instantly thanks me for it.

"Danny, I don't need to get checked over."

"You could have a head injury."

"I'm fine, I promise. Just take me home, please."

"I'm not taking any risks."

"You're so cute when you're mad."

"Sophia, I'm not mad. I'm worried." A muscle ticks in his jaw, and he white-knuckles the steering wheel.

So cute. So easy to love.

I try to erase the last thought that popped into my head. Maybe I do have a head injury, after all.

"You're lucky," Dr Khan, the emergency room doctor, says after examining me.

After a brief consultation and the relevant diagnostic tests, she's ruled out any serious injury.

"You could have potentially been looking at a broken bone or dislocated shoulder, so congratulations on your ability to fall off a bike correctly."

I shoot Danny a pointed look to say, "I told you so."

"I'm happy to send you home, but I will ask that someone stays with you for the majority of the time, as other injuries may become more apparent in the coming days."

"That's no problem, she can stay with me."

Erm...what now?

"What should we be looking out for, Doctor?" Danny asks.

"While the shoulder injury is quite visibly painful right now, you may start to notice pain in other areas of your body; your muscles, ligaments, soft tissue. It's completely normal, but I just want you to be prepared."

Dr Khan takes a deep breath, and smiles underneath her surgical mask. "The good news is that this is temporary, and will most likely be relieved by taking a few days to rest and recover. A combination of ice and over-the-counter pain medication will help to reduce the pain and inflammation, then you should be right as rain. I'd also strongly advise that you take a few days off work, just until the swelling subsides. If it takes longer than seven days, your GP can issue you with a fit note."

"Thank you, Doctor."

"No need to thank me. I'm just glad it wasn't serious for you. Take care of yourself, and make sure you keep nice and warm."

"I'll look after her. Thanks again." Danny says.

En route, we stop off at my house to pick up a couple of changes of clothes, my phone charger, toothbrush and contraceptive pill. With Stefan and James both working, Danny manages to convince me to stay with him for a few days while he works from home. It makes sense, and in all honesty, I don't have much of a say in the matter. Unsurprisingly, Stefan and James are totally on board.

They've been riding that Danny train since that first night in Lilura.

Along the seafront road, we pull into a private estate, through a gated driveway, then park up outside a large, white and grey three-storey dwelling. Again, I question my life status because I feel like I've died. This house looks like it belongs on a Pinterest board or one of those Instagram home accounts.

As soon as Danny opens the front door, a cream-coloured golden retriever comes bounding towards us.

"There's my beautiful girl," he says, bending down to pet her. She looks so happy; I swear she's smiling. "This is Penny."

"Nice to meet you, Penny," I say, bending down and adopting a light, friendly voice, like I'm speaking to a small child. With a closed fist, I offer my hand to her, and turn to face Danny. "Like Johnny's partner in Dirty Dancing?"

The golden-haired pup makes my acquaintance, then fusses over Danny once again, wagging her tail so hard, it looks like it's about to fall off.

"Weird take, but no. Like Penny Lane."

"The Beatles song?"

"Exactly."

The space is vast, with a large, open plan kitchen and living area with dark oak flooring, white furnishings and white walls throughout, and a staircase with glass panels leading up to a mezzanine area.

Even though I feel like I've just walked into a Home and Garden magazine photoshoot, the cream and taupe accents create an elegant, homely feel. Still, I don't want to sit down or touch anything for fear of breaking something, and I have no idea how dirty I am from the fall.

"I know, baby girl. Daddy's home early."

It melts my heart to see this side of him. Father figure. Animal lover. Budding economist. God, this man.

He scratches Penny's ear for a few moments, before she bounds off again, and leaps onto a chunky knitted blanket on the sofa. He glances at his watch. "Actually, not that early. Have you eaten anything today?" he asks me.

I think about the limp salad that stared me down while I listened to my mother sobbing on the phone. It's the last thing I ate—and I'd barely touched it. "Not really."

He loosens his tie, pulls it over his head and undoes the top button of his white dress shirt, then cocks his head towards Penny. The shock must be having an effect, because my body temperature has skyrocketed. It's a wonder I'm still alive after that display.

"Will you be okay here while I take this one for a walk? I'll grab some food on the way back. Anything in particular you fancy?"

"I'll come with you."

"No, you heard the doctor, you need to rest."

Considering we've known each other less than a month, I find it hard to believe that he trusts me to be alone in his house. Which goes to show how wary I am of people.

"Then something food-shaped and delicious will do," I say, smiling.

I take up residence on the couch, and before Danny leaves, he prepares a small stockpile for me; the remote control, an ice pack for my shoulder, a glass of water, a cup of tea, and a blanket—even though the weather outside is stifling. He shows me the direction of the bathroom, and leaves his number in case I need to call him.

Our earlier conversation regarding the origin of Penny's name sparks nostalgia, and I feel inspired in the form of eighties romance movies. Imagine my surprise when I find Dirty Dancing, one of my favourites, on a streaming service, and the discovery dampens every urge I have to snoop.

Ninety minutes later, Patrick Swayze's iconic line feeds through the surround sound as Penny bounds through the front door and jumps onto the couch beside me. She gives me a little sniff and a nuzzle, then settles on her blanket while I stroke the back of her neck.

"I'll be right back," Danny says, briefly checking both us girls are okay before he disappears again. When he returns a few minutes later, he sets down a takeaway pizza box, and a small, rectangular deli box on the coffee table.

"Off," he says to Penny, holding a chew stick under her nose.

She jumps off, and he rewards her with the treat. After wolfing it down, she settles on the floor with a toy.

"Are you crying?" he asks.

I couldn't wipe the zany smile, nor the tears from my face if I try. "It's the film."

Sure, Patrick and Jennifer's legendary performances are partly to blame, but so is the fact that Danny had made the effort to seek out my favourite deli. I open the box and shoved a slice of mushroom, olive and pineapple pizza in my mouth. One bite, and I realise how ravenous I am.

"I thought I'd see what all the fuss is about," he says, referring to the pineapple. After grabbing a slice and a napkin, he makes a dent on the couch beside me.

I breathe in, and the scent of citrus, woods, and sea water fills my lungs, and all I want to do is climb on top of him and lick the salt from his skin. I dismiss my traitorous thoughts, instead turning my attention to Johnny and Baby's infamous lift.

"This is a great movie," he says, pointing the pizza at the screen. I side-eye him, giving an incredulous look. "I'm serious. My mum was obsessed, so I sort of grew up watching it. I must have seen it a hundred times."

"Me too."

"I think you and my mum would get along."

We share a smile.

"The fact that Hollywood cast an actor with a distinctive nose meant a lot to mini me. Obviously, I wasn't thrilled when I found out Jennifer Grey had surgery afterwards, but I don't blame her to be honest. I probably would have done the same if I had the money when I was younger."

"You don't like your nose?"

"I mean, it's not Jessica Alba's."

"It's perfect."

We share a smile, and again I bat away the image of straddling him on the sofa.

It doesn't take long to polish off the pizzas, along with half the box of Italian pastries he had surprised me with. By the end of it my stomach is beyond full, but I'm not completely satisfied.

Along with his adorable canine apprentice, Danny gives me the grand tour, starting with the kitchen. It's modest compared to the size of the living room, but it's beautiful and contemporary, with a white brick island, handle less cupboards, and bi-fold doors that open out to a vast back garden, leading straight onto the shingle beach.

The attention to detail is exquisite throughout, right down to the ceiling panels, spot lights and stove fireplace. I desperately want to ask how he could afford such an incredible property, but I don't have to.

"My parents actually built this place. My mum was an architect working in London, and my dad was a builder. They met working on a project together."

"That's so sweet," I say, following him upstairs while Penny retreats to her bed.

On the landing by the mezzanine is a separate, more relaxed living area, with two small white sofas and a glass coffee table. The décor is almost identical to the downstairs lounge.

Coastal artwork lines the walls, and a tall bookcase stands in the corner filled with travel guides, coffee table books and succulent plants. I zero in on a photo that looks a little out of place amongst the arty prints.

"Is that you?" I ask, inspecting the photo.

Danny lets out an embarrassed laugh. "Sure is."

The photograph shows a young Danny, around eighteen or nineteen years old, with a long, shaggy haircut, wearing a green parka jacket.

"That look is a whole mood," I say, sardonically.

"I told you we wanted to be the next Oasis."

He opens the door to a guest bedroom, which has no more than a bed and a nightstand with a lamp, and bi-fold doors leading onto a balcony.

"My grandparents helped them set up their company in property development just after my brother was born. We would always come down to Brighton when we were kids. When I was five, my mum had a TIA, which is like a mini-stroke, so they made the decision to move out of the London smog—away from all the stress."

"I'm so sorry, Danny. Is she okay?" I ask, quietly hoping that it was nothing sinister and my questions don't upset him.

He nods, closes the door and makes his way across the hallway. "The move did them a world of good. This was their final project before they retired a few years ago. They bought the existing property, knocked it down and turned it into this. They loved this place so much that they didn't have the heart to sell it, so they kept it and let it out as a holiday rental," he says, opening another door.

I peer in to see another guest room. It's almost identical to the first, but it looks a little more lived in with a stack of books housed on a small desk, and a rail of clothes hanging in an open wardrobe.

"I moved in here when Belle and I separated. This is my niece's room." I have a flashback to the little girl holding Belle's hand. "She goes to Brighton University, so she stays here during term time. My brother feels better about her having a home from home. That way they can save a bit of money, and know she's safe."

And the mystery of the little girl continues. "Do you have any other nieces or nephews?" I ask, trying my best to sound casual.

"Amelia's the only one on my side of the family, but I have two little nieces on Belle's side; a six-year-old and eight-year-old."

Mystery solved.

After he shows me around his office and the large, white bathroom, he leads me towards another door in the centre of the landing. Turning to face me, he palms the handle, and says, "this is where the magic happens." His hazel eyes spark with a wink as dimples deepen. "And by that, I mean the magic of sleep."

For a moment, my mind escapes to fleeting thoughts of other women in his bed, but they vanish as soon as he opens the door. Like the rest of the house, the Pinterest-worthy room carries a neutral colour palette, with homely touches that make it feel cosy and luxurious. Crisp, white cotton lays on a king-sized bed, with an arrangement of cushions and a taupe blanket styled neatly across the bottom.

Patio doors open out onto pale grey decking and a glass balcony, with panoramic sea views over the English Channel —it completely takes my breath away. The entire house has a whispering scent of citrus; fresh and full of warmth, like sitting in an orange grove on a sunny evening to watch the sun set.

"How do you keep this place so tidy?" I ask.

He shifts his weight and runs a hand through his hair. "Would you judge me if I tell you I have a housekeeper?"

"Why would I? There's no shame in having a helping hand. You're busy, and you're creating a job for someone. I'd say that's a win."

"Very true. So, what do you think?" He sounds like a real estate agent trying to make a sale.

"It's beautiful, I love it. You even have those tiny, posh seagulls over this way."

I admire the dainty, pretty birds, which are small in comparison to the giant sky pirates closer to town.

"You're beautiful."

I meet his honey-green gaze, and he tucks a strand of hair behind my ear. My heart stops for a full second as butterflies swarm my belly.

"Sophia, I—"

"Ouch."

Pain sears through my shoulder blade, and my hand shoots toward the injury. I curse the timing. His hand immediately follows, and I move mine away to welcome his warmth on my skin. Instantly, the pain eases and I relax.

"What can I do?" he asks, his palms moving lower down my arms. I breathe him in. An intoxicating cocktail of bergamot and sandalwood, and summer nights on the coast.

"Kiss it better."

Chapter Twenty

♥

I LOOK INTO HIS eyes, then, biting my lip, draw my gaze down towards his mouth, and kiss him. Instantly, I melt against him. Residing in the moment with my hand resting against his chest, my body stills, and the pain eases.

"Are you sure this is what you want?" he asks, against my mouth.

Pulling back, I search his darkened eyes. "Are you?"

"Do you realise how much I want you?"

Smiling, I kiss him again, urging my heart to stop racing as he guides me down onto the bed. I shift backwards, and prop myself onto my elbows. With his knee between my legs, he undoes the buttons on his shirt and peels it off, releasing a burst of his scent as it falls to the floor. His sculpted body is even better when I'm not looking at it through a car wing mirror. Infinitely better because, this time, he's close enough to touch.

Leaning on my good arm, I reach out. Between breathless kisses, my fingers slide from the dark wisps of hair on his chest, down his athletic abs to his tan leather belt. I tug on his waistband, and he climbs on top of me, claiming my mouth. A bolt of heat shoots through my centre as I savour the taste of him.

He runs his thumb along my lower lip, and I focus on the weight of him on top of me and the movement of his hand as it drifts lower down my body. He trails kisses down my neck, chest, then gives my injured shoulder some healing attention. It's a nice touch, and one I won't forget in a hurry. He could kiss everything better for the rest of my life, and I would have no objections.

Resting his fingers at the apex of my button-down tea dress, he draws in a sharp, deliberate breath, and shakes his head.

"Tsk-tsk, so many buttons," he says, a playful smile on his lips, the warmth of his breath on mine.

I laugh, and closing my eyes, part my mouth as he draws me into his embrace. Our tongues dance in perfect rhythm, and he lifts my chin to deepen the kiss. His body, heavy and warm, is a weight I could forever bear. Being so close to him, yet so confined, is pure intimacy, innocence and freedom wrapped into one. Here in our bubble, our force field, no one and nothing can break us.

His mouth leaves mine, and I tip my head back to soft, slow kisses that follow the trail he's already made down my neck and chest, then he returns to my lips, sending bursts of electricity shooting through my veins. Another round of kisses, then he starts to unbutton the front of my dress.

Opening my eyes again, I tuck my chin towards my chest and watch with adoration as nimble fingers skilfully unhook each button, stopping after each one to kiss the skin beneath it. Every drag of his lips across my skin makes my breath hitch.

"Is this okay?" he asks.

"Yes. God yes."

Rough fingers brush my skin—all the way from my neck, down the length of my torso, and over my stomach.

Carefully, he opens the dress, letting it pool beneath me. I prop myself up again, sliding it over my shoulders and down my arms, then I lay supine.

He cups my face, pulling my lips back to his. A sheet of goosebumps creeps across my skin with the sweet, gentle touch. His kiss trails down the side of my neck to my chest, and in one swift movement, he frees my breasts from my black lace bra.

Taking one in his mouth, he swirls his tongue over and around one nipple, and I buckle under his touch, feeling the fire spread throughout my body. With his free hand, he cups and circles my nipples with his thumbs.

"I want you, Danny," I say, breathless and rasping, reaching up towards him. It feels so good to be bold.

"Not yet. I need to taste you first. Is that okay?"

Fuck.

"Okay? Yes Danny, yes I think I could cope with that."

He slips a hand between my legs, and I draw in a sharp breath as his fingers make small circles over my underwear. Breathing deep and steady, I close my eyes and savour his sweet, slow caress. His mouth returns to mine as he pushes my underwear aside, circling his fingers over my slick centre.

Sliding down my body, he trails kisses along my skin, leaving goosebumps in their wake. When his face reaches my centre, I raise my hips to meet his mouth in an attempt to soothe the deep ache in my stomach. After a small taste— an appetiser—he pauses to flash those adorable dimples and perfectly sexy smile, then he slides down my underwear and buries his face between my thighs. I melt, urging him to never stop.

With measured precision, he slips a finger inside, and I rock against the perfect rhythm of his mouth. He picks up speed, driving goosebumps with every flick and turn of his tongue.

Opening my eyes, I watch deft fingers move over my body, and I struggle to control my breathing when my legs begin to shake. I want to hold on, to make this last as long as it can, but I don't have it in me.

"Danny," I pant.

His name is like a driving force to my pleasure. As soon as I say it, my entire body quivers, bucks and shakes. I close my eyes and arch my back, letting the warmth consume me as I crash against the bed, revelling in the sweet release.

Moments pass, breathing slows naturally, and together, we bask in the serenity of my aftermath. When it passes, I'm suddenly aware that he's collapsed right beside where his mouth had been only minutes ago. I feel naked, vulnerable and exposed. In a way, I want him to see me like this, in my purest form, because the innocence I feel with him hasn't been there for such a long time.

"What are you thinking?" he asks, propping himself up on an elbow.

It's the age-old question that I always dread, because my usual train of thought goes something like how-the-heck-am-I-going-to-get-out-of-here, but this time is different. This time, I want to avoid giving an honest answer, because I never want to let him go. My greatest fear in this moment is him realising that I'm a mistake.

I bite my lip and take a leap of faith. "That it couldn't have been more perfect."

His furrowed brow morphs into a raised one, and his downturned mouth is replaced by a smug half smile. I lean down to kiss him, and he crawls up the bed to meet me halfway, his arousal hard to ignore as it digs into my hip.

"Is it greedy of me to admit that I still want more?" I ask, eyeing up the bold display in his trousers. His line of vision follows mine, and so does his hands. He starts to undo his belt, but I stop him. "Wait. Can I do it?"

He nods.

I kneel beside him and carefully undo his belt and unzip his trousers. My fingers don't make quick work like his do, because weirdly, with all my experience, the thought of undressing someone has always felt far too intimate, and after everything, he still makes me nervous. Usually, the clothes are on the floor within seconds, but with Danny, I want to take my time.

Savour the moment. Go slow. Remember everything about it. Feel the vulnerability and the newness of it all and just be.

He pulls a condom out of the bedside drawer and hands it to me.

"I can't promise I can be what you want," he says.

The unprompted display of vulnerability only makes me want him more. His sweet, gentle side turns me on just as hard as that hot, infuriating alter-ego of his.

"You are everything I want, and we've waited too fucking long."

I smile widely, and when I free his cock from its restraints, it broadens.

Holy shit. That is the most handsome dick I've ever seen in my life. Well-groomed, sizeable and hard, his perfectly-proportioned cock stands proud and ready for me, and I can't stop myself thinking about how much I want to taste him. I push his clothes and underwear off the edge of the bed, and he shuffles up towards the headboard, propping his head on a pillow.

I climb onto his lap and kiss him so deeply I can feel the air being sucked from my lungs, while his warm, hard cock teases my opening. The temptation to guide him inside is too much, but I hold myself back. I need to taste him first. This man could easily kill me and I wouldn't care. Nothing will ever come close to this; I've never felt this safe with anyone.

I slide down his body, kissing his neck, chest, torso, until I reach that perfect appendage between his muscular thighs. This I can't slow down, no matter how hard I try. I want him too much.

Butterflies swarm my tummy as I wrap my mouth around the tip and take his entire length in my mouth. Using my hands, I work in a rhythm. Usually, I would use some fancy technique I read about on some Instagram post, but I don't need that.

I use my intuition, listening to his body the way he listens to mine. With his pleasure as my own, I'm finely tuned in to his wants and needs, and it feels amazing to be so connected to someone at last.

The moans that escape him are the sexiest noises I've ever heard. He buries his hands in my hair, and I keep going just to hear him again and again. Using my touch and mouth to make him come undone is so sweet and satisfying, I've forgotten how it feels to want to be someone's everything.

"I want all of you," he rasps.

I'm grateful, because I can feel the pain shooting through my shoulder. I'm already wet from his tongue, but hearing those words and seeing him in all his rawness completely consumes me.

I unwrap the condom and glide it on, then slide back up the way I came. Warmth fills me when I lower myself onto him, taking charge as I guide him inside, and I revel in the stretch. A perfect fit.

I contort against him, wanting to feel every inch of his skin on mine. His low, guttural moan is pure satisfaction and music to my ears when I ease all the way down his length. Sliding against his body, I moan into his mouth. Our breath becomes one as I rock back and forth, feeling every muscle harden against me, finding a rhythm. Weak whimpers escape my throat as I focus on the brush of my hard nipples against his chest and the friction of his calloused hand as he slips it between us and palms my clit.

Quickening the pace, our kisses become sloppy and reckless. Kissing him without restraint is the sexiest thing in the world. It's freeing. Organic. And so right. My fingernails dig and rake his shoulders until I can't hold back any longer. My whole body shakes, and I clench around him, sending me crashing into euphoria once again. Within seconds, he's gripping my hips and losing control before I feel him throb and release inside me, his breath hot against my mouth as I fall into him, our bodies slick with sweat.

Exhausted, I pull the throw from the end of the bed and loosely cover myself, giggling as I flop down beside Mr Handsome Dick in a blissful haze.

"What's funny? he asks, while he discards the condom.

"Nothing. Sometimes I giggle if I have really good sex," I say, trying to catch my breath. The reality is, it's been a long time coming.

Danny quirks an eyebrow. "Watch out, Miss DeLuca, I'm going to keep you laughing all night."

"Never say that again."

Like the lines around his eyes, his dimples deepen.

"Thank you." My face draws a serious expression.

"For what?"

"Making me forget."

Tenderly, I kiss him, and our faces linger closely for a second, before I retreat and grip the throw closer to my body.

"Is it your shoulder?" he asks.

I shake my head, and a single tear falls down my cheek. Quickly, I wipe it away.

Why, of all times, do I have to get emotional now? I blame the orgasms.

"Nothing, I'm just worried about Kiki, that's all."

"Do you want to talk about it?"

I hesitate for a second, but I know I can trust him. I know he genuinely cares, and I feel a pull to open up to him. "It's just...it doesn't make it go away. I'm not naive. I know this will probably be the rest of her life. There are no quick fixes with mental illness. I just wanted her to have a better life than I did. I can't help but feel partly responsible for the way she is. If I hadn't been so difficult, if I had been there, there would have been no need for her to do this to herself."

"Do you honestly think that? You can't blame yourself."

"But she's my sister, Danny. I never wanted her to be like me."

"What's so wrong with you? You're kind, you're beautiful, and you make everyone around you feel important. I mean, you've just had an accident. You could have been seriously hurt and here you are thinking about your sister still. She's lucky to have you."

"I'm sorry," I say, smiling through another tear.

"Don't be." He kisses me again lightly, and all I can taste is the saltiness of my tears between our lips.

"But I'm not those things." I pause to collect my thoughts.

"When Kiki was born, my mum had complications. They stayed in hospital, and my dad took the week off work to take care of me. I was twelve or thirteen at the time, and I thought it was ridiculous. It was the summer holidays, and I thought I was an adult, that I didn't need my dad to babysit me. We went to the beach every day. We ate fish and chips, dinky doughnuts and Mr Whippy ice cream. We swam in the sea at low tide, picked periwinkles and built sandcastles. We walked for hours, talking about nothing in particular, or sometimes saying nothing at all and we trawled the shore looking for sea glass. He took me to the Sea Life centre and won me this ridiculous otter stuffed toy from the grabber machine, and he told me that otters were special. That the older ones take care of their younger siblings, and as long as their parents were alive, otter siblings often never part. I was so in awe of my dad, he was this beacon of information, like he seemed to know everything without ever needing to Google. He just knew things. It was the best day ever when he won me that toy."

Danny listens to me in silence, and the rise and fall of his chest tells me he hasn't died of boredom yet.

"When mum finally brought Kiki home, it was like I had disappeared, or rather my dad had. It sounds ridiculous, but it felt like the instant she was born, all his love for me had been projected onto her. That week we spent together was the best ever, but it was bittersweet because I felt like he was saying goodbye. I mean, imagine being jealous of a baby? I resented her for taking my dad away from me for a long time. I was so used to being an only child, then suddenly, I had to share my parents. Why did she get to have him and not me?

"People can be there physically, but it doesn't mean they're with you spiritually and emotionally. My dad left me the moment Kiki came home, and I've spent a lot of time trying to work on myself to be the daughter he'd be proud of. And I guess that's why I have such low expectations of men. That's why I let Ryan cheat on me, and why I turn a blind eye to him cheating on Chrissy. I've spent the best part of my twenties believing that party girls don't get hurt. I closed off the parts of me that felt good because it felt better to be numb."

Danny tucks a loose strand of hair behind my ear, and meets my gaze. Before I say what I'm about to say, I hesitate. But I remind myself that this is a safe space. Our force field.

"I don't want to be numb anymore."

He searches my face, then pauses briefly before opening his mouth to speak. "I hope you know I would never hurt you, and I'll never leave you," he says, and then he pauses, before saying, "Can I tell you something?"

I meet his gaze, awaiting some kind of confession.

"I'm low-key obsessed with you," he whispers.

I swear to God my heart is on fire when I kiss him, and as we talk, doze, spoon and slow fuck into the early hours, I realise I'm done chasing cheap thrills. I'm done using men and hurting myself in the process just to get over the last one. I'm exactly where I want—and need—to be.

Chapter Twenty-One

♥

T HE LITTLE SLEEP I have is restful, but I wake up in agony, and my shoulder hurts like an absolute bitch. I glance towards Danny, who's facing the opposite way, but judging by his lack of movement and steady breathing it doesn't take a genius to figure out that he's asleep. Maybe I did finally bore him to death.

Taking care not to wake him, I slide out from underneath the covers, find his shirt on the floor, and wrap myself up in the crisp white cotton. His muted Riviera scent lingers on the fabric, giving me the comfort I don't know I'm craving.

Quietly, I step out into the hallway and make my way downstairs to grab my phone on the coffee table where I left it. Penny bounds towards me for a morning cuddle, then she makes a beeline for the kitchen, pawing at the bi-fold door. I open them up and let her outside, then drop a quick text to Stefan and Lauren, and call my mum for an update on Kiki.

Once Penny has relieved herself and is back inside, I lock up and creep back upstairs. Before I make it back to the bedroom, the door clicks open, and Danny emerges looking deliciously vulnerable with his adorably dishevelled bedhead and day-old stubble. His white socks and boxer briefs finish off the look perfectly. I stop in my tracks, drinking in the sight of him, my mind triggering those magical memories of last night. He meets me halfway by a narrow wooden staircase that I hadn't noticed yesterday.

"Morning you," he says, a lazy smile spread across his face.

"Morning."

He eyes the phone in my hand. "Any news?"

"She's eating, which is a huge relief. They're running tests and taking bloods today, so it's essentially a waiting game. But my mum seems pretty positive that she'll be allowed to come home."

"That's great," he says.

I force a smile, but my heart fills with sadness. As if he can see right through me, he closes the gap between us, cradles my face in his hands and kisses the top of my head. It's exactly what I need.

"She'll be okay," he says.

I've never wished for anything to be more true. "I should go. Visiting hours start at ten."

"Want me to come with you?"

I shake my head. "It's fine, you don't have to. Besides, you've already done enough."

"I want to."

In this moment, those three words mean everything to me, and although the sadness isn't completely lifted, I can't help the smile from spreading across my face.

"Let me give her a text and see if it's okay first. But I'm pretty sure she'd love to meet a real-life rock star."

Danny quirks an eyebrow. "Well, if I'm going to get into Rock star mode, I'm—and I hate to say this because it looks so good on you—going to need that shirt back."

"You just want to see me naked. Perv." Laughing and rolling my eyes, I reluctantly hand it over, and his scent leaves me. When he puts it on, I have visions of a young and iconic Tom Cruise sliding across the floor in Risky Business.

"Fact. I am a perv, and I'll never have my fill of seeing you naked. So much so, that before we head out, I'm going to run you a bath and tend to your wounds, and you're going to love every second of it. Right after I let Penny out."

"I let her out already. I think she was ready to burst, poor thing."

"You know, if you didn't stink right now, you'd be pure perfection."

"That's probably true, but I smell like you. So technically, you also stink."

"She's such a charmer," he says, flashing his dimples. "Bathroom. Now."

Danny washes me while I lay there, letting the warm water cleanse and heal me. Immersed in his touch, his pure, wholesome act is the most beautiful, sensual and intimate thing I've ever experienced. Like he said he would, he tends to my wounds, treating me with the utmost care, respect and compassion. He's every ounce the perfect gentleman, and I'll be damned if I could fall any deeper than I already have.

·♥·♥·♥·♥·♥·

"I still don't know why you insisted on bringing your guitar," I say, as Danny and I walk hand in hand in the hospital corridor.

"How else am I supposed to win her over, without demonstrating my mad skills?"

"You might want to start with never using "mad skills" in a sentence ever again."

We're almost at Kiki's room when I spot my parents walking towards us. Instinctively, I drop Danny's hand, and immediately curse myself for being so paranoid.

But the last thing I want is for Mum to start bombarding Danny with embarrassing questions and dropping hints about how she can't wait to see me settled down. When they see us, she almost breaks into a run to give me a hug.

"Hi, sweetie," she says.

"Hi, mum," I say, my voice muffled and distorted in her embrace.

I wince as the ache in my shoulder magnifies from the pressure. Mum holds me at arm's length and looks at me, then turns to face Danny.

"Hi, Mrs DeLuca. I'm Danny."

He holds out his hand to shake, but she pulls him into a hug. "Please, call me Ale."

After the most awkward hug I've ever witnessed, Danny holds out his hand towards my dad, and the two men embark on an even more awkward handshake.

"What's wrong?" Mum asks me.

She always knows when something's up, but now is not the time to mention my little accident. I don't need her to fuss over me when all our focus should be on Kiki.

"Nothing, I'm just tired." It's not a total lie.

"We're just on our way to grab some coffee, I'll get you something. Danny, would you like anything?"

"I'd love a cappuccino, please."

He reaches inside his back pocket for his wallet, but my mum stops him. "Please, it's on us."

She shoots my dad a kind and knowing smile, and turns back to face Danny and I. "We'll see you soon."

I'm hoping that the caffeine will fix the pain, but in reality, I know it probably won't. Slowly my shoulder is getting worse, but that's exactly what Dr Khan said would happen, so I'm not worried. When my parents are out of sight, I pop two painkillers and pray for the ache to end.

"Your parents seem pretty cool," Danny says, when they're out of earshot.

"My mum isn't a regular mum, she's a cool mum," I say, glancing his way to gauge his reaction. "Sorry, Mean Girls super fan right here."

"Oh, I know. I've seen it."

"Well aren't you full of surprises?"

"You underestimate me, Miss DeLuca." He smirks as we approach the door.

"Wait here," I say.

The temptation to kiss him is too much, but I hold back.

"Hey, Kiki Bear." I say, leaning in the doorway.

I try my best to sound upbeat, but it's difficult. Kiki's spark has disappeared almost overnight. Again.

Deathly pale and fragile, she shivers under a mountain of blankets, even though the weather outside is warm enough to ripen a tomato. I perch on the edge of the bed, hold Kiki's cold hand, and lower my voice. "Are you sure you don't mind me bringing Danny here? I can ask him to wait outside—"

"No, it's fine," she says, smiling.

I study her face for any uncertainty, but I don't see any. I grip her hand tighter and call towards the door. "Come in," I say, and Danny enters.

"Hey, Kiki. It's good to finally meet you. I'm Danny. I've heard so much about you."

"I've heard nothing about you."

I clear my throat as Danny greets her with a warm smile, not letting her rudeness bother him. After sitting down on a chair beside the bed, he props his guitar against the wall.

"You're three members short of your barbershop quartet," Kiki says, dryly.

I stifle a laugh. It's nice to see she still has her sense of humour.

"No prizes as to where you get your sass from." He shoots me a pointed look.

Kiki shrugs and says, "I learned from the best."

"I'm sure you did." Danny picks up his guitar and pulls the strap over his head. "What kind of music are you into? I used to teach, so I'm sure I can learn a song or two."

"I doubt you'd even know who they are."

"Try me."

Kiki sighs. "Travis Scott, The Weeknd, Drake..." she trails off.

"I'll let you in on a secret." He lowers his voice. "I sat behind Drake at Wimbledon...twice."

Kiki bolts upright. "No way."

"Way. So what you got?"

Kiki scrolls through her phone, and Drake's In My Feelings plays through the speakers. Danny listens, gradually picking up the right notes to play, his confidence evident in the way he throws himself into the music.

"I hope one of you can sing," he says, "because I'm tone deaf." A blatant lie.

Kiki giggles, then turns to me, suddenly self-aware. "You start," she mouths.

I look at Danny, then flash a "here goes nothing" smile.

My singing voice is nothing special. It isn't sweet and melodious like my sister's, but ever since Kiki was a baby, she's loved it when I've sung to her. Finally, Kiki joins in with a harmony, and after a while, Danny starts singing too. He's right, his Drake impression is way below par, but the three of us vibing like this has me all in my feelings. I can't help but smile.

The song never ends, because all three of us erupt into laughter at the state of Danny's terrible attempt at rapping.

Once we calm down, Kiki quizzes Danny on his music tastes. "So, what kind of music do you like?" she asks.

Danny shrugs. "Let's just say my music taste is a little more...classic?"

"Oh yeah? Like who?"

"The Beatles, Queen, The Rolling Stones."

"Wow, you must be really old," Kiki says.

Danny laughs. "That's what your sister tells me all the time," he says, and gives me a wink.

Butterflies swarm my tummy. How does he have this effect on me with one look? Not that I'm complaining.

My parents return, along with an auxiliary nurse, who checks Kiki's vital signs, then escorts her to Radiology for a bone density scan.

We sip coffee in mostly silence and small talk, while awaiting news on Kiki. When she returns twenty minutes later, Danny steps outside to give us some privacy while the nurse explains that the results can take up to two weeks. Shortly after, we say our goodbyes, and allow Kiki to rest.

Chapter Twenty-Two

♥

ON THE DRIVE HOME, I manage to convince Danny to show off his teaching skills, so we take a detour to the studio.

"Welcome to Guitar 101."

I smirk at his stern-but-sexy teacher voice.

"Something funny, Miss DeLuca?"

"No, Mr Pearce."

"Mr Pearce is my dad; you may call me Sir," he says with a wink, observing my cross-legged seating position on a rug by the couch. He walks over to the wall lined with guitars, bypassing the electric guitars and unhooking an acoustic one from a bracket on the wall.

"The fuck I will."

"Please refrain from using profanity, Miss DeLuca. Will you be sitting like a hippie for the duration of the class?"

I nod. "Is that a problem, *Sir*?" I smirk.

"No problem. But it's more comfortable on a chair."

"Is that so?" I can't help myself; Danny is by far the hottest teacher I've ever had. He plays a scale to check the guitar is in tune, then he bends down and hands it to me, quirking an eyebrow when he gives me the same plectrum I used when I fucked myself.

"Are you right-handed?"

I nod.

Danny fetches himself another acoustic from the wall, then sits on the couch and checks the tuning. I rest mine on the top of my thighs, positioning my left hand on the neck and my right hand over the sound hole, while he briefly explains strings and frets, and demonstrates an E chord oh-so-effortlessly.

"This is E Major," he says.

"Can't you just teach me Wonderwall, or something?"

"No, Wonderwall is overrated. Plus, it doesn't work like that."

I pout.

"There are better Oasis songs."

"Like what?"

"Live Forever. Slide Away. Focus."

"I haven't heard that one."

"No, I'm telling you to focus. I'm a leftie, so essentially you can mirror me. Index finger on the third string, first fret. Second on the fifth string, second fret. Third finger on the fourth string, second fret. Relax your fingers a little." Pausing, he leans forward to readjust my placement. "Now, press down and strum."

The sound that leaves my fingertips sounds passable, but I'm no expert.

"Again."

The second time sounds slightly worse, but I don't know why. As far as I'm aware, my fingers haven't moved. He props his guitar against the couch and kneels behind me.

"Relax your wrists."

I do as he says. The heat from his breath sends a sheet of goosebumps down my spine, and warmth floods every inch of my body. Gently, he guides my elbow away from my body, into a loose right angle by my side, then cupping my hand in his, he eases the neck towards me, so that it sits straight across my body.

"Now try. Press your second finger down a little more, and try not to touch the first or second strings."

Slowly, I strum the chord again, and the sound it makes is infinitely better, almost perfect.

"Good," he says. "Keep going."

He's the perfect distraction, but I try not to let intrusive thoughts of our close proximity lead me astray. I continue to play, finding a rhythm, finding calm in the chaos of my racing heart, experimenting with different levels of volume, and finding that I prefer the sound when it's soft, slow and controlled.

"How do your fingers feel?" he asks.

"Not as good as yours."

Oops, did I say that out loud?

"Is that an invitation, Miss DeLuca?"

"It's whatever you want it to be."

From behind, Danny feels his way to the apex of my dress, his fingertips lightly aligning with my sternum, while his other hand dips below the cotton-clad curve of my hip. Fire ignites throughout my body when his touch settles an inch above the waistband of my underwear.

It's difficult to concentrate on anything else, and I try everything in my power not to grab his hand and guide it underneath my dress.

"*This* is E major," he says softly, as he adjusts his index finger to slightly offset the other two. "Would you like me to keep going?"

"Please," I breathe.

My injury objects to the declaration hanging in the air, and instinctively, my hand moves to my shoulder. In an attempt to ease the ache, I tilt my head away from the pain.

"You're hurting," Danny says, his voice barely a whisper as his words brush against the exposed part of my neck, sending more goosebumps across my skin.

"I'm fine, it's this angle."

Placing the guitar on the floor beside me, I close my eyes, and uncross my legs. Sinking my hips back onto my heels in a Vajrasana pose, my hands softly graze my knees, and I breathe deep into my injury.

With the rise and fall of my chest, Danny's fingertips follow the curve of my belly around the back of my waist, tracing a line from the bottom of my spine to my nape. Slow, measured kisses follow the shape of my hairline to the back of my ear. He buries his hands in my hair, gripping my scalp and softly dragging his teeth along my lobe. My breath hitches as he gently pulls my head towards him, the stretch a simultaneous mixture of discomfort and relief.

"Does that hurt?"

"No, it feels good. Keep going."

"You Summer girls are something else," he breathes, and it instantly gets me wet.

He kisses the tender spot on my shoulder, the warmth from his mouth instantly easing the ache, but the one between my legs remains. "Heat and ice are key principles to healing. So is rest, elevation, movement, and compression."

"Where are you going with this?"

"I want to try something. It could be dangerous if we're not careful, so I need you to trust me. It might help, but it might hurt, and I don't want to hurt you."

Anything.

"Fuck it, I'm just going to say it, and if I scare you off then I'm sorry, but something tells me you might be as perverted as I am."

He's right of course.

He pauses, and within seconds, he's kneeling in front of me, his golden-green gaze fixated on mine.

"Ever since I saw you picking up that glass on the second day we met, I can't stop thinking about having you bound, on your knees, and fucking you any way I can."

The heat between my legs turns into fire, and I'm pretty certain my underwear is soaked through. The power his words have over me is unbelievable. It's a lot to digest, but all I can think about is giving myself to him in all its entirety. Summer, Sophia, and everything in between.

"Why would that scare me off?"

"Because it's not conventional."

"What *is*? Last I checked, kink shaming wasn't cool." I pause, looking through my lashes. "I'm in."

All of me is one hundred percent yours, Danny Pearce.

A slow smile spreads across his face, and he kisses me hard.

"First, we need to see if you can move your arms behind you—to see if there's any pain there. You'll never trust me if I cause real damage. Then again..." he pins me with those hazel green eyes and a shit-eating grin. I know exactly what he's thinking, and I would be completely obliged for him to do his absolute worst to me.

I move my arms slowly behind my back. It aches a little, but it doesn't hurt.

"Is that okay?" he asks, and I nod. "I'm going to tie you up with a guitar strap, promise you'll tell me if you're in pain?"

"I promise."

He searches my eyes, presumably to make sure I'm being truthful. "I'll be gentle. Think of this as a trial run. Do you know what a safe word is?" I nod. "Pick one."

My gaze falls to his hands. "Southpaw," I smirk, and he treats me to those dimples and a wide, filthy smile.

"Wait there," he says, after gracing my lips with a quick, hard kiss.

Making his way towards the guitar-lined wall, he removes the strap from a Gibson, then picks out a pair of wireless headphones from a storage hook, and hands them to me.

"Put these on."

I comply, and he kneels behind me.

"I've never done anything like this before," I say. I'm apprehensive, but excited. And I trust him—that has to count for something.

"Neither have I," his voice is muffled, but I can still make out his words. "We'll go slow. Try to focus on the lyrics."

It's the last thing I hear before the music starts. In my kneeling position, the heavy, syncopated beat of Muse's Undisclosed Desires sets the tone and mirrors the pounding of my heart while he wraps the distressed leather of the guitar strap around my waist. It's tight, but comfortable, with a little give, and my pulse quickens with anticipation.

Slow, measured kisses land between my shoulder blades, working their way towards my nape, his erection evident as it presses against my back. Long fingers sweep the length of both my arms, leaving a trail of flames in their wake.

Easing the plectrum from my grasp, he gently guides one hand behind me, feeds it through a loop, and repeats the process with the other one. A quick tug of the leather releases its distinct, oaky scent as it tightens around my wrists. It's soft and warm, and has enough give to keep the pressure in my shoulder from mounting.

From behind, Danny runs the tapered end of the plectrum along my lower lip. I close my eyes, focusing on its roughness as it trails down, scratching my chin, neck, and chest, finally resting at the apex of fabric meeting flushed skin. He leaves it pressed against my sternum long enough to make a mark, and I appreciate the small ounce of relief I feel from the discomfort.

With the plectrum discarded, Danny's deft fingers unbutton my dress. My breath hitches with every twist of his fingers. This is pure agony. His body radiates so much warmth, but our proximity will never be enough. I tip my head back into his closeness, resting it on his shoulder, and he meets my lips with soft, slow kisses, reminding me of that infamous Spiderman kiss, while his hands follow the trail he made with the plectrum previously, down my chin and chest, then between our lips.

Oh, fuck.

His fingers brush my skin, from the dip in my neck down the length of my torso, and over my stomach. Carefully, he opens the front of my dress, reaches into my black lace bra, and circles his thumb over my nipple.

"Keep going," I think I say, but Matt Bellamy's vocals drown out the sound of my voice.

As Danny explores every inch of my body, over and under fabric, I focus on the words, on his touch. Every lyric, every breath, every caress, is a carefully curated masterpiece serving to stimulate my senses and heighten my arousal, and under his control, I have no reason to feel anything but safe.

Heat spreads rapidly between my legs as Danny moves the lace of my bra down, and his palms alternate between both breasts, giving me all the attention that I crave. Reaching a hand between my legs, he finds my centre, and I draw a sharp breath as his fingers make small circles over my underwear.

With my eyes still closed, I focus on the sweetness of his touch, a stark contrast to the spellbinding sound of Imagine Dragons' Believer hitting my eardrums. I savour the fire in his fingertips, every skip of my heartbeat, every butterfly that tickles my belly. The odd feeling of not being able to hear myself, or him, but through my heightened awareness of his presence, everything is magnified.

Reaching around, he pushes my underwear aside, moving his fingers in the same circular motion over my clit, keeping a steady rhythm while my pulse races. Raising my hips, I rock against his palm, unfolding under his expert touch.

Oh, God.

I open my eyes, mesmerized by his eagerness to learn my body in a way that no one has bothered to before. Slow, measured caresses make my legs shake, and my lack of a volume button means that I can't hear myself moan, or pant, or scream, and it leaves me wondering if any sound has escaped my lips.

Every fibre of my being wants to hold on, to make the feeling last longer, but I'm so close. As if he can read my mind, he slows, then stops, and I instantly regret my train of thought. I need the release, and the waiting is agony.

It feels like an hour has passed since I've felt his touch, but I know it must have only been a few minutes, because the next song begins, and a rough hand grazing my inner thigh startles me in the most delicious way. But the surprise only serves to heighten my need. This time, he makes quick work, making no hesitation to slip a finger inside, then another.

Fuck. Fuck. Fuck.

I struggle to focus on the words like he asked, when all I can think about is having my fill of him. Again, I lean back against him, against the haven of his warmth and the length of his fingers as they curl and pump inside me.

Arctic Monkeys' Do I Wanna Know kicks in. Using his free hand, Danny gathers the bottom of my dress and tucks it into the leather around my waist. His breath, hot and heavy on my neck and his cock pressed against me pushes me closer to the edge.

I hold my breath as he pulls down my underwear to the back of my knees, and eases his length inside me. Arching my back to better accept him, I lean into the resistance binding my waist, while Danny grasps the strap to keep me upright and close to him. Finally, I feel like I can breathe, and let out a long overdue exhalation.

With a soft gaze, I open my eyes, and notice a small device in Danny's hand. It's round and thin, like a watch face. He holds it against my clit, a constant beat pulsing like a metronome, teasing every sense, every nerve.

Oh my fuck.

While his other hand explores the rest of my body, I slide against his warmth, breathing in the scent of citrus, leather and wood as the pressure builds inside and around me. Gradually, I can feel Danny losing control as he drags his teeth across my neck, his breath like fire on my skin. His entire palm covers my breast, squeezing, pulling, scratching, as his strong arms keep me anchored to him.

Muscles contract and pulse, and he doesn't hold back. It's hard to tell where he ends and I begin. But I don't care. Every part of my entire being belongs to him. One final sprint towards the edge sees me crashing into oblivion, the release tearing my body apart into a beautiful, shaken mess.

I collapse onto my knees, my head against the edge of the sofa, drawing heavy, ragged breaths. Somewhere in the afterglow, my ties have been freed, the music has stopped, and the headphones play nothing but my shallow breath and the slowing pound in my chest.

Danny, quiet in all his glistening glory, kisses my shoulder before easing my dress back around my body, and he buttons me up with the same level of care he had shown before. After he helps me onto the couch, he covers my legs with a blanket, removes the headphones and hands me a bottle of water before pulling me close and wrapping his arms around me.

"How do you feel?" he asks, with a soft, gentle voice.

I try and fail to think of a word that even comes close to the way I'm feeling. But there isn't any one word to describe it.

Glowing, amazing, exhausted, intoxicated, elated.

"Euphoric. Like being underwater," I say. I pause to have a drink and gather my thoughts. "So, what happens now?"

"I'm going to take you home, light some candles, give you the best bath you've ever had, and make you dinner."

I meant with us.

The question is never far from my lips over the next three days of complete bliss we share together. Three days of teasing, fucking and making love in every room and in any position that doesn't cause my shoulder to seize up. Three days of being bathed and fed, nurtured and cared for, with plenty of Penny cuddles. Three days of the incredible view and the sea air on my doorstep, listening to him play covers of my favourite songs on the balcony at sunset—like he's curated the perfect summer playlist just for me. His rendition of Watermelon Sugar puts Harry Styles to shame, but maybe I'm biased. And even though Danny still draws the line at playing Wonderwall, I never imagined in all my wildest dreams that I'd ever know what life with someone I love would look like. The first person to ever make me feel like I'm enough.

Yes, I am undeniably and unapologetically in love with Danny Pearce.

Danny perches on the sofa's edge to tie his shoelaces, while I stand by the front door waiting for him, as I mentally and physically prepare to leave. The bruising has subsided, but my shoulder is still too tender to cycle home comfortably, and I haven't yet had my bike checked out, so we agree to leave it at Danny's house until I'm fully healed.

"I want us. I want this more than anything. But we still need to be careful," he says, after I finally pluck up the courage to ask him what I really wanted to.

He rises from the sofa to join me by the door. I want to say that I understand, that I'm willing to wait. But at the same time, I want him to be mine, and only mine. I'm already done with the fact that, after two years, Belle still casts a shadow over his life. I'm done sharing him—even though it's indirect—and I know how selfish that sounds. My heart fills with sadness, and my gaze falls to the ground in an attempt to hide it, but he sees right through me.

"Hey."

Light fingertips gently coax my chin towards him.

"Any day now. Then we can be together properly."

Sadness turns to hope, and I lift my gaze to meet his.

"I mean what I say."

Instantly, I'm lost in his honey-green gaze. I want to believe him, but I've been let down by people I trust so many times before. He glances at the large gym bag by my feet. "Why don't you stay?"

With those words, the hope in my heart merges into complete subordinate love. "I can't. I have work, and—"

"So we'll stop off at yours and get more clothes. I'll drive you to work."

"I can't ask you to do that."

"I'm offering." He edges towards me, so that our lips are barely touching. I cast my eyes downwards again, savouring the closeness and his fingers on my skin.

"At least until your bike is fixed."

Chapter Twenty-Three

♥

IN THE TWO WEEKS that follow, Kiki's test results come back clear, and she comes back home. With a mixture of acupuncture and physiotherapy, my shoulder pain has significantly eased, and although I'm back at work and cycling, I'm still living out my staycation romance with Danny, he even gave me a key. I've definitely gotten used to this dog-mum life a little too easily.

"You look nice," I say, walking into the kitchen, but Danny doesn't hear me.

His white polo, tan chinos and signature summer scent screams Riviera man-snack as he sits on a bar stool with his back turned, and I want nothing more than to rip his shirt off. I'm about to wrap my arms around his waist and go in for the kill when I notice the glass of whiskey. My eyes dart to the piece of paper he's holding.

"What's that?"

"It's a decree absolute," he says quietly, meeting my gaze with a sombre expression.

"Meaning?"

Rising, he swipes the sheet of paper from the kitchen island and hands it to me. "It means I'm officially divorced."

I scan the document briefly and breathe a sigh of relief. Thank fuck it's finally over. "Are you kidding? That's great news."

I leap into his arms, but he doesn't return the gesture. My elation dampens. "What's wrong? Aren't you happy?"

He shakes it off, and I retreat, searching his vacant features. "I think I'm just a bit shocked, that's all."

He smiles, but it doesn't reach his eyes.

A million questions scream inside my head, but when he pulls me into a hug, they mute themselves before I feel his body stiffen. I can't find the words to say, but the way he holds me feels forced and insincere. Still, I let him, silently willing him to never let go. But after a few moments, he does.

"I know it's short notice, but my parents invited me for dinner for their anniversary tonight—"

The fear of rejection threatens to creep up on me again, but I push it away. "That's okay, I'll look after Penny. It's not like I've never been here alone before," I say, that familiar lump of rejection hitting the back of my throat.

He brushes my offer aside. "No, I want you to come with me."

Relief comes first, followed by a dose of fear. He's already met my parents, so what's the harm in meeting his? The sparkle returns to his eyes, telling me all I need to know.

"I have nothing to wear," I say, mentally scanning the small pile of clothes I brought with me.

"I have a whole wardrobe of my niece Amelia's clothes upstairs. I'm sure we'll find you something."

After an epic movie-style montage, I opt for a sage floral tea dress. I ditch my usual white trainers in favour of heeled sandals, and wear my hair down in loose waves. I'm relieved to find that his niece has a similar style to mine, and the fact that we share the same size makes it easier to find something to wear.

The water on Brighton Marina glistens as we stroll hand in hand along the boardwalk. Prana is a relatively new restaurant and lounge, serving world influenced small plates and cocktails. The waterfront seating area is stunning. Lined with tall, skinny trees dressed in an abundance of leaves and lights, creating the perfect backdrop for a calm and romantic setting. When we arrive, an older couple are quick to spot us. They wave us over. Judging by their smiles and the way they hold themselves; I assume they're his parents. They look expensive in the same way that Danny does.

My heart races—a mixture of anxiety and the niggling feeling that Danny is only with me physically, and not mindfully. I can't shake it off, but I plaster on a smile anyway. With a squeeze of my hand and a flash of his dimples, my heart races in a different kind of way.

"Happy Anniversary," Danny says, giving his mum a kiss on the cheek and his father a handshake. "Is there room for a little one?"

They seem shocked to say the least, but after a beat, a smile spreads on both their faces.

"Well of course. Sit down, dear," his mum says, gesturing to an opposite chair.

"I'm so sorry to impose. Happy Anniversary. I'm Sophia."

His parents introduce themselves as Richard and Christine. Danny sits beside me, and I reach across the table, shake both their hands, then sit back down.

"So, you're the one who's been stealing all my son's time?" Christine says, taking a sip of what looks like a martini.

"You'll have to excuse my wife, she's already on her third one," Richard says. He flashes a cheeky wink, and I can tell where his son inherits his charm, but it doesn't prevent me from feeling uneasy. With a glance towards Danny, I clear my throat and wait for him to say something. I assume he will at least tell them the good news, but he doesn't. Maybe he doesn't want to spoil the festivities.

"So, how long have you two been married?" I ask, trying my best to remain unphased. I instantly thank my job. Small talk is the peak of my comfort zone, and I know I can use it to my advantage to slice the tension in the air.

"Forty-three years," Richard says.

"That's incredible, what's your secret?"

"It's a formula," Richard says, lifting his glass and studying the liquid inside. "Like the perfect cocktail, it needs the right amount of communication, independence and romance."

As the conversation flows, Danny becomes quieter and more distant, and I can't help but wonder if he's starting to regret diving headfirst into a new relationship. My smile remains tight-lipped as I nod along, but I can't deny my discomfort.

"That dress is positively lovely, my dear," Christine says, before turning towards her husband. "Doesn't she look wonderful?"

Richard nods.

"I'm sure my daughter-in-law has one just like it."

"Oh?" I say, expecting her to tell me about Danny's brother's wife.

"Doesn't Belle have a dress just like that, Daniel?"

A lump lodges in my throat the moment she says her name. This is beyond awkward.

Richard makes a discreet attempt to silence his wife, but it doesn't go unnoticed. My pulse is racing. I feel ridiculed, like I'm the only person at this table who isn't in on some private joke.

Surprise, Sophia. You've been fooled again.

Please don't let it be true.

"No, mum. It's Amelia's dress," Danny says, softly.

I wonder why it's taken him so long to answer.

Christine touches her temple as her expression falls, confusion etched on her face.

"No, no. I distinctly remember seeing Belle wearing that dress. I have it in a photo album somewhere, I'm sure."

Richard places a hand on Christine's with pleading eyes.

"She really is the most beautiful woman, and an excellent cook. Remember when—"

Danny's chair screeches across the floor.

"I'm going to the bar. Would anyone like a drink?" he asks, his tone terse.

I've never heard him speak like that before. He's angry, and I want to know why.

"It's table service, darling," Christine says, with a wave of her hand.

He stands, completely disregarding her.

"I'll come with you," I say, rising from my chair.

I'm desperate to question the sudden turn of events, to gain some clarity from the confusion, but I can't confront him in front of his parents on their anniversary. Somehow, I don't think he wants me to, either.

"No, it's fine. Prosecco okay?"

I nod, and sit back down. I feel like I've just been told off. It doesn't sit right with me at all. Within moments, his behaviour has made me feel small and insignificant again, like that little girl pushed aside all those years ago. Christine must sense my sadness, because she offers me a sympathetic look.

"I'm so sorry, dear. I get confused sometimes."

"It's fine, really. It happens," I say, offering a sincere smile.

I can't help but wonder if Christine is right. It's too late, I'm already starting to question everything our relationship is built on. There's only one way to find the answers. I have to know the truth.

I excuse myself to go to the bathroom, my sudden pallor and dizziness a viable reason. In the stall, I sit and scroll

Belle's Instagram feed, feeling ridiculous the entire time. I never want to be the girl who Insta stalks my man's ex, but here I am, and there Belle is, wearing that same sage-green floral dress three summers ago.

Bile rises in my throat as all my fears are confirmed. There's no denying now that I'm wearing Belle's dress. Suddenly, I'm questioning the validity of our entire relationship. I've never felt so embarrassed, so powerless. But I need answers.

I slam my purse on the bar while Danny knocks back a shot. "Nice of you to tell me that I'm wearing your ex-wife's dress."

"What? No, it's—"

"Your niece's? Right. Somehow, I don't believe you."

I show him the photo, which only adds to the ridicule. Woman scorned is never the brand I aspire to be.

"Can we talk about this later?"

"Actually, now seems like a pretty good time as any."

"Just drop it. Please." His jaw clenches, and I can sense the anger in his voice. If riling him up is the only way he'll listen, I'm going to try my luck.

"I can't believe you dressed me up like your ex; do you not realise how sick that is? I don't know whether you're still in love with her, or you just don't want to be with me, but either way it's not good enough. You didn't even tell your parents that you were getting a divorce!"

My statements are met with excruciating silence.

"I never have been—nor will I ever be—her, and I won't apologise for being who I am."

"I said drop it."

"I'm not a fucking child."

"Then stop acting like one," he spits, pausing to compose himself.

Something in his body language tells me he's already defeated; he isn't going to fight for me. The realisation cuts worse than any spoken word could. It's too late, anyway. My internal controller has already selected party girl mode, and my proverbial walls assemble faster than a fuckboys finishing time.

"It's cool. I'm out of here," I say, defeated.

I throw my hands up and walk away. I don't wait for him to speak, because I fear that he won't, and I can't take any more blows to my heart.

Outside, his parents fawn over a beautifully presented seafood platter, and the nausea hits worse than before.

"I'm so sorry, I'm really not feeling well. I'm going to head home. It was lovely to meet you both."

"Oh, darling. Maybe you just need to eat something." Christine gestures to the platter. The sight of the food turns my stomach.

It's not that I think Christine is a bad person, or that she had intentionally tried to humiliate me. But the fact that Danny didn't come to my defence made me feel small, cheap and insignificant.

"I would offer to take you home, but I've had a couple of vinos. I'd be happy to call you a taxi?" Richard asks, retrieving his phone.

"Thank you, but it's fine, I don't live too far."

An hour of walking in heels is nothing compared to innate urge I have to take flight. I need to get the hell out of here. "Enjoy your night."

Turning on my heel to leave, I catch sight of Danny in the corner of my eye, the weight of his gaze forcing me to pick up speed.

I stop when he calls my name. But the battle between my head and heart insists that I carry on. I haven't the strength to fight, not when the rejection is a constant pummel in my gut.

Thanks to him, I finally know my worth, and I'll never be somebody's second choice. But I never thought he'd be the one to make me feel completely worthless. A tear rolls down my cheek with only the sound of my heels pounding the boardwalk for company. Alone again, naturally.

Chapter Twenty-Four

♥

WHEN I THROW OPEN the doors of Lilura forty minutes later, I'm barefoot, holding these ridiculous heels, and my hair is a wild mess from the humidity. The first person I spot is Lonely Guy nursing his usual. I check myself in one of the many mirrors on the wall. I look like shit.

Still wary, I perch a few stools away from him and swing my legs around to see Luke leaning across the bar. Aside from a couple of businesspeople types, we're the only ones there. Sunday evenings are eerily quiet, it doesn't even look like the same place.

"Changed your mind?" Luke smirks, leaning across the bar.

I eye him up and down, and roll my eyes. The old me definitely would have, but too much has happened now. He holds up his hands in mock defence. "I'm messing. What can I get you?"

I cock my head towards Lonely Guy. "I'll have what he's having."

I may as well join him in feeling sorry for myself. When I do, I realise I've gone full circle. Lonely Guy and I are pretty much the same person.

"Whiskey? Really?" he asks, eyebrows raised and arms folded.

I shrug. "Sure, why not."

He swipes a bottle of Lagavulin from the bar and serves it neat alongside a glass of water, with a packet of baked cheese-flavoured crisps.

"This one goes nicely with Roquefort, but these will have to do. The general idea is to taste it neat first, then—"

Before he can continue, the amber liquid is down my throat. It's disgusting. How do people drink this stuff? I grimace, then chase it with the entire glass of water. "Nope. Never doing that again."

"I'll get you the bartender special."

He winks, and grabs a few bottles from behind the bar. I check my phone. Who would guess that no messages on the screen would be such a punch in the gut? I check my socials, then set my phone down on the dark wood and continue my pity party.

"Do you have any Tabasco?" I ask, as I open up the packet of crisps fully, and lay the foil plate in front of me.

"Sure." He grabs a bottle of pepper sauce, and sets it in front of me. "So, what's the deal? Did your date stand you up? You look royally pissed off."

I shoot him a pointed look, then douse my snack in Tabasco. "Me? A date? Do you know me at all?"

"I just thought...you seemed different the last time I saw you."

I shake my head. "Nope. Once a party girl, always a party girl."

The words taste bitter on my tongue, even worse than the whisky. "Fair enough."

A group of three young men in suits approach the bar. The stench of aftershave is nauseating, I have to turn away. I scoot over a little, towards The Lone Ranger.

"So, have you heard from Alex?" he asks.

I shake my head. "No, have you?"

"He's kind of gone off the radar. I think he's shooting a campaign in like, Dubai, or something."

"Good for him," I say.

I couldn't care less.

He wipes the bar with a dry cloth and sets down a fresh napkin and a new drink—a short, heavy glass filled with golden liquid with a foamy top, garnished with a lemon slice and a cherry on a stick.

I take a sip, letting the smooth, citrus flavour roll over my tongue and slide down my throat. I close my eyes to savour the taste. "Mmm...so much better."

"Thanks. I'm working on my sours."

"It's really good. Hey, have you gotten any further on having your own place?"

"I might have something in the pipeline," he says, then excuses himself to serve the stench next to me.

I eat my crisps and finish my drink, checking my phone constantly, but there is still no word from Danny, or anyone for that matter.

"Can I get you another?" Luke asks, returning.

I search for the answer in the bottom of the empty glass, shaking my head. "I should probably head home."

I leave him a tip, and it reminds me of the night I met Danny. Is this what it will be from now on? Constant reminders of what never was, but could have been? Would we have met under different circumstances? After all, we've been going to the same gym for years, and I'd never seen or noticed him.

During the hour or so that I'm in Lilura, the wind has picked up and the air feels marginally cooler, and I'm grateful to have called a taxi.

I half expect to see Danny waiting on my doorstep with a giant bouquet of flowers and an apology. But things like that only happens to nice girls in movies, and I prefer plants, anyway.

No Danny.

No bouquet.

No plant.

I've always prided myself on being self-sufficient, and I was naïve to think that I had something worthwhile, or worth fighting for. Still, I can't shake off the last few weeks, and how good—and right—it feels to be with Danny, in every meaning of the word. If tonight has taught me anything, it's that first impressions always matter, and the only person I can rely on is myself.

I barely make it through the front door when I see the blonde hair of my arch nemesis sitting across from a sombre looking Stefan at the dinner table. What the fuck is *she* doing here? A surprise, nonetheless, but not the one I'm expecting, and certainly not a welcome one.

Stefan's fork hovers between his lips, and Chrissy turns around like she's waiting for me to say something. Summer would have raised an eyebrow at Stefan, daring him to take a bite, but I'm defeated. Exhausted. And I'm so sick of fighting. I completely disregard the both of them and head up the stairs.

"Sophia, wait." Chrissy rises from her chair. "Please. I just want to talk."

My mind immediately thinks the worst, that something has happened to Ryan, but when my eyes meet Stefan's, I know that's not the reason she's here.

"I have nothing to say to you. Not now. Not ever."

"Do you have to be so childish?"

Hearing Danny's words again is a punch to the gut.

"Funny you should mention it, actually. It wouldn't be the first time I've heard that today."

"Always with the sarcasm. You know, I came here to say I'm sorry. But I'm not sure you deserve my apology."

"You mean, you've actually climbed off your high horse and regard me as a person now? Whatever did I do to deserve your kindness?"

I roll my eyes and continue to walk up the stairs. I've waited twelve years to have this out with Chrissy, but the timing is so off, I haven't the strength to argue.

"Just hear her out," Stefan says.

"Why should I?" My heart races and my head spins. With shaking hands, I clutch the banister.

"What the hell is your problem?" Chrissy spits.

"My problem? With you?" I throw my head back and laugh. "How much time do you have?"

The hurt conveyed in Chrissy's eyes is fleeting, but it's clear and genuine. Maybe there's more to her than I think. Maybe Queen Bees have hearts, after all.

"Look. I know I've been a bitch. But can we just talk like adults? Please."

I throw my hands up. "Fine."

I make myself a warm tea to soothe the ache in my chest, and we each sit on separate couches, while Stefan busies himself in the kitchen.

"Look. I don't expect us to be best friends. I never have," Chrissy starts. "But I want us to get along for Ryan's sake."

"So that's why you're here. Because he asked you to?"

"He misses you guys."

"Does he? That's nice. But I'm done with toxic behaviours, and that's Ryan to a T. Even the way he treated you; we might not get along, but no one deserves to be treated like he's treated you."

Chrissy shakes her head, eyes downcast. "No, you're right."

Moments pass in silence, her eyes turn glassy, and a tear falls down her perfectly contoured cheek. I want to tell her my reasons for protecting myself, but I can't trust her enough to open up to her, and I'm still not sure that she deserves my honesty.

"But no matter how much he cheats and lies; I can't let him go," she says, finally.

I can't decide which is worse, the fact that I feel sorry for her, or the fact that despite everything Ryan has put her through, Chrissy will never stop loving him. I realise that everyone is powerless in their own way. But she's owning her shit, and I respect the hell out of that.

"Only you can decide what to do with your own life. I'm not trying to dictate at all. All I'm saying is our friendship doesn't fit anymore."

"I'm sorry," Chrissy says.

"For what?"

I know exactly what she's apologising for, but I want to hear her say it.

"For being so mean."

I shrug in mock nonchalance. "Karma's a bitch."

Chrissy meets my gaze through tear-stained eyes.

"I'm messing. It's fine. Over it already." I wave a hand away and take a long sip of my drink. "Come on, I'll pour you a glass of Fuckboy Tears." I pause, rising from my seat. "And strictly off the record...I'm sorry, too."

Chapter Twenty-Five

♥

SUMMER'S WELL AND TRULY over, and for the past two months, I've avoided my bedroom. Aside from a multitude of "*I'm sorry*" and "*Please talk to me*" texts in the first few days of our fallout, I haven't heard from Danny. The freshly laundered outfit—Belle's outfit—mocks me every time I open my closet. I know I have to return it—and pick up my bike—at some point. But I'm not ready, and a lump catches in my throat whenever I think about it.

Every time I turn on the TV, I'm reminded of him. I can't even watch a dog food commercial without welling up. Somehow, I manage to link everything back to him. I've withdrawn from my friends, especially April—I hate keeping her at arm's length, but it hurts too much to see intimate photos of her and Ollie. I go to the gym, but I can't stop shifting my gaze towards the water machine in the hopes of seeing him there, and unhelpful images of him in tennis whites run through my mind at every opportunity. I can't even stomach a slice of pizza, but there's always an endless supply of ice cream in the freezer. It's ridiculous. I'm ridiculous. When did I become such a cliché?

I post selfies to keep up appearances, but it all feels so fake, and no amount of validation fills the gaping hole that's left in my heart.

Concern for Kiki's return to school has kept me occupied, though, and although it was a mostly-smooth-if-not-slightly-anxiety-inducing transition, I still worry and keep tabs on her daily. I'm grateful that I'm now two months into my teacher training course, and when I'm not working or studying, I'm busy jotting down ideas and creating a business plan.

With the help of my yogi friends, I planned a twenty-four hour Hip Hop Yogathon fundraiser for Beat—a charity for disordered eating—and it was a smashing success.

Life is better, more productive, and for once in my life, I feel like I finally have a purpose. At least that's what I keep telling myself.

A few days after the fundraiser, I check the donation page again, and an anonymous contribution flashes onto the screen.

"I'm so proud of you," the message says.

The words cut right into my skin and etch their way into my heart. Initially, I think it's from my parents, but when I see the amount, I realise it's not. My parents are financially comfortable, but there is no way they could afford to donate that kind of money. There's only one person I know who could.

I pace the living room. Everything in my gut screams Danny's name. Confusion turns into anger, then guilt. Is this his *apology*? Emotions scroll through my head at speed, like those Instagram filters that guess which Disney character or meaningless object you are. On a whim, I video call Ellie. Beautiful Ellie with her cards and her wise words—she would know what to do.

"Hey, is everything okay?" Ellie asks. I'm so happy to see her face.

"Actually, I need your help."

I tell her everything, and she couldn't be any more supportive.

"Let me pull you a card."

I guide us through a quick meditation to clear our minds, and Ellie lays out the cards face down in front of me, panning the camera lens over them so that I can choose one.

"Queen of Cups. Interesting," Ellie says, turning the card face up. A slow smile spreads across her face. "It's telling you to pay attention to your intuition, and trust your feelings. Don't be afraid to lead with your heart, not your head. Feel those feels, even if they scare you. Fear holds us back in so many ways. You're one of the strongest people I know, even if you don't believe it sometimes, and you of all people deserve to be happy."

With Ellie's suggestion, I buy Danny flowers, and, if I'm honest, I feel a little ridiculous about it, but it seems like an innocent gesture to show my appreciation. I deliberately avoid lilies, with their pollen relentlessly insisting on staining everything they come into contact with.

Instead, I opt for a small, non-toxic bouquet of seasonal flowers in an autumnal colour palette. I imagine that the shades of cream, taupe and burnt orange would compliment his decor perfectly, and I hate myself for even considering how they would look in his house. I even wonder where he would display them, and give myself a less than gentle reminder to snap out of it.

Dress. Flowers. Bike. Leave. That's all you have to do. Don't fucking cry.

The back and forth in my head is a constant the entire taxi ride, and as the car crawls to a stop and I see the open gates and the nearly brand new Audi parked outside, my heart pounds. I would happily stew in here like a teabag in the back seat with the tinted windows rolled up for the rest of the day, but over-steeping leaves a bitter taste, and I know what I have to do in order to feel at peace.

Somewhere between paying the cab fee and wrestling with a jammed passenger door, the heaven's open. The taxi pulls away, and as I glance up through rain-soaked lashes, I freeze when I lock eyes with a pretty, petite brunette standing with Penny by her side in the doorway. The dog whines and pulls, but her efforts are ignored as I follow the woman's gaze to the dress I'm holding, and I remember why I'm here.

When I look back up, my eyes lock with Danny's as he comes crashing into the woman. I can see her a little more clearly now, and I realise that the woman isn't Belle like I initially thought.

Through the rain, I can't quite place his expression. Shock? Anxiety? Confusion? Whatever it is, I'm positive I feel all of those magnified and more.

The pounding in my ribcage clouds my vision, making it infinitely worse. That familiar feeling of being underwater, but this time is completely different than the last, and the time before that. The physical pain from my accident could never compare to the unwelcome ache in my heart. My instinct is to run, but I know I have to tackle the problem head on. Be a grown up. Get my bike back and get on with my life. Between us, the rain is a veil, a shield, protecting me from them.

As I walk towards them in what seems like burning slow motion, Danny says something inaudible to the brunette, and, within moments, she and Penny are out of sight. Taking Florence Welch's advice, I shake it off, remember who the fuck I am, and tell myself that Summer isn't over.

"I just came to get my bike and return the dress," I say, the second I approach him in the doorway. "I won't keep you."

No matter how badly I want to.

The door between us is the perfect metaphor. Wide open, how a heart should be. He opened mine, and in turn I opened up myself to hurt, grief, and love. As much as I want to close it, the desire to keep it open is stronger now. To be able to experience the greatness of love, even if it isn't supposed to be with Danny.

"Sophia, I—"

My name on his lips are the only word I want to hear for eternity. I blink back tears, and hand him the bouquet, along with the dress hanger.

"The flowers are for you. I wanted to say thank you for your donation, it's going to make a huge difference." I'm trying so hard to be brave, that there's no room to be bold. His mossy, amber eyes are glazed and guilt-ridden. "But you can't throw money at something and call it an apology."

Inside, my heart is breaking, but I wear my brave face well.

"I deserve that."

"Can I just have my bike back, please?"

"Will you at least wait inside?"

"No, it's fine. I can see you have company." I fold my arms across my chest, and for a moment, his eyes narrow.

"That's Amelia. My niece."

"Of course it is." I roll my eyes.

"I wasn't lying before. She really does live here in term time."

Oh.

"I'm sorry. I just thought...because of what your mum said. That it was Belle's dress this entire time, and—" And now I want the ground to swallow me.

"My mum feels terrible about what she said. She has memory problems, and she gets confused sometimes because of her TIA."

"It's not your mum's fault. I overreacted."

"You didn't. I was being a dickhead. The reason I didn't say anything was because I didn't want to start any drama. My entire life I've avoided stressing my mum out, because I'm terrified she'll get sick, but it doesn't excuse the way I acted that night. It was like I was on autopilot. I was so deep in my own shit, that I wasn't even thinking about you."

He looks behind me to the rain, which hasn't eased up. I now look like a drowned, depressed mess. "I was selfish, and I should never have disregarded your feelings like that. I should have said something as soon as my mum started talking about Belle, and I genuinely didn't realise she had ever worn that dress. I'm so sorry for everything."

Penny barks impatiently in the background.

"Please come in."

Reluctantly, I follow him inside. The house already holds so much history, and I'm not sure if it's possible to keep my emotions in check. As soon as I step over the threshold, Penny is at my feet. God, I've missed that adorable little face, the loving licks on my hand, and her soft golden fur. I introduce myself to Amelia, who's sitting on the sofa with her nose in her phone, and continue to play with Penny.

"I missed you, girl," I whisper.

Awhile later, Danny returns with my bike.

"Thank you." I bend down, choking back tears as I say goodbye to the pure joy that is Penny. Who knew I could get so attached to that bundle of fluff so quickly?

"You know, that's not the whole reason I made the donation."

I spin to face him.

"I donated because it's important to you. And what's important to you is important to me."

Our eyes lock, and in this moment, nothing else matters.

"What are you doing tomorrow?" he asks.

I don't know what to say. But just knowing that he hasn't given up on this sends a rush of butterflies to my stomach.

"Working."

"When aren't you working?"

He pins me with those hypnotic golden-olive spheres. My heart is racing. "Sunday."

"Keep it free."

"Why?"

"I want to do something we've never done before. I never got the chance to take you on a real date."

"Danny, I don't know."

I don't know how many more apologies I can handle before I completely surrender to you.

"Give me a chance to fix this. Please." His hold on me is so strong and undeniable that I can't convince myself to say no. My subconscious guides me to an earlier conversation of ours.

"Music is like an anchor. It's a feeling, a surrender. Music has the ability to capture, bind and free you all at the same time. It's healing."

No matter how much I deny it, Danny is all those things to me, and I'd be doing myself a disservice if I didn't lead with my heart and give him a chance to redeem himself. He's far from perfect, but so am I. What we had was real, I'm sure of it. Our journey together brought both of us growth and healing, and whether my pride allows it or not, I need him.

"Fine."

The look on his face is victorious, and adorable, like a kid who's won a Blue Peter badge.

"I'll pick you up at ten. Bring your wellies."

Chapter Twenty-Six

♥

S UNDAY ROLLS AROUND QUICKLY. Butterflies, nausea, and excitement settle in my tummy while I get ready, but it's nothing a quick meditation can't fix. The mid-October weather is surprisingly warm, so I opt for high-waist jeans, a crop top and smart white trainers, and I carry a brand-new pair of wellington boots, because who out of the equestrian or dog-walking world owns a pair of wellies?

I watch Danny's car pull up on the curb outside the townhouse, and I grab a light bomber jacket on my way out, then shout goodbye to Stefan and James.

"Get in loser, we're going winkle picking," Danny calls from the rolled down window.

I laugh, his comment instantly putting me at ease. I can't believe he remembered my throwaway Mean Girls reference in the hospital. Then again, I bet he's been dying to say that. I slide into the passenger seat and throw my jacket into the backseat next to a couple of souvenir shop bucket and spade sets.

"You weren't kidding, were you?"

"Nope. The tide is on its way in, but we should be good for an hour or so."

Twenty minutes later, we're parked up in his driveway. Armed with our buckets, we walk through the house to the beach, taking Penny with us. Danny weaves his way over an abundance of seaweed, rock pools and stones to a large cluster of rocks.

I fall into step with him, while Penny laps up the glorious ocean. The underside of a rock houses an abundance of periwinkles, Danny shows me what to do, and we pick them off one by one, putting them in the buckets, making sure to leave plenty behind for reproduction.

"You know, this feels completely backwards," I say.

"What does?" Danny asks.

I follow him against the rocks, always one step behind, making patterns with our footprints in the sand. "I mean, after everything that's happened."

He turns to face me, eyebrows raised.

"Don't you think I owe you at least one date?"

"You don't owe me anything."

"No, you're right. But you deserve better than the way I treated you."

My bucket is already halfway full by the time he's made the declaration. I try to distract myself by trying to find more winkles, but his realisation hangs heavy in the air, and I can't ignore it.

"It's fine. It just wasn't meant to be."

It hurts more than I realise to say those words aloud. Danny stops.

"Do you really believe that?"

The golden green intensity behind his eyes is blinding, lighting my soul and sending a sheet of goosebumps across my skin. The wind whips around us and I break contact. No is the short answer.

"You know, I've always lived without regret; every experience in life is a learning curve, and nine times out of ten, it leads to better things. But I regret everything about the way I acted that night with my parents. I should have fought for you. I was too busy in my own world, sulking and being a fucking coward."

He sits down, raking his fingers through the sand. "I was hurting, and for some reason I had this unexplainable feeling of guilt and shame."

I kneel beside him, the wet grains of sand pushing against my knees.

"I never expected divorce to feel like...grief. I thought I had dealt with my demons through the separation. I thought it would lift the weight from my shoulders, but receiving that letter made me realise I had been in denial for a long time, and then the anger hit that night. I was angry with her, myself, my parents."

"Do you regret leaving her?"

He shakes his head. "God, no. I could never—"

He doesn't finish, and I don't encourage him to. The constant sound of waves lapping the shore fills the silence.

"I'll never be her," I say, quietly.

"I wouldn't want you to be. I'm in love with *you*."

It's the first time he's ever said those words, but in my frustration, I dismiss them. "You're in love with an alter ego."

"Why is it so hard for you to let me love you?"

"Because we had a taste of it, and then you hurt me. You really hurt me. And I realised that trying to keep up with your idea of perfection proved that I'll never fit in with your lifestyle. Maybe I'm not the type to stay in one place. Maybe I should be living some kind of nomadic lifestyle, dancing to the beat of my drum, or something. You think I don't realise that I'm completely replaceable? All I wanted was to be good enough for you."

I trusted you.

"Replaceable?" he scoffs. "Do you even realise what a fucking force you are? What you do to me?"

He pauses, dropping his bucket. Penny sniffs around it as he turns to face me, meeting my gaze with an intensity I haven't seen before.

"You're like a summer storm. Something completely unexpected that I never knew I needed. When I'm with you, all the heaviness, the weight, is lifted and I can finally breathe."

He steps closer like he's gearing up for a fight, and my breath hitches. We're so close, I can almost taste the salt of the sea on his breath.

"You're my favourite season."

His declaration leaves me speechless. Butterflies swarm my tummy, and my lips are tingling, begging to be kissed. But I will him to finish. I need it.

"I want all of you, Sophia. I want to feel the sand of every beach on every continent between my toes with you beside me. I want to kiss you in every ocean. I want to watch you as you are right now, with the wind in your hair and the sun on your face. I want to build sandcastles with you and get sick eating our bodyweight in dinky doughnuts and Mr Whippy ice cream. Fuck it, I'll even let you have my flake. I want you, forever."

The pounding in my heart propels me forward, close enough for the tip of my nose to graze his. All I want to do is touch him, and hold him, and tell him how much I love him. But the doubt in my head tugs the leash on my heart tighter.

"Please say something."

The light behind his hazel eyes dulls when he reads my expression.

"I can't, Danny." I blink back a tear. "It's not easy for me to let people in. With you, it all seemed so natural. But you hurt me when I trusted you not to. You promised me, and I can't forget that. And trying to relive happy memories isn't going to fix it."

For the smallest moment, he looks completely defeated. My heart is shattered.

"Well can we at least finish the date? I had it all planned out, and it would be a shame to let the weather go to waste."

Here he is, the man I love, making the best out of a bad situation.

Positive vibes only.

I hate myself. I completely and utterly despise these intrusive thoughts I have and everything about myself that holds back my happiness.

The cool tide infiltrates the space between us, jolting us back into reality. I deserve it. Deserve to be completely washed away, devoid of every trace, because I feel like a monster.

"Fuck it. Let's do it," I say.

In my mind, this is our final goodbye, and I never want it to end.

After Penny has her fill of the ocean, and the buckets are overflowing with shellfish, we make our way back to the house.

"Where's Amelia?" I ask, carefully removing my wellies and leaving them by the back door.

I hand Danny my bucket, and when his fingers graze mine for a sweet second, I remember how good it feels to be touched by him. He doesn't seem to notice. Or if he does, he has an excellent poker face. "She's out with her friends."

"Do you mind if I borrow a hairdryer? My jeans are soaked."

"Sure, help yourself. It's in a storage box in the wardrobe. Left hand side."

"Thanks."

After I start to climb the stairs, he calls my name. I turn to face him.

"I still have all your clothes here."

Of course. How did I forget about those? I make a mental note to take them back with me when I leave. How I'll do that while cycling is beyond me.

After my jeans are warm and dry, and I've checked my makeup, I join Danny downstairs, where he's busying himself over a pot of boiling water in the centre of the kitchen island. I perch on a bar stool facing him and peer over the stove.

"How long do they have to cook for?"

"Just a couple more minutes."

He holds a couple of metal pins over the fire of a gas ring, and places them on a tissue.

Once the periwinkles are cooked, he strains them and sets them aside in two batches; one for each of us. He sits down next to me with an empty bowl between us, and shows me how to prise them out of their shell casing. We sit in silence while we're tasked with filling the bowl with the small, slimy, molluscs.

"Have you tried one yet?" I ask. They don't look particularly appetising.

He shakes his head. "I'm sure they'll be just like escargot."

"I forgot you were fancy," I smirk, and he retaliates with a bite of his lip.

My eyes focus on his mouth for far too long, but I manage to push my thoughts aside.

"Want to do it together?"

I pick out two plump, juicy ones from my bowl and hand one over to him. I mirror him, my mouth open as he brings it to his lips, and sucks it from his fingers.

Fuck. How can he make something so gross look so sexy?

I chew once, then swallow it whole. The texture is odd, slimy, but they're surprisingly sweet, with a salty aftertaste.

"Did you enjoy that?" he asks.

"I did, actually. Maybe I'd fit into your world after all."

I cement my passive aggressive comment with a trip to the sink to fill a glass of water. When his hands grip both sides of the basin around me, I drop the glass, and I'm lucky that I don't end up with a hand full of broken shards. I turn around, and instantly sink into the depths of his hazel eyes. The water maintains a steady stream as he gently presses me backwards with his body until there's nowhere left for me to go.

"What part of any of this feels wrong to you?"

He leans in, pressing his body against me. I try so hard to ignore the ache in my chest and the heat pulsating throughout my body, but it's pointless. I inch closer, leaning towards his lips.

Just one more time. Then we're done.

Bang. The front door opens, then shuts, and Amelia catches us mid-embrace. She raises an eyebrow.

"Don't mind me, I'm not staying," she says.

Neither am I.

I knew the moment we were alone it would lead to bad things, or extremely good things, depending on how I look at it. How could I let myself get sucked in again? His poor niece can't climb the stairs quick enough, and before I know it, we're alone again, and the brief interruption had done little to dampen my desire to taste him.

Reaching around my waist, he turns off the tap and retreats.

"Careful. We don't want to waste water, Miss DeLuca."

Fucking tease.

"Now put your shoes back on, the date isn't over yet."

Chapter Twenty-Seven

♥

THE AMUSEMENT ARCADE IS full of teenagers, and I'm the oldest person here by at least eight or nine years, so I dread to think how old Danny must feel, but he seems completely at ease and in his comfort zone. I admire his ability to adapt to any environment, like a sexy, sarcastic chameleon.

Tucked in a corner are two grabber machines with identical canine-themed prizes. I take the one closest to the fire exit, and point my aim towards a Dalmatian toy.

"I hope you know I'm choosing to ignore your comment earlier about reliving happy memories," Danny says.

"Why is that?"

"Because I want you to have the best day you've ever had. I don't want you to compare it to any other day you've had in your life, because every day should be as new, exciting and unpredictable as the last."

I don't say anything, because I don't need to tell him that he's already won. My eyes focus on the prize, and after minutes of trying and countless attempts, the claw prongs wrap themselves underneath and around the spotty leg, drag it over the Perspex screen and drop it down the chute.

What are the chances?

"I've won! I actually won something."

I'm so happy, I bounce straight over to Danny with my prize and wrap my arms around his neck. His citrus scent brings back so many memories, and I curse my olfactory nerve for coaxing me into almost forgetting where I am. In my mind, it's just the two of us, and the rest of the world doesn't exist. When I let go, my eyes fall to the floor, and I use the time to compose myself. When I look up, I'm treated to his kind hazel eyes and wide smile.

"You went for the Dalmatian, huh?"

"They're my favourite breed."

"Oh? Since when?" I give him a pointed look, as if to say stop teasing, then I dart my eyes over to his machine. "What are you trying to catch?"

"Other than you? I've got my eye on the King Charles...for obvious reasons."

I scan the Perspex box, and buried underneath a Jack Russell is the Cavalier. "You picked a hard one."

"Doesn't matter how hard it is, I want what I want."

Heat floods my cheeks, and courses through my body. He's making himself damn hard to resist, and if his smirk is anything to go by, he knows it too.

Fifteen attempts and countless change later, Danny is still at a loss, and I can sense his frustration. In that time, he's managed to move the Jack Russell out of the way, and is making short bursts of progress in lining up the King Charles for the chute.

"Hey, take a break," I say.

"I've almost got it."

I sigh and lean against the glass. My tummy rumbles, making me wish we had eaten earlier, instead of setting the rest of our seafood forage aside in the refrigerator to reheat later. The fire behind his eyes makes it clear he isn't ready to call it quits anytime soon.

Minutes pass, and by the umpteenth attempt, I finally sense his gumption waning, like a marathon runner hitting their proverbial wall. I should have told him after the first few pound coins he dropped in that his machine was clearly rigged—the claw on his one has a much looser grip than the one I used.

"I think it's about time you cut your losses, cowboy."

"Just a bit longer. I promise," he says, sweat beading his brow.

His eyes never leave the glass.

"Look, I'm all for being your personal cheerleader, but I'm hungry, and it's pretty clear that machine is a scam."

He slams his hands on the navigation buttons in defeat. I jolt, and his eyes fall to the floor.

"I just want—no, I need—today to be perfect."

"I don't need some ridiculous stuffed animal, Danny."

I place my hand over his, and he looks up to meet my gaze.

I need you.

He looks as vulnerable as the day I met him at the rehearsal studio. All I want to do is to hold him and take care of him, like he had done for me.

"Let's go. The day isn't over, right?" I flash him a smile, and the one he mirrors indicates his surrender.

Outside, the setting sun hides behind a huge, grey cloud, and we walk along the wooden planks of the pier as tiny water droplets kiss my cheeks. Behind my veil of rain, I can be bold.

"Hold on a minute." We stop, and I take a deep breath, drawing strength from the rain and the kind concern behind his honey-green gaze. It's never going to be easy to admit my feelings, and it doesn't help that I've chosen the background noise of rainfall to shout over, but I can't go another second without facing my truth.

"What I meant to say in there was that I need you. I need us. I've always looked for clouds in clear skies, but you calm the storm in my soul, Danny. You taught me how to love and respect myself. I tried so hard to protect myself, but it only proved pointless. I don't regret anything that did or didn't happen between us. The tears, the pain, the emptiness, the heartbreak. All of it was worth it. Because I experienced what it was like to be without you, and I know that's the complete opposite of what I want. You gave me back my power, and above all, you helped me feel safe again."

He looks at me like it's the first time ever, like everything about this is brand new. We could start again.

We can do this. Be bold, Sophia.

"I love you. So much," I say.

He cups my cheeks, pressing me up against the cool metal railings overlooking the ocean. Soon, his hands are tangled in my damp hair, and he's kissing me hard, warming my entire body with every flick of his tongue.

By the time we come up for air, we're both rain-soaked and completely smitten. Running through the downpour, we find shelter in his car.

With a dripping wet face, he turns to face me. "Are you hungry, DeLuca?" His voice is barely audible over the blanket of rain on the windscreen.

"I could eat. You?"

He flashes his dimples. "I could eat you."

"Is that a promise?" I ask, brows raised.

"Absofuckinglutely."

With Amelia still out, we made good use of the kitchen island, the couch and the bedroom, and didn't waste any resources making up for lost time. I barely had time to bask in my afterglow before Danny had me chopping garlic and parsley in the kitchen while he filled the shells of a mini muffin pan with the periwinkles, topping them with garlic butter and toasted breadcrumbs—seemingly right on schedule. While we wait for them to cook in the oven, he prepares a salad, and I set the table.

"This is nice, cooking with you," I say, cutting a slice of sourdough ciabatta and eating it. The loaf is delicious, the perfect balance of soft and crusty, and the salty tang makes my mouth water.

"I think I'm in love with this bread."

"That hurts. Also, that bread starter is probably older than I am."

"You and your fancy carbs."

"Fancy and delicious."

"Just like you." I grin, and bite off another chunk as I watch the rain out the window subside. The timer chimes, indicating that dinner is ready. Steam and the smell of garlic perfumes the kitchen when Danny opens the oven door, and I sit on a stool, salivating while he dishes up and hands me a plate. I take a bite. The sweet, buttery, garlicky goodness is enough to make me squeal in delight. "I think I'm having a mouthgasm. This is incredible."

I tuck in, dipping a chunk of bread into the garlic butter. Danny takes a seat next to me.

"Buon appetito," he says, in his best Italian accent. It's terrible, but I kind of love it.

"Eat up, the final part of our date awaits."

"There's more?"

"If you have room for dessert."

Everything is dark, but I trust him implicitly. The next surprise requires a blindfold, and only Danny's guidance to lead the way. As soon as I step outside, the coolness in the air nips at the exposed parts of my skin, and I wish I'd worn something a little warmer. Pebbles crunch under my feet, and I stumble numerous times as Danny guides me across uneven terrain, then after a few minutes, he helps me down onto the ground.

"Wait here," Danny says.

I shift to make myself comfortable. The darkness and uncertainty has me feeling on edge and tempted to remove my blindfold, but the sound of waves crashing against the shore grounds me and gives me comfort. I wait, eventually feeling Danny's weight next to me.

"Okay, take off your blindfold."

My eyes adjust quickly to the warm orange glow emanating from candles anchored between pebbles, and I soak up my surroundings. A scattering of cushions lays against a stack of rocks, and a picnic basket is nestled amongst them on top of a large, circular blanket. I can't quite believe what I'm seeing. It's like something from a movie, a little cheesy, but also entirely perfect, and I'm blown away. I blink hard, making sure I hadn't fallen asleep and entered dreamland somewhere along the way.

"I can't believe you did this," I say, finally focusing on Danny, his silhouette shrouded in candlelight. The moon, stars and ocean create a perfect backdrop to the sound of the waves crashing against the shore, and an acoustic guitar lays between us.

"Do you like it?" Lifting the strap above his head, he checks the tuning with his fancy watch gadget.

"It's beyond perfect. Thank you."

He smiles gracefully, and I melt a little more. How could I ever think I could be without that smile?

"Welcome to "Beat the Intro: Summer Edition."" He lowers his voice in an attempt to sound like a game show host. "With a little twist." He snaps the tuner off his guitar and clicks it back onto the watch. "I thought if all else failed today I could serenade you. Never fails. Girls love musicians."

Stop. It.

It's ridiculous how he doesn't even have to try to turn me on.

The song kicks off with clean, crisp, open chord strumming. I try to focus, but the thing about acoustic covers is that the intro usually sounds nothing like the original produced song. After the opening bars, Danny starts singing the first line of lyrics before I have a chance to guess the familiar tune. As soon as I hear the first line, I know it.

"Latch," I say.

He stops singing, but continues to play.

A soft, sweet smile spreads across his face like he's holding onto a memory. I lean across, gently pressing my lips to his, and the song fades out.

"This song was playing the first time you kissed me," he says. With his hand behind my neck, his smile widens, and he pulls me in for another raw, emotionally charged, perfectly imperfect, all-consuming kiss. "You really left your mark on me that night."

Suddenly, there's no need for a blanket.

"Next one," he says, smiling, his breath warm and inviting against my mouth.

He shifts onto one leg, and pulls a plectrum—*the* plectrum —out of his back pocket. "Going to need my lucky pick for this one."

My stomach flips, a knee-jerk reaction to those dimples that will never get old, even when we are. Deft fingers move effortlessly across the strings. The melody is so incredibly beautiful, that I don't even care for the name of this song, or the fact that I suck at this game. I just want to hear him play. As soon as he sings the first line, I recognise it instantly.

Will You Still Love Me Tomorrow? from Johnny and Baby's blissful post-coital scene in Dirty Dancing.

Danny's version is stripped back, slowed down and mellow, and like the last kiss that graced my lips, the song is completely full of raw, unfiltered emotion. A tear falls freely as my perception heightens, consuming every tiny detail of our perfect moment. The final note hangs in the air, and Danny gently lays the guitar beside him.

"Thank you," I say.

Danny shrugs. "I had a load of spare time when I was being an asshole. I spent every day learning songs that reminded me of you."

"You weren't an asshole. You were hurting."

My heart aches for the time we lost to pride.

"Regardless, I had a lot of grovelling to do. How else was I going to get you back? Other than food...which brings me to my next trick."

He reaches for the picnic basket, lays it between us, and opens the lid. Inside is a small-scale version of the Italian celebration cakes reminiscent of my childhood. Frosted sides are studded with crushed almonds, and a handwritten message is scrawled across the top of white icing.

Tomorrow, it says.

"Tomorrow?" I ask.

He nods. "I want this...us. Tomorrow, the next day, and the next...and every day after that." He holds my hand. "Look, I know forever is a scary word, but today was incredible. I want more of those, if you do? No more running, no more fighting, no more hiding. Taking each day as it comes and living in the moment. That's what I want."

He squeezes my hand to his chest. "You're the Yoko to my John, the Cady to my Aaron...the Buffy to my Spike."

I can't help but smile.

"I can work anywhere in the world, and once you're qualified, you can too. I want to experience everything with you like it's new, and I want to give you everything you want. We can be nomads together, what do you say?"

I pause for a moment to consider his proposal. "You know, I always thought I had to dress a certain way, or act a certain way to belong, and I wasn't sure if I'd ever fit in with your lifestyle. But that's okay, I've made peace with it."

The warmth in his honey-green gaze is pure kindness and love.

"Danny, you're the only person who's ever made me feel comfortable in my own skin, and all I want is to be where you are. Tomorrow, and always."

He plants another soft, sweet kiss on my lips, and glances at his watch.

"Think we have time for one more song?"

I nod, and recognise the intro to Oasis' Wonderwall instantly, and as we sing and sway under stars and moonlight, I'm happy, I'm safe, I'm home.

Epilogue

♥

*O*NE *YEAR LATER*
       "Drumroll please."

Danny enters the attic room in the beach house the moment I finish filming a segment for my YouTube channel. After our beach date, we dedicated our free time to turning the unused upstairs bedroom into a yoga studio. Lush green plants and sea views provide the perfect backdrop for filming, and my audience of one—the Dalmatian teddy —is always the perfect cheerleader.

"Well? Don't leave me hanging. How much did we raise?" I ask, sweat dripping from my forehead.

"Twenty-six thousand."

"Are you serious? That's twelve grand more than last year." I leap into his arms, elated, and he spins me around. "I need to call my parents. Kiki will be so happy."

I retrieve my phone from beside the Dalmatian and video call my parents. On the third ring, my mum answers.

"Hi sweetie, how's it going?" she asks.

It' so refreshing to see my mum looking so radiant and well-rested, like all of her worries have disappeared.

"Where's dad and Kiki? I want you all here for this."

An adorably wide grin spreads across my mum's face. "Is this what I think it is?"

My mind races to diamonds, pretty dresses and flower arrangements, instantly dulling my mood. I moved in to the beach house with Danny pretty quickly, but I have to keep telling myself that any further commitment will happen when the timing is right. In the meantime, I manifest an abundant life for all of us, and it seems to be working.

"Just get them, please."

A moment later, three beaming faces grace my screen. Kiki is still in recovery, but she hasn't relapsed since she ended up in hospital over a year ago. She looks healthy and happy, and my heart bursts every time I see her glowing like that.

"We raised twenty-six grand for Beat."

"Honey, that's amazing."

"Nice one, sis," says Kiki.

"I'm proud of you, tesoro." My father's comment catches me off guard, lodging a lump in my throat. Mum's eyes sparkle as she looks to my dad with approval.

"We're all so proud of you," she adds.

"Thank you, you have no idea how much that means to me, but I couldn't have done it without Danny and all of you."

I look up to see my Riviera man-snack leaning in the doorway, with a twinkle in his eye. My heart skips a beat, and I still can't quite believe that this man is all mine.

"I have to go, but we'll celebrate soon."

I hang up, and Danny raises his eyebrows.

"Couldn't have done this without me, huh?"

"I said what I said." I make my way over to him.

"This was all your idea. Take the recognition," he says.

"My idea, *your* contacts. The media would never have covered this story if you didn't have contacts at the BBC.

And Monty's shout out on his Instagram live? That was a nice touch."

"You did all the work though. I mean, I'm not complaining. Watching you in those poses can do things to a man. But twenty-four hours of it? I'm surprised I didn't die of a heart attack."

"Next thing you'll be telling me you practice self-love to my videos."

"I do…and I'm not ashamed to admit it."

I scrunch my face and give him a playful slap on the arm, but he knows that his perverted alter ego is one of my favourite sides of the multi-faceted Danny Pearce.

"You know, you really should pay for your porn."

"Why would I want that when I have my beauty and brains standing right in front of me."

"Well, aren't you just full of it?"

"Would you want me any other way?"

"I want you every…single…way," I growl, biting his ear.

He claims my mouth, but before we get carried away, he retreats.

"Good, because I have a surprise for you." He leaves the room, and a beat later returns with a fluffy companion in his hand. "I thought your pup was a little lonely, so I got him a friend. Now you have two cheerleaders. An even number. Like you and me."

He places the stuffed Cavalier King Charles next to the Dalmatian.

"You went back for it?"

"I've been keeping that thing a secret for the last six months. But like I told you, I want to give you everything you want. Tomorrow, and always. So, I kept telling myself to wait for the right time to do this. Remember what I said, about taking each day as it comes?"

I nod.

He reaches into his back pocket, pulls out a box, and on one knee, he presents me with a simple, beautifully crafted marquise diamond ring. My palms sweat and my heart swells.

"The right time is right now, and I don't want to waste another second without you being my wife. So, without further ado, Miss Sophia DeLuca, will you marry me?"

I pause to admire the dainty and understated, but beautiful, ring. For a moment, I can't speak. And even though the next words to come out of my mouth are scary, I know there is no other way to answer.

"Just to clarify," he says before I can speak, "the diamond is one hundred percent ethical and sustainable."

"It's one hundred percent perfect," I say, smiling. A tear rolls down my cheek.

"So is that a yes?"

Without wasting any more time, I smile, then simply say, "Yes."

He beams, flashing those panty-dropping dimples that I will never tire of.

"Well then, I guess you'd better call your family back. But before you do, there's something I want."

He doesn't have to spell it out. Ever since we made our relationship official, we could barely contain our greed for one another, seizing every opportunity we had to sate our hunger before we could be interrupted by a twenty-something student or a dog barking.

As my hand slides under the hem of his Henley, my fingers dance along the waistband of his jeans. The warmth of his body and that captivating scent drives me wild. But as quickly as it begins, it's over.

"Not that." Danny reaches for my hand, taking it in his own. His golden green eyes twinkle with mirth. "Not yet, anyway."

"What are you doing?" I ask, confused.

I haven't quite recovered from my lustful haze when I'm faced with the front camera of his phone.

Damn, my horny face has one hell of a smize.

"Smile," he says, beaming those glorious dimples as he takes a snapshot and reviews it.

"Hmm. It's a bit blurry. Let me take one on mine," I say, remembering his words from the night we met. I raise my eyebrows, daring him to make the next move.

"Nice try, perv," Danny says, rising to the challenge.

"Don't flatter yourself," I laugh, tossing the phone in the direction of the stuffed animals. I can't wait any longer. I close the door, and christen our new status as the future Mr and Mrs Danny Pearce.

Acknowledgements

♥

First and foremost, I want to thank JL Peridot, Sarah Smith, Stefanie Simpson and Skye McDonald for taking me under your wings. I can't even express how grateful I am for all of your support and advice. You are all angels. I love y'all to pieces, pastries.

To Jenna Britton and Joshua Edward Smith; thank you for reading the hot mess that was my first draft, and for all your feedback that inspired me to carry on, even when I didn't feel like it.

Tova Opatrny and George Carlton; thank you for taking the time to read my manuscript and for your vital feedback.

Ali Williams; I'm so glad we met, my Italian sister-from-another-mister. Thank you so much for being an amazing editor and friend. Here's to many more days out in Brighton!

Torie Jean; you smashed this cover out of the park. I couldn't have done this without your talented eye and attention to detail. Thank you for putting up with my indecisiveness, and for all of your support. You're truly a gem.

Natasha Hanova; I really appreciate the time you took to break down my first chapter, and for all your feedback and advice. Thank you for believing in this book.

To Tina, Daniella and Gina; each and every one of you are a pillar of strength in your own beautiful way. I don't tell you enough, but I have so much love and respect for all of you. Thank you for all your encouragement and guidance.

Mum and Dad; thank you for believing in me. I love you.

Sebastian; thank you for your patience. I love you.

Arlo; thank you for teaching me unconditional love. You're my number one for life.

Finally, I'm so grateful to the Writing Community on Twitter, and for you, dear reader, for taking the time to read this book. My gratitude goes beyond the stars. I hope you love this story as much as I do.

About Author

♥

Sonia Palermo writes fun, sexy, steamy contemporary romance with sex-positive, sassy-but-soft heroines and cinnamon roll heroes.

She lives in a village on the South Coast of England with her partner and son.

Printed in Great Britain
by Amazon